Alex Through the Looking Glass

Alex Higgins

with
Tony Francis

PELHAM BOOKS
LONDON

Alexander Gordon Higgins

1949	Born 18 March Belfast
1968	All-Ireland Amateur Champion
1971	Turned professional
1972	World Professional Champion at first attempt
	Irish Professional Champion
1978	Champion Benson and Hedges Masters
1980	Married Lynn Robbins
1981	Champion Benson and Hedges Masters
1982	World Professional Champion
1983	Coral UK Champion

'Statistics won't tell you much about me. I play for love, not records.'

First published in Great Britain by
PELHAM BOOKS LTD
27 Wrights Lane
London W8 5DZ

© Alex Higgins 1986

British Library Cataloguing in Publication Data

Higgins, Alex, *1949–*
    Alex through the looking glass.
    1. Higgins, Alex, *1949–*   2. Snooker
    players—— Northern Ireland——
    Biography
    I. Title   II. Francis, Tony
    794.7'35'0924   GV900.S6

ISBN 0 7207 1672 1

Typeset, printed and bound in Great Britain by
Butler & Tanner, Frome, Somerset and London

Contents

Illustrations

In a few cases it has not been possible to ascertain the copyright owners and it is hoped that any such omissions will be excused.

Introduction

There was no shortage of sympathy when friends discovered that I was compiling the life story of Alex Higgins. It is some story. An unrelenting saga of domestic strife, drink, women, tantrums and – yes, moments of pure sporting brilliance. No-one who has lived that way would surrender the secrets of his soul easily. Alex possesses an almost childlike ability to block from his consciousness experiences he has no wish to recall, to the extent of convincing himself they didn't happen. His suicide attempt, recounted in these pages for the first time, is a case in point. Until forced to come face to face with it, Alex had banished it from his memory. Only grudgingly did the facts emerge. I suspect he will read it again and persuade himself it must have happened to someone else. The pursuit of truth (rather than his perception of it) was not the least taxing part of this operation.

I am certain that his capacity for self-deception coupled with an unswerving self-esteem have brought him through troughs of despair from which frailer mortals might not have resurfaced. There are, as readers will discover, several Alex Higgins. The one whose mind is distorted by alcohol can be insufferable. He is capable of inflicting mental and physical scars on those dearest to him. His estranged wife Lynn has seen the violent rages. I would submit that they are the single most important reason for the marriage breakdown. A few hotel keepers, publicans, restaurant owners, girlfriends and fellow snooker pros have seen them too. Del Simmons, his manager for ten eventful years between 1976 and 1986 has felt the unprovoked lash of his tongue so often that he has become immune to it. Frequently it would be in the dead of night when Alex was crying out from his own private hell and the telephone was his only companion.

Next day, the incident would be forgotten. Every day is a new day

1

to Alex Higgins. The slate is wiped clean. Whatever abominations occurred yesterday evaporate into thin air. That can be as enchanting as it's sometimes exasperating. An appointment will be missed, a promise unfulfilled but, by the same token, a grudge instantly forgotten.

Just before Christmas 1985, during a particularly harrowing period, he called me with a tinge of desperation in his voice. There were but a handful of shopping days left and the Festive Season had caught him by surprise.

'Can you get me a BMX bike for Jordan?', he inquired. It was more a command than a question. 'Get it on the train to Stockport for Lynn to collect.'

'Hold on a moment,' I interrupted, 'does Lynn know about this?'

'No,' came the reply, 'we're not talking to each other. You'll have to sort it out with her. I've got a match tonight. I won't get another chance to buy him a present. Do what you can for me.'

I couldn't raise Lynn, but ordered the bike (with a sizeable discount); arranged payment; sorted out Red Star parcels and train times – all at considerable personal inconvenience. When I got through to Lynn to relay the details, she was astonished.

'I've already got a bike for Jordan. I don't know what Alex is playing at. Can you cancel it?' There was no mention of the conversation when I met Alex the following day.

Over the 16 months I worked with him on the book, I found him at different times unreliable, rude, aggressive, selfish, charming, hilarious, but never dull. For all his faults you cannot fail to like him. Whether you'd choose him as a bosom pal is another matter! My research coincided with a year of unparalleled trauma, even by his standards. Alex reached hitherto unscaled heights of notoriety. In January 1986 he was headline news in one national newspaper or another for 20 days without a break: a host of past acquaintances came out of the woodwork to sell their stories. Lynn tells me she was offered £75,000 to blow the whistle on her husband. I have no reason to disbelieve it.

Alex kindly offered to put me up one night at his Prestbury home during the 'black eye' scandal. It's an experience not easily forgotten. The house in which he'd intended to make a fresh start with Lynn and the children was now an empty refuge; dark, forlorn, cold and abandoned. A monument to his impossible dream of reconciling family and business. In the corner of the cavernous, still unfurnished lounge stood a wilting Christmas tree, encircled by fallen pine needles, incongruously hung with coloured baubles and topped with a Christmas fairy. The work of his new girlfriend who'd moved in and been moved out. On the mantelpiece, Christmas cards from his sundry supporters, and one from his adoring mother, Elizabeth with the message: 'To a wonderful son.' Whatever else Alex is or becomes, he'll always be that.

He'd pitched camp in the middle of the floor. Around him his essential belongings; television set, settee, electric fire dragged from its customary position in the hearth, ashtrays, cans of lager, and, literally at the end of its tether, a telephone which never stopped ringing.

I wondered what his fans would think if they could see him now. Their hearts would certainly have gone out to him. Alex was suffering, but stoically. He didn't want sympathy. He knew deep down that most of his misfortune was self-inflicted. I was surprised by the brave face he put on life. He talked cheerily of hiring a housekeeper to tackle the mess, of buying a washing machine to reduce the Himalayan collection of laundry building up in the utility room and blocking the rear entrance to the house. He was, he confessed, down to his last shirt.

People have often asked me whether Alex and Lynn will make it up again. Who knows? It's a curious relationship, even when it's dislocated. They can neither live with each other nor without each other it seems. In his darker moments, Alex would do anything to repair the marriage and have the strength of the family around him. At other times, he appears happy to go his picaresque way. Lynn, at the time of writing sees little hope for them. Against that, she looks forward to, even relies on, his visits and telephone calls. She admitted inventing a phantom boyfriend to incur his wrath. He reacted by flinging a glass of lemonade in her face. That little cameo, I think, tells you a lot about both of them.

I've seen him hurry to get out of the house when the kids were playing up; curse his wife for deliberately growing fat before his eyes, then go to extraordinary lengths to appease her. It was on just such a day that Alex and I were in the executive club at Manchester Airport for another recording session. I guessed there was something afoot when he offered to carry my briefcase on the way out. (Not the behaviour you expect from the legendary Mr Nasty.) The realisation slowly dawned as Alex pointed to a towering cheeseplant which over-shadowed the British Airways desk. 'See that plant?' he queried (as though I could miss it). 'I've bought it for Lynn and I want you to carry it home for me.' I did as I was told, naturally. No point alienating the chap over a simple thing like a cheeseplant. It was, I might add, rather heavy. Alex had taken a shine to it on our way through the concourse and inveigled the bewildered ground hostess into knocking it down to him for £35. The place looked quite denuded without it. My car, on the other hand, became a mobile botanical garden as we headed back to the Higgins residence, an uncomfortable fifteen miles away. I'm still brushing John Innes Number 3 out of the car. All I can say is I'm glad I had a sunroof!

It fell to me from time to time to book him into hotels and I soon understood why. In most major establishments in most major towns, Alex was persona non grata. Embarrassed hoteliers would hint at some dark deed in the past and explain, apologetically that there was no room at the inn. I've seen restaurant owners and waiters reduced to jibbering wrecks as they vainly attempted to satisfy his outrageous demands. Alex fancies himself as a gourmet, particularly when it comes to Oriental food. If the China tea isn't offered on arrival, he'll want to know why. And if the assortment of exotic concoctions he chooses to order doesn't in any way match up to what's available, well ...! 'Call yourself a Chinese restaurant? This is just a khazi!' Once, having found little satisfaction at a respectable and popular restaurant just outside Nottingham, he called for the owner, and put the poor chap through the ultimate test.

'Do you know the Chinese godfather?' Alex shouted across the bar, referring to a well known Mr Fixit in the north of England. I cringed as a pale shadow of despair crossed the owner's face. Was his peevish customer joking, or was this perhaps the name of another special dish he had neglected to include on his menu?

'No,' came the reply, 'velly solly, not know Chinese godfather.'

'You will,' said Alex, 'you will.'

I'd love to see the man win another major title. It would be a victory for artistry over science. Alex is one of the top students at the Wayward Genius School of Sport. He's in good company. Fellow scholars include George Best, Ian Botham, John McEnroe, Ilie Nastase. Their sublime talent can lift you out of your seat. It springs from a wonderfully uninhibited spirit but one which carries the seeds of its own destruction. The opposite school belongs to the steely-eyed grinders: Steve Davis, Bjorn Borg, Geoff Boycott. Fiercely committed, highly successful but frequently uninspiring.

Alex is loved, I suspect, by far more people than he's detested. His incessant mailbag shows that his appeal cuts across all age and class barriers. It's quite astonishing how many well-to-do middle-aged women follow him wherever he plays and maintain a regular stream of correspondence. He brings out the maternal instinct in them. They close their eyes to the bad things like you would with a naughty child. For them, snooker without Higgins would be like night without day.

I prefer to think of Alex not as the wretched figure shivering beside the two-bar fire because he couldn't figure out the central heating; nor the boorish prima donna who takes no responsibility for his worst excesses. I prefer to think of him as the master showman jesting with the live audience as another long pot scuttles home; the incorrigible hustler taking a fiver from another *ingenu* as he did at the Wilmslow Conservative Club one wintry afternoon which sticks in my mind.

Alex had boasted that he could hit the cue ball across the table and flip a ten pence piece off the side cushion into a glass balanced on the edge. Twice I watched him line up the shot and fail miserably as the sceptical challenger rubbed his hands in anticipation. Alex waited until the fellow slapped his fiver confidently on the baize. At the third and final try he pinged the coin unerringly into the glass, smiled, collected his winnings and said: 'Come on, Tony, we're going.' Pure theatre.

Tony Francis

1
On Reflection

When I look into the mirror I see the indistinct outline of an enigma. A man who's been misunderstood for most of his life, and presumably always will be. The face betrays the ravages of a life packed with drama and stress, victory and defeat: eyes that have perhaps squinted too long down a snooker cue, but are still as sharp as ever, and inside the clothes, a tired, under-nourished body which would blow away in a strong gust of wind. Yet this frail little man set the world alight didn't he? Whatever they say about me, they'll never forget me. My name is burned into the annals of time. When they made the Hurricane, they must have broken the mould. I'm a one-off; a mystery man who would drive the world's most eminent psychiatrist to his own consulting couch!

Without snooker, there would be no Hurricane. Like Beethoven without his music, or Picasso without his canvas, life would be empty. It's the one thing that sustains me as well as tearing me apart. Sometimes I wake up in cold sweat wondering what would happen if I was forced out of the game; if physical injury deprived me of what I love best. That's the biggest fear. Not because I'd be destitute, but because I wouldn't know what to do with myself.

Playing big match snooker can be as great a turn-on as sex. There's nothing more exhilarating than walking into a room bursting with people to challenge my old enemy, Steve Davis. I know there's another ten million watching on television, a vast audience who were never interested in the sport until I came along. In situations like that, the adrenalin pumps through my body like rocket fuel. I feel something wash over that I can't analyse. It's as though a racing driver has found an extra gear. I know there's a switch inside which sooner or later will turn itself on. When it does, stand by! The fluency pours from the cue. It's an extension of my arm. I can't tell where one begins and the other one ends.

An outside force takes charge and I know I can't miss the pots. The last ball might just be nestling in its pocket when the next is on its way. My mind is turbocharged. I feel so alive I'm part of another world. There's nothing on earth that can stop me.

Part of the magic is the animal rapport I have with the live audience. The electricity is so strong that if you were to walk between us you'd probably get a few thousand volts through you! I turn crowds on like no one else can, and they have the same effect on me. I need that public acclaim to feed my ego. It's a very hungry ego. I have such a quick brain and such quick eyes that I can sense in an instant what the crowd is thinking and feeling. Usually, I don't even have to look. It's instinctive and it transmits itself to my play. My feeling for the game is raw. Never mind the coaching manuals – I hit the balls while I'm still on the hoof. I go for 'impossible' pots no one else would consider. Pure, basic, instinctive snooker; the hunter hunting and the crowd baying for more. It's like being high.

All close relationships are built on love and hate and my relationship with snooker is no exception. I love it, but hate the demands it makes of me. I resent the time needed to practise. Without practice, there's no future, however gifted a player might be, but it can be stultifying hitting shots for hours on end. I'm the type of guy who needs to play for real. If that means giving someone a 100 start and playing him for a fiver in the local Conservative club, so be it. Heaven knows, I've spent nights on end playing all-comers in precisely that fashion. The money doesn't matter, but the competitive edge has to be there.

When I was younger and single, I could run with the pack like the modern-day player does, but family commitments and the loss of motivation which arrives with age have prevented my devoting the necessary time to the game. In any case, where are all the hustlers today? Today's player competes for prize money and that's his be-all and end-all. Once an up-and-coming player has won a slice of loot for reaching the last 16 or whatever, he hoards it away and goes home. He'd do better seeking superior competition to improve his game. Perhaps he hasn't got the guts to take the knocks and bounce back. It took guts to play in the snooker halls of Belfast when I was a kid. Guts and self-belief to carry on while the old boys were beating me and taking my spending money; and to persevere until I could beat them at their own game.

That's the kind of challenge I relish but unfortunately the kind you don't find any more. The days of the hustler have disappeared now that the game has moved onto a bigger stage. It's an inevitable evolution. Snooker players are all better off for it, but the excitement has gone. The thrill of the raw duel where you lay down the challenge, back your judgement with pound notes and fight it out there and then. No fancy theatre, no television cameras, no dinner jackets and bow ties ... just a cue, a bottle of gin, a packet of fags and a game.

It's the gunslinger mentality. Find the fastest cueman in town, beat him, take his money and move on. That's the life I've been used to. Living by your wits. One false move and you're dead. I reckon I'd have been at home in the wild west. The freedom; the call of the wild. Nice dream but equally I have to live in the real world of mortgages and pensions and family commitments and plumbers and carpet fitters. The Lone Ranger never had those problems!

It's no secret that I'm struggling for motivation these days. I blow hot and cold about tournament play although my love for the game will never die. It has to be something really special to spur me on, not like the early days when I'd play all day and night and still come up for more. It was the only way I knew of filling the time. Of course I'd run out of partners, especially in those lonely twilight hours when I was wide awake and the rest of the world was fast asleep. Few people could stay the distance with me. After the midnight chimes, I come alive ... like Dracula. That's when you see the real Hurricane. As soon as daylight starts creeping in, it's time for me to go. I've always been very highly strung. A cat on hot bricks. But I have never let nerves get the better of me. I know that switch inside me links everything up, channelling nerves and energy in the right direction. If you could channel it all the time you'd be a genius. Like harnessing electricity. Every human being could be an achiever if you could do that.

Relaxing has never come easy because of the lifestyle I've become used to, and sleep is an intrusion. I very rarely want to go to bed unless, I'm absolutely exhausted. I don't need sleep like most people. When I'm away at hotels, I seldom get back until the early hours, usually when I've run out of partners. Even at home I can't go to bed before two or three o'clock in the morning. That's my norm. Instead of winding down, I get more and more alert. My daughter Lauren's the same. When she was younger we used to give her a warm bath in the night to try to relax her and get her back to sleep. My body clock was thrown out of rhythm years ago and it'll never recover. Even when I do doze off, I toss and turn all night and talk in my sleep. A hyperactive mind never rests. As a schoolboy, I'd get up in the dead of night to make myself bacon and eggs. When I visit my sister, Isobel, in Australia, I'll sit up all night watching the television movie (you can in Australia). Attempts to wake up the rest of the family usually fall on deaf ears, however good the film. The only one who has the stamina to stay with me is my niece, Julie. I used to entice her out of bed with a supply of ice lollipops.

One advantage of getting older is that I can cat-nap in the middle of the afternoon. Generally, though, I find it impossible to unwind. Occasionally I'll settle down to a book, but on the never ending carousel of train journeys up and down the country, it's been extremely difficult. There are too many interruptions. My favourite read is Robert Ludlum. I've read every one of his books, some of them two or three times. *The Bourne Identity* is the best book I've read or will read. Ludlum's so wealthy he hasn't had to write anything for three years!

On the other hand, music is not an important influence in my life. When I've a few friends around, I like to play heavy rock, but I couldn't tell you the names of the groups. They come and go, don't they? Classical music appeals in short bursts, though I wouldn't pretend to know anything about it. I guess if I was cast away on a desert island, most of the records I'd take would be soul. Singers like Tina Turner, Diana Ross, Dionne Warwick, Gladys Knight ... all the ladies you notice.

To the outside world I'm a hellraiser; a temperamental genius always on the lookout for trouble. Well, that's not the real me. My mother and sisters think they're reading about a stranger when they pick up the newspapers. Underneath it all, I'm a shy, placid person, no different from when I was a kid. With people I can trust I'm nothing like the monster I'm reported to be. Unfortunately, there aren't many people I can trust. Hangers-on, yes; people who like to be seen next to me – but genuine types, not too many. I've made a point of not trusting anyone unless I'm absolutely sure. If you put your trust in yourself, you don't need anyone else. In every sense of the word, I'm a loner – happy to be in my own company and like a prodded cobra if someone invades my privacy.

From the day I set out alone at fifteen to see the world, I've learned to fend for myself. How many kids leave home at that age for another country? It takes a certain kind of person to do that. As the years rolled by and I became public property, I was forced to erect a bigger fence around myself. That explains the aggression in my make up. Is it really surprising that I've hit the roof a few times? Put anyone in a goldfish bowl and it's bound to happen. It means that for me, true friends are hard to find, because people flit around like moths attracted to a light bulb. I can sort them out quickly now. If you go through life and collect half a dozen people you can honestly call friends, that's enough.

I have a few close friends I can trust. Mostly they're from other walks of life. I understand the hazards of their profession, and I think they respect and understand the hazards of mine. People like Andrew Chandler the golfer, Willie Morgan and a couple of others. They're people I've known for ten years or more, people who would not desert me if I wasn't famous. On the snooker circuit, my best friends are Jimmy White and Kirk Stevens. We can relate to each other; have a laugh; go through the problems of the day and offer each other encouragement or sympathy depending on the circumstances. I've kept things to myself on my lonely wanderings over the globe. Unlike footballers or cricketers with back-up teams and colleagues to commiserate with, I've never had anyone to turn to. I wouldn't know what it's like to be cossetted.

In many ways, there's a similarity between myself and another famous Irishman, George Best. Over the years I've bumped into him several times and a nicer more genuine bloke you couldn't wish to meet. Apart from being Irish, we share another commodity ... a shining talent that made people jealous and turned them against us. Okay, there's a basic weakness of character there as well, but everyone has those. All too often the outstanding ability goes hand in glove with the fiery temperament and the self-destructive streak. But I know one thing – people like George and me coming onto the scene today would be wrapped up in cotton wool and handled like precious stones because that's what we are. You shouldn't set out to destroy a rare talent, you should do everything in your power to protect it. If that had been the case with us, maybe we wouldn't have abused our ability.

I'm a decent enough fellow, but I've been driven to ground by the press pack and a few vindictive people in snooker who seem bent on destroying me. They have a habit of putting you on a pedestal so that they can knock you off. I don't deny that publicity helped to put me

11

where I am, but I was my own biggest influence. John Pulman, the eleven-times world champion was my hero, though to be honest I knew very little about him. His was the name which conjured up a magical world I hadn't even glimpsed. Others I look up to are Lester Piggott and Muhammed Ali (I prefer his original name, Cassius Marcellus Clay). He was truth. The greatest athlete that ever lived. He had a profound effect on me. He displayed supreme ability, and had that rare gift of being able to lift people out of the drudgery of their everyday lives. He gave enjoyment, entertainment and laughter. When he got older and took the blows, he showed another side of his personality – courage. Clay had every trait a world champion should have. When he was beaten, he went away to retrain and rethink, returned with a new strategy and overcame fighters who'd beaten him. A lesson for everyone.

In Clay's great days, I would go out of my way not to miss his fights on television, or closed circuit cinemas. Once I arrived for an exhibition date in Southampton, checked into the hotel, shaved and changed and went downstairs to ask the receptionist which cinema was showing the fight. When she told me it wasn't being shown in Southampton, I paid the cancellation fee, repacked and checked out. I made three century breaks during the exhibition, won a bottle of champagne each which I exchanged for my favourite tipple, vodka, and caught the last train to London. I made it to Leicester Square and spent the rest of the night watching the fight on closed circuit. Clay's last fight in Las Vegas left me in tears. Tragic to see such a great talent laid low. I'm glad I haven't met him since then. I prefer to remember him as he was. The greatest. I'm not the sort of person to hero worship anyone, but at times I've deliberately set out to copy Ali's behaviour and philosophy. There could be no finer teacher.

I also love John McEnroe. He's a character. Tennis without McEnroe would be like snooker without Higgins. I can understand his outbursts. The people who complain about him are hypocrites. They're the ones who queue up to see him next time. It's just the same with me. Sport is showbiz now, and it's all about entertaining the crowds. Where I can sometimes pot a ball which looks mathematically impossible, McEnroe can hit a shot down the line with such precision that it stays in by a fraction. Then the idiot of a line judge who's half asleep calls it 'out'. No wonder McEnroe explodes. The only other influence in my life has been God. That might surprise a few people. They don't know me.

12

Our family was very Church of Ireland. It didn't mean I went to church every day. I never have and never will because a prayer in church is no different from a prayer in the garage. You take your church around with you. There have been times when I've prayed for help at the snooker table. There have also been times when I've cursed myself for expecting too much from God. I've won a lot in my life and should be thankful for that.

The basis of my popularity after ten years at the top is the appeal I have for the working man. I'm proud to be 'The People's Champion'. I can't think of a more satisfying title than that. I'm conscious of the man in the street who's paid his fiver to see me play an exhibition. I get a kick out of making him happy and brightening up his life. The nucleus of modern snooker players come from a working class background like mine, so I'm not the only one in touch with the grass roots. What's different about me is that I've gone out of my way to identify with the bloke who knocks in a few balls at the British Legion. This is the bloke who works hard for a living down the pit or in the factory (if he's lucky enough to have a job) and he deserves to be entertained. Equally he respects someone who's had to work just as hard at his profession. He can see how much effort I've put into snooker over the years; he can see my undying love for the game and that's why he never deserts me, even when I'm going through my bad patches.

That's how the title 'People's Champion' came about. Travelling around the country performing one-night stands, I built up a big following. These are the folks who come to watch me play from all corners of Britain. When I'm struggling they're even more behind me, which is the test of a loyal supporter. That's why the audience is so boisterous when I'm playing tournament snooker. You've seen the following I get on television. No one else can command loyalty and support like that. They know I'm the back street kid from Belfast who got myself out of the rut and sat on top of the world. That must be a good example to any under-privileged youngster. I proved that if you're determined and devoted, you can reach the top from the most inauspicious beginnings. I wouldn't go so far as to say I consciously carry a torch for the working classes, but I think that's the way they see me. And because there's a flamboyance about my style of play, and my style of living, it gets them on the edge of their seats. They can see sportsmen like me, Muhammed Ali, George Best, and Lester Piggott deriving real pleasure out of what we do, and it's an inspiration to them. If somewhere along the way I've helped someone to escape from his dreary working environment, then that's not a bad achievement is it?

I still keep in touch with the people I met on the way up. I might not see them for years on end but I never forget, and I hope they don't either. Some of my happiest times have been spent at the local working men's club. I can relate to people like that. It happens less and less now because I'm finding it harder to appease people who demand my time. The bigger the game has got, the harder it is to find peace and quiet and a place to practise. I'm pestered everywhere I go. I appreciate their attention and know that every autograph signed for some youngster is another convert to the game. Sometimes, though, I'd give my kingdom for some privacy. The permanent dilemma is that I can't practise properly without an audience, yet when I get one, it doesn't let me practise. It's catch 22. I'm no nearer solving it now than I was fifteen years ago!

The greatest thing would have been to turn that crowd support into some practical use for the sake of my country. Barry McGuigan has proved that it can be done. He's done what the politicians have failed to do since the dawn of time in Ireland – bridge the sectarian divide. The plight of the ordinary man in Belfast worries me. Things weren't so bad before. What I see today makes me weep. We've got one of the nicest cities in the world, full of close-knit families and warm folk with hearts as big as dinner plates. People who care about each other and about their neighbours. Yet they're tearing each other apart. I'm only a humble snooker player so I wouldn't know how to stop the violence and hatred. It's not that I wouldn't like to try, just that I'm not sure what help I could be. I haven't got that same driving commitment that McGuigan has. I admire him for that.

Travel has shown me other parts of the world with troubles too big to comprehend. Some of the poverty in India and the Far East is ridiculous. It can't help but upset you. I've had tears in my eyes seeing little kids in conditions unfit for pigs. It's a world away from my life of jumbo jets and five star hotels, and yet there it is on the doorstep. Bob Geldof's doing great work for Ethiopia, but what about the real poverty five miles out of our own city centres? Doesn't charity begin at home? There's an awful lot of people out there on the breadline. I know, I've seen them, talked to them, played snooker with them.

One conclusion I've come to as I've wandered through most continents of the world is that we shouldn't have given the British empire away. History tells us that the world is all about the survival of the fittest. Being liberal has made us weak. We've gone to extreme lengths to give help to others and now we can't even help ourselves. I'm an unusual mixture politically. True blue in the sense that I believe in encouraging people to stand on their own two feet (echoes of Maggie), but with a strong feeling for the working classes. I don't think the two sentiments are irreconcilable. Some people need help, but there are many more who can help themselves if they really want to.

Plenty of people have suggested that *I* needed help during some of my wilder days. One or two have recommended more drastic measures too, but I honestly couldn't care less what the old fuddy-duddies say about me! I know I put the game on the map and they can't take that away from me. It wouldn't be a bad epitaph would it: 'He was a bit of a lad, but he gave a lot of people a lot of pleasure'?

I'm a product of the sixties which spawned a few wild characters. It was a time when young people broke free from convention and did their own thing. I suppose I grew up with a lack of respect for authority and it's been with me ever since. If there's one thing I won't tolerate, it's people ordering me about, especially when they've never achieved anything in life themselves. I've been off beam hundreds of times, I don't deny it, but don't run away with the idea that I'm some sort of nutcase. Because I've been in the spotlight, my misdemeanours have been exaggerated and embroidered almost beyond recognition. I could have made a fortune suing newspapers. Once the *Sun* did a front page story about me giving the 'V' sign to an audience. In fact I'd done nothing of the sort. My gesture was to gee the fans up, that's all. It was deliberate mischievousness by the newspaper and I could have taken them for thousands. The trouble is to have done that would have given them even more to write about.

I will happily confess that I'm no angel! At times I've behaved abominably. I've hit people, thrown things at them and been rude in fits of temper, but who hasn't lost his rag on occasions? Many's the time I've behaved like an immature kid, but don't forget that in the early days that's just what I was. I came through a tough school, as you'll hear – a school where you had to stand up and be counted or get trodden underfoot. Many of my outbursts can be attributed to the pressures of being on the road, rushing to keep appointments despite the best efforts of British Rail and hotel managements to make life as difficult as possible. All the travel and the late hours, the snatched meals and the delays have made me a more irritable person. I was aggressive to begin with. Put together a cocktail of aggression, anger, inconvenience and fatigue and what have you got? – Dynamite!

There are a lot of things I don't like about myself, but I can't rake over the truth and start again. There are an awful lot of things I've done wrong. Things that make me cringe when I'm reminded of them. But I have to live with them. I'm Irish after all, and fairly short-fused, so many of those occasions were inevitable, however hard I tried to avoid them. There's one *good* thing about me (at least). I don't harbour grudges. When I've been in the wrong I've gone out of my way to apologise. If the victim understood the spur-of-the-moment outburst, he accepted the apology. If he didn't, well there's nothing more I could do. These blow-ups usually happen during tournaments when I'm supposed to have my mind on the job in hand and some busybody gets in the way. That's the worst possible moment to interrupt me with petty requests or demands. That's when I've snapped and told them to bugger off (or something fiercer!) People should have more consideration.

They say you reach your peak at this game when you're thirty. If that's the case, I'd better get my second wind quickly! The game's so different now. Everything's a five furlong sprint so you've got to get into the swing of it quickly or you're dead. I've packed my life with action, and I'm not so sure I don't want to rest on my laurels now. No one can go hell-bent all the time. I've done it for longer than anyone. It's taken its toll. Now I've got to decide which course to take. Am I the responsible adult who should be taking things easier and enjoying the fruits of his success, or am I still the hustler's hustler? I wish I knew.

2
The Good Life?

Snooker has given me everything I could dream of: a comfortable lifestyle; money in the bank; investments; an unlimited supply of tailor-made clothes and a nice house in the country. To be truthful, it means very little to me. Material possessions have never dazzled me. Money is a way of securing the future – that's all.

Lynn and I sold the bungalow in Cheadle in the summer of 1985 and paid a quarter of a million for a five-bedroomed house in the Cheshire stockbroker belt. It seemed like natural progression, and a good investment and was planned to give our marriage a fillip. I like the place but I don't stand in the drive admiring it. I don't pull back the curtains, survey my estate and feel that I've done pretty well. Nothing like that. I probably won't appreciate it until I'm older. When I'm in my mid-forties maybe I'll be able to take things easy and enjoy the house and garden. Maybe I'll buy a gundog and go off across the fields ...

As a naïve twenty-two-year-old I was very impressed when Oliver Reed invited me to his forty-seven-bed mansion in Surrey. One day, I thought, I'd have something like that. How things change. I wouldn't want a home that size now because I'd have to put a management team in to look after it! Delveron House is big enough. It has two acres of ground backing onto farmland and woods and an oak panelled snooker room with its own bar. The table is from the 1985 world championships. It has more or less the facilities I've always wanted. I couldn't wish for a nicer place to practise. When I was younger and purer of heart, I'd have been in there several hours each day.

The other trappings of success are flashy cars, but I've never had a craze for that sort of thing. I like cars, but that's all. My father

17

didn't teach me to drive and I've not bothered since. Most kids learn from the age of about sixteen, but I was at the stables by then, trying to hold down a job, and driving seemed irrelevant. I can't imagine ever getting around to it now. There's a Mercedes in the garage, but it was just for Lynn to carry the family around, nothing pretentious about it. I don't own boats or villas abroad and I still travel everywhere by public transport. It would be nice not to have to spend so much time on trains, but I'm not in Barry Sheene's league. I can't afford my own helicopter. In any case, you can't land helicopters on top of snooker halls!

I could exist day to day on very little money. There was a time when I might have had a taste for caviar and champagne, but not any more. Most meals I eat at restaurants taste awful to me. I suppose a lifetime of snatching quick meals has turned me off food. The meals I enjoy best are the ones Lynn and I prepared ourselves. I'm no mug in the kitchen. You could say the greatest pleasure I get in life today is knowing that my kids are catered for. Money means that my daughter can look a million dollars. She can have all the things I never had. Jordan as well, though he's a bit young yet. I want to give them five-star treatment including boarding school education, though Lynn disagrees. Lauren's a real poser. If she wants to be an actress, with my money behind her, she's free to take that chance. Money buys freedom. Ultimately both of them will have to find their own way in life, but thanks to snooker, there's money assured for them whatever happens.

People sometimes ask why, in my late thirties, I still punish myself with a heavy schedule of one-night stands. The truth is that, I don't have the money to down tools. I'm not financially independent for a host of reasons, so I have to keep treading the boards. There are so many things I have to do to keep my ship on an even keel that I can't sit back and relax – running two houses for instance. Lynn always said I should slow down, but it isn't possible ... not yet. The crux of the matter is that I didn't earn anything like as much as I should have done after winning the world title in 1982. It was a great relief to beat Ray Reardon because it seemed to be the answer to all my financial worries. The prize money was only £25,000 (which no one was going to retire on), but we calculated that the commercial spin-offs should net a further half a million pounds. That would have secured mine and the family's future and enabled me to concentrate on tournament play. I felt the pressure was off after five or six years of indifferent play, and that I could start something approaching a normal family life – spending time with my children and putting in the odd round of golf, my other sporting passion.

I had another think coming. It wasn't a bad year, but the income never came close to expectations. Why? Well, perhaps my reputation didn't do me any favours. People were reluctant to use me commercially because of my so-called 'wild' personality. The fact that I wasn't the man the papers depicted and that I hadn't missed a single engagement for ten years counted for nothing. It's there in the records. Unless physically impossible, I turned up and played no matter what happened. How many players can say that?

It was disappointing to be the 'People's Champion' and not to command the financial rewards that should have been mine. People in powerful places probably didn't like the way I went about my life and work, although the consumer, the man on the street couldn't get enough of Alex Higgins and still can't. There's no doubt my fiery nature made a rod for my own back, but I wasn't as bad as they made out. Surely, in the right hands, I was a highly marketable commodity? The world snooker champion, and the most popular player on earth? The world should have been my oyster. I don't want to blame my management unduly, but I never felt I was in the position where I could get on with the snooker and leave someone else to look after the 'shop'.

Watching Steve Davis doing his coffee commercials and marketing his own aftershave, I wondered why Hurricane Higgins missed the boat. When I'm dressed up and shaven, I'm not a bad-looking bloke. It wasn't my job to come up with marketing ideas. I'm only a snooker player. Davis and Barry Hearn have the right partnership. It means Davis can earn as much money in his sleep as he can at the table. I've never been in that fortunate position. Ian Botham, a mate of mine struck rich because he found a manager who not only loved cricket but saw the market potential of his personality. Although that turned sour, it is ironic that Tim Hudson, his manager at the time, ran a business just round the corner from my house. Whereas I could have been financially secure years ago, I'm still searching for that elusive state. I've had a series of agents who weren't frankly quite up to it. I remember saying to one of them, Geoff Lomas that I was sure I could win a major title any time if only there was someone to take the pressure off and make sure I earned a good living outside the game. It was the new way of doing things in the late seventies. Each of the

19

managers I've had, Geoff, John McLaughlin, Dennis Broderick and Jack Leeming were good in their own ways, and so was Del Simmons. But I've still had to flog around the country to make a decent crust. That speaks for itself. Hopefully, under my new manager, Howard Kruger, it will all change.

I reckoned that a certain London agency who were well respected in sporting circles did a pretty poor job promoting me as a snooker player. It was their idea to have Tom Gilby, one of the leading fashion designers of the day, dress me in brightly coloured co-ordinates. When I say bright, I mean it – red or green waistcoats and lurex trousers in white, green and red! There I was strutting up and down Tom's shop in Sackville Street like the proverbial peacock. I think Mr Gilby had his mind more on the pop luminaries of the time; people like Mick Jagger. I went along with it because the agency thought it would be a novel idea to brighten up the game's image. I turned up to one tournament in green evening dress and was promptly fined £100. The whole business was farcical. People were trying to turn me into something I wasn't. They did their best, but I was hopelessly miscast.

I reckon snooker's earned me well over two million pounds in the past fourteen years. My best season was 84–85 when I topped £100,000 prize money for the first time. Funnily enough, I didn't have a resounding season by any means – it's just that the prizes had risen so sharply that a few quarter-final and semi-final appearances were all you needed to hit the six figure mark. On top of that I suppose I must have collected another £60,000 or so from exhibition work. Mind you, the overheads are high. I paid my manager 20% of all takings, and I could spend between one and two thousand pounds a week travelling to the venues and staying in hotels. The demand was there for seven nights a week, but I'd have killed myself trying to do that. It would have been possible when I was much younger. In fact I'd often manage five or six nights a week. In those days, though, I wasn't charging £2,000 a time. It was more like £150. The clubs couldn't afford any more. After my world championship win I actually *reduced* my nightly rate from £1,000 to £500 for a whole year to keep faith with my fans. Commercial suicide, but, as I've said, money isn't everything.

It's interesting to see how the prize money has increased since television came along and snooker exploded. I received £480 when I beat John Spencer in the 1972 world final in Birmingham. Now, as we know, it's gone sky high. Sponsors are trying to outdo each other with bigger and bigger offerings. I think that first prizes of £50,000 or more for a major tournament are perfectly justified. Not many sports are as rigorous or as mentally demanding as snooker. To be at the top for any length of time at this game you have to be an exceptional sportsman. The pressure alone is enough to make you wilt.

On top of that, the snooker player is constantly surrounded by people offering him drinks. By the very nature of the event, alcohol is an essential ingredient. You're expected to drink with the sponsors. It's part and parcel of the scene. And yet drink is sometimes the last thing you want before a big match. It's a game built around functions. When you're not playing, the sponsor's tent can be the only refuge. We're grateful to them for making the tournament money so attractive, but I wish they'd give a little more consideration to the players' needs. It seems that as long as the drinks are flowing and their customers are being fed and watered, that's all that matters. Players aren't exactly discarded but I feel we are too often left to pick our way through the debris.

The winner's worth every penny he can screw out of the sponsor. Make no mistake, he deserves it. Not only is he a sportsman but he has to have the discipline to produce his best in front of millions with a virtual party going on around him. It's as hard as Seb Coe or Steve Cram bidding for world records and gold medals, except that it's us, not them who endure the loneliness of the long distance runner. Most of us only have ourselves for guidance.

A lot of things came unstuck around the late seventies. I made the mistake many people make when they suddenly find their pockets bulging with money they've never had before – I nearly blew the lot. I got badly in arrears with the taxman and it took me two painful years to catch up. We didn't have accountants in those days. Nowadays, you wouldn't dream of not having one. The only saving grace was that the really big money hadn't arrived, otherwise I might have blown a fortune! There's no two ways about it, I was a silly young man with no idea of the value of money. I suppose you could say I had a good life in return – girlfriends, night clubs, travel all over the world – though it wouldn't be my cup of tea now. I still like a wild night now and then but I'm getting older and less energetic. What seemed a good time then seems unnecessarily wasteful now. I should have been looking after the pennies. It would have eased a lot of the pressure on me today. People accuse me of being tight with my money these days. Cautious I'd say.

I would never spend as much now on booze, gambling and taxi

fares. In fact I haven't been in a casino for four years. I'd think nothing of a £100 taxi ride cross country just to catch some race meeting; ridiculous. My other big mistake was lending people money, I was a soft touch and too many knew it. Most of that money I never saw again. Equally, there were some outstanding friends who were generous with me. I have to reserve a special mention for a couple called Sheila and Tony O'Beirne who were like a second mother and father to me when I was seventeen and in London struggling to make ends meet. They travelled all the way up from Guildford to give me £50 for an air ticket to Belfast so that I could fly home for a break. In the sixties, that was a lot of money. The sad thing is that Sheila and Tony didn't get an invite when I was the subject of *This is Your Life*. If anyone should have been on the show, it was them. Unfortunately, Lynn, who helped draw up the list of guests, had never known the couple. It wasn't anybody's fault but I always felt that Sheila and Tony were insulted by that.

My consuming vice was gambling. It would be normal to lose £7,000 or £8,000 in a day at the races! The worst was at Wolverhampton in 1976 when I lost £13,000 in one afternoon. I was a pretty good judge when I was reading up, but this particular day, I had to rely on a few tips and every one was a loser! In despair, I had £3,000 on one of Piggott's mounts in the last race. The damned thing was two lengths clear with a half a furlong to go when I went into the bar. I figured there was no need to watch the finish, I couldn't lose. When I came out with my vodka and orange, the horse had lost. I was speechless. At 7–4 that would have put me nicely back in pocket.

As luck would have it, I got my £13,000 back next day. My old friend, Desie Cavanagh gave me a couple of red hot tips and I turned £250 into £13,000 in two days – the difficult way! You wouldn't catch me gambling like that today. Depending on how much cash I'm carrying, I'll have £100 or so here and there, but the difference is that I don't need to gamble any more. If I won £10,000 at the racecourse, it wouldn't change my life would it?

The big gambling went on in Australia where I was a habitual visitor to the races after winning the second world title. I got in with a bunch called the Legal Eagles. They were solicitors who made more money out of the horses than out of the law. A great collection of characters they were. The inspiration was a lawyer called Peter Wake who was best man at my first wedding. It would be par for the course for me to go to Ranwick, the race track at Sydney with four or five thousand Aussie dollars in my pocket. One day I only carried a thousand and that was quickly whittled away. Down to my last 100 dollars, I decided on drastic action. There was an interstate race at Melbourne which was to be televised at Ranwick so I fought my way through the crowds to the tote van. The favourite was a horse called Nearest but I wasn't going to have 100 dollars on a 5–2 chance, so I decided to split on the two outsiders (or 'roughies' as they call them down under), hoping they'd finish second to the favourite. No sooner had I placed the money than they were off. The Aussie commentators, in their inimitable fashion went through the fifteen horse card like a dose of salts and to my astonishment, one of my nags, Repetition was in the lead.

I couldn't see the TV picture, just hear the commentary. On the line, they said, Nearest was 'flying' and seemed to have got the verdict over Repetition. I strolled back to the members bar to wait for the result of the photo, and tried, unsuccessfully, to lay off some of the fifty dollars I'd placed on Repetition. Just then, I got a tap on the shoulder and the news that my horse had beaten the favourite. The price was 58–1 or something preposterous and I came away with more than 2,500 dollars. From then on I couldn't do anything wrong. On the last race, I had two bets. Three thousand dollars went on a 15–4 shot and one thousand on a 'saver' at 7–1. The 15–4 came in first and the 'saver' second. It was the Midas touch all right. By the end of the day, I was 24,000 dollars in pocket – about £16,000. Needless to say, that was my purple patch! It's not the end of the story, however.

A year later, I was at Ranwick again and having a scotch in the men's bar with Phil Wilson, the racing correspondent of the *Sydney Sun*. Nearby, a couple of guys were having a run of luck and one of them told me he fancied Devereux in the three o'clock. I had a look at the card and what should be in the same race but Repetition! I had a hundred dollars at 6–1 and would you believe, it won the photo finish again!

They were the good days, but like most punters, I lost hand over fist in the end. I used to bet on anything that moved. If I wasn't otherwise engaged in an evening, I'd pop down to the local casino in whichever city I was and gamble away a couple of hundred quid on roulette, no problem. Then there were the card schools. I reckon at one stage, gambling, womanising and drinking was accounting for every penny of the £15,000 a year I was earning!

It definitely stunted my growth. Think what I could have done with all that capital if I'd been more level-headed. Nowadays, I don't make a move without consulting my accountant and financial advisers. I wouldn't say I'm obsessed about security, but I'll be relieved when I attain it. Not for me so much, but for the others. You might not think so to judge by my reputation, but I'm more worried about the future of the people close to me than my own. I've got the consolation that I'll always be remembered in the history books for what it's worth, but I'm determined to do right by my children, my wife and my mother. I'm grateful to mum for what she did for me. Hers was the original sacrifice to help me on my way and I'll never forget that. She had a hard life, but didn't once ask for money from me. It was always me asking her.

One thing you could never accuse me of is flaunting wealth. Some people get a kick out of that. It confirms their success and reassures them that they are important, but that's not for me. I don't drip with jewellery for instance. I've had some nice pieces in my time, but usually they were given away or misplaced. Other little eccentricities I allow myself are a wine cellar. It's nowhere near full yet – in fact I drink the stuff as soon as I get it. I like antiques and paintings and have always admired any sort of craftsmanship. Everywhere I go I'm on the lookout for bits and pieces. I invariably go to the bottom of the barrel to find a bargain. You wouldn't see me paying a fortune for an antique. The thrill is to pick up a good piece for a snip, I've got a good friend in the painting line whose advice I value because I wouldn't trust my own judgement.

One exception to this was an old honky tonk piano I snapped up for £30. At the auction, there was a £75 reserve on it and we missed it. It went to a dealer, but by applying a bit of the old charm, I got him to knock it down to me for a mere £30. He only made a £4 profit, including delivery! Lauren will have lessons on it. Perhaps Jordan too.

I love buying surprise presents for the children and, in the past, for Lynn. For a while after tournaments, I got out of the habit of joining the drinks circuit and would go out and buy toys for the kids or something special for Lynn. They deserved it. From my point of view, you might say it eased the conscience of a father who was too often away and not able to do things with his children that most fathers do. Lynn didn't think I plunged into the mink market often enough, but there you are. The last time it cost me £4,500 for a full length mink. If you're going to buy one, it might as well be full length! It won me a kiss for Christmas, but as soon as the holiday was over, Lynn was down at the shop exchanging it.

I don't take expensive holidays so much now. When we were first married it was a big attraction. We'd go to Spain and other tourist haunts, but the truth is that I'm spoiled with all the travelling I do in the course of my job. There's hardly a corner of the globe I haven't been to. My idea of getting a suntan now is out on the golf course. I like active holidays.

A few years ago, I planned to become a tax exile in the Far East. I fancied the idea of being the wild colonial boy! The idea still appeals in a way, though it's more likely that I'll stay in England. The north west was my first port of call on the mainland and has become a second home. Despite the crippling tax laws in this country, I have the privilege of living in the best place on earth. Australia is a marvellous place to bring up kids and enjoy the fresh air but I couldn't live there – not even on £200,000 a year for sitting in the sun!

The year 1989 will be my watershed. I've promised myself that I'll finish the one-night stands by the time I reach forty. I'll play tournaments only, and be selective about those. At that age, I'll still be in the top ten I promise you, possibly the top four. It's good that so many young players are ready to inherit the earth, but I can hold them off for a while yet – just long enough to bow out gracefully. After that I'll become one of the veterans like they do in tennis and golf. I couldn't possibly retire from snooker for good. Even if I was financially secure, I wouldn't be able to resist the temptation of the occasional exhibition. I love the feeling of a crowd around me. I suppose I'd feel naked if they took it away for good. There's life in the old dog yet, you'll see.

My business interests take care of themselves. I've invested in a couple of factory units in Salford, I've a half share in three racehorses, a quarter share in a snooker club in Oldham and a thousand acres of forest in the north of Scotland I've never seen. With more foresight and better advice, I might have been into my umpteenth million by now with a chain of snooker halls across the country.

3
Schoolboy Hustler

'Sandy told me he had this marvellous gift and he had to
follow where it took him. I said: "Go on, son, you must do
it." '

(Mrs Elizabeth Higgins)

For a council estate kid from Belfast, I haven't done too badly for
myself. I was born with no prospects, left school without a single
qualification and made it completely on my own to the top of the tree.
I came into the game a little too early for my own good. A decade
later and the streets would have been paved with gold.

The snooker bug bit me at the age of nine. Some bite, wasn't it? I
had no time for school. I'd discovered the Jampot, old Harry McMillan's back alley snooker hall where the tobacco smoke hung thick
around the lamps and the light was so dim it could have been night.
Very often it was. Even at that tender age, my mother had to wait up
until midnight for me to come home. Leave the Jampot before they
threw me out at 11 pm? Never! *That* was my school. I learned more
there about myself, about life, about the business of survival than I
could ever have picked up behind the ink-stained desks of Kelvin
School. I was forged in the fiery furnace playing grown men for money
when I was barely out of shorts.

The schoolboy hustler, that was me. I had the brashness to go
anywhere, play anyone and the supreme confidence in my ability to
triumph in the end. I'd have played on the floor in those days. I loved
the game. No one ever taught me. Not consciously anyway. But I was
a great watcher. When the older guys used to make us mark for them,
I would turn that to my advantage by studying every move.

I have a photographic memory and like the Japanese, anything I see, I take home and improve upon. I'd watch Geordie Kirkwood, slowly and deliberately chalking his cue before planting those bony fingers on the baize, arching his knuckles and gently rolling the blue into the middle pocket. Geordie would collect the cigarette butt he'd left dangling over the edge of the table, suck deeply on it then turn to me and say: 'It's a simple game, son. Just treat 'em like eggs.'

The Jampot was my natural habitat day in, day out for the next few years. The hall was tucked away behind a row of terraced houses off Belfast's Donegal Road. Like most snooker halls then, it was a spit-and-sawdust establishment though Harry did his best to keep it clean. It was also a fire trap. Underfoot were bare wooden boards scrubbed down with disinfectant because they had to serve as a universal ashtray as well as a floor! Goodness knows why the place never went up in flames. The hall was too close to the school for comfort. Lunchtime used to stretch into the afternoon and it became harder and harder to go back to class. As the passion grew, I'd make good my escape from the classroom, nip across the Distillery football ground, up the terracing and over the wall straight into the Jampot.

To begin with, my parents didn't know I was spending so much time in the snooker hall. It wasn't until the school inspector called at our house one day that the penny dropped with my mother. She didn't let me down. She told the inspector I was ill in bed – not a very convincing alibi since I'd already missed thirty-four days schooling in the year. Luckily for both of us, the inspector swallowed it. Maybe he realised he was onto a loser. Mum was petrified in case he asked to go upstairs and check. Great lady, my mother. Her father died at sea and her own mother died at the age of thirty-four, leaving her to bring up her brothers and sisters. That's where I get my survival instinct from. She was afraid of nothing and no one and still isn't. I'd back her to find her way across the other side of the world without batting an eyelid. She wore the trousers in our house. My father, Alexander was handicapped by a terrible accident as a boy. He was hit by a lorry and it left him with residual brain damage which prevented his ever learning to read or write. These days, you'd get three quarters of a million pounds compensation. Dad didn't receive a penny. He did what he could to help me.

My three sisters, Ann, Jean and Isobel had to act like law enforcement officers to get me out of the Jampot. They'd come looking for me at mealtimes and stand at the door of the hall shouting into the smoky blackness: 'Sandy, your tea's ready. If you don't come now, mum'll kill you.' I knew there was no substance in threats like that. Mother was too soft-hearted. Neither she nor dad ever tried to dissuade me from playing snooker. They must have realised there was little else on offer for a young lad growing up in Belfast. In any case, it had to be better than hanging around on street corners or vandalising tower blocks.

(*Isobel:* **He was always asking for money, even after I got married. He was always skint. I was a sucker every time. I coughed up because he had that way of charming people. In any case, I loved my brother.**)

Mum gave me five shillings a week school dinner money, little realising that four fifths of her hard-earned gains would be subsidising my extra-curricular activities. I bought one dinner ticket – for Fridays, on the assumption that by the end of the week I'd be well and truly skint and in need of a square meal. For the rest of the week, dinner was a Mars bar, a Coke and snooker. When she found out what I was up to, she carried on giving me the money just the same. You might say mine was the archetypal misspent youth, though I'd argue that ultimately, it wasn't misspent at all. They tried to warn me at school. Stewart Love, my old maths teacher used to repeat *ad nauseam*: 'Keep playing snooker, Higgins, and you'll end up nowhere.' I don't blame him for that. He had no way of knowing that a restless talent was building up to gale force. Just as well I paid no heed to his strictures. If they'd allowed me to practise on the staff room snooker table, they'd have seen for themselves. But they wouldn't let me use it. Kelvin School must be about the only place I haven't put on an exhibition!

I felt sorry for Mr Love. He was a good sort really – just weighed down with the responsibilities of trying to teach kids who didn't want to know. He would pace up and down rather like I do now – anxious, biting his fingernails, unable to get it together at all. I can't say I blame him considering some of the n'er-do-wells he had in his charge. He took an interest in me despite, or perhaps because of, my waywardness. I wasn't exactly the cissy of the class, but I was different from the herd. I was expert at sitting on the fence, weighing up the pros and cons of any given situation, then jumping off at precisely the right time. The calculating sort. I even had a minder. He was a big bruiser called Norman McCreery whom I took everywhere with me.

Snooker didn't attract my exclusive attention. I was, and still am, keen on soccer, though I was a touch on the puny side for bodily contact sports. A teacher knocked the wind out of my sails when I was a sensitive twelve year old. My mother had bought me a full set of new soccer kit, but I was five minutes late for the games period on the day it made its debut appearance. (I guess I must have been at the Jampot.) I got changed in record time and ran to the touchline looking resplendent and full of eager anticipation. The teacher took one look at me and bellowed: 'Higgins, get back in the dressing room!' It was a heartless thing to do to a kid.

If Stewart Love was a good chap, so was Harry who owned the Jampot. Strictly speaking, you had to be fifteen to get in, but he turned a blind eye if a kid had talent. He was one of those rare creatures – a baptist with a billiard hall, very religious, but equally at home in those seedy surroundings. I didn't get a 'buzz' out of playing kids of my own age. That would have been too easy. Mum once told me she overheard two of my contemporaries from school chatting in the Donegal Road. One of them said he was off to the Jampot for a game of snooker, but the other lad warned him: 'Don't you be going down there. Higgins is there. He's a shark and he'll swallow you up!'

My reputation was spreading! What I loved doing best of all was hustling the men. They had no qualms about taking my half-a-crown spending money. I guess they needed it wherever it came from. I didn't begrudge them. It was only a matter of time before they were paying me. The living legend was a guy by the name of George McClatchey. They called him 'the Bug'. Unfortunately I never saw him, but the name caught my imagination.

There was a class structure at the Jampot. On the lesser tables, they'd be playing for sixpence a time. Table eight was the one to aspire to. That's where all the money was and where all the best players gravitated. Instead of sixpence it was a pound. You had to graduate – and it was a long apprenticeship. Much tougher than anything the kids of today have to face, but perfect character-building stuff. Because the games were always for money, there was that extra edge of competition. It would be a couple of years yet before I started winning regularly, but I beat my first adult when I was twelve and could build breaks of 35–40 by then. They were rubbish players. I used to give them 80 start and still take their money. I could pick up £6 or £7 a week. Not bad for those days. They resented getting beaten by a kid so I had to keep out of their way. That could well have been the

29

origin of my 'hurricane' style of play. You had to play your shot and clear off quickly before someone's cue caught you round the back of the head! There was one fellow there called Jim Taylor who had an ugly growth on the back of his hand. He was such a bad loser that you knew his cue would be hovering overhead while you played. He might have caught me once or twice, but no more. I was too fast.

The chances to play were few and far between. Most of my time was spent scribbling down other players' scores on the back of a cigarette packet. It was the only way to earn enough to get back on the table. When they won players were supposed to give their 'markers' threepence. Sometimes, they were too tight-fisted in which case you had to make do with a penny. It could take a long while to save up half a crown. There was a cash flow crisis every week, relieved occasionally by visits to nearby aunts and uncles who could usually be counted on to give me a couple of shillings. When the mood took me – not often – I'd make a few extra pence chopping firewood and selling it in bundles from door to door.

It was around this time that mum had her prophetic visit from the gypsy fortune-teller. People in Belfast are suckers for fortune-tellers, especially my mother. She found it difficult to turn anyone away. The gypsy virtually held mum to ransom, demanding thirty shillings for reading her teacups. She was no fool. She knew well enough that superstition prevented my mother turning her away. Eventually, they agreed on a compromise payment of three shillings. When the scruffy visitor predicted that someone in the family would be famous, my mother was beside herself. She'd always hoped that my sister, Ann would make it as a ballad singer. It never crossed her mind that *this* little bundle of mischief would be the famous one!

I was getting itchy feet. My school reports confirmed that I was more than useful at English, geography and woodwork, but there seemed no reason to stay on for 'O' levels. I'm sure I could have been an academic given half a chance, but the prevailing atmosphere at school didn't encourage those sorts of thought. Job prospects in Belfast for an ambitious youngster were negligible. I didn't fancy the shipyards. Snooker didn't appear to offer a way out. It was just a hobby. If anyone had suggested I could make a career of it, I'd have said they were mad.

So, at the tender age of fifteen, I left school and Northern Ireland to seek my fortune as a jockey. It seemed a good idea at the time, though, looking back, it was a daring, not to say rash course of action.

I'd always been interested in horses. You could trust four-legged animals. My weight was just right for racing – seven stone of skin and bone. Until then, I'd never even ridden a horse, but I'd watched others and fancied my chances. I answered an advertisement in the *Belfast Telegraph* for a stable lad at Eddie Reavey's stables in Wantage, Berkshire. I was accepted for a month's trial.

Without pausing to think, I packed my things and set off across the water to be the new Lester Piggott! It was a big blow to my mother and father. Mum has never wanted me out of her sight to this day. I'm her son and she takes that very seriously. It probably hurts her now that she's getting on and seeing very little of her boy. At the time it tore her apart, though she didn't tell me till afterwards. Both of them took me to the docks to catch the boat to Liverpool and they were fighting to hold back the tears. Me? I was happy-go-lucky. Off I went with my new suitcase and the whiff of freedom and excitement in my nostrils. Dad apparently broke up when I was out of earshot. 'That's my only boy, and now he's gone.' Mum said they both cried themselves to sleep that night. If I'd known what was in store, I'd have done the same myself!

It was on the Belfast to Liverpool ferry that I tasted my first drink – half a pint of beer. After a long journey by train across England I reached the stables at Wantage and prepared for a month's trial. I was sacked six times for shirking, but they must have liked me because it took two years to get rid of Sandy Higgins! The basic problem was that although I loved horses, I didn't like what they did when they got up! Shovelling horse muck wasn't my idea of a good time. And it was very inconvenient getting up at five in the morning. I wasn't used to that at all. Breakfast in bed and screw the dole was more my scene!

There was an assistant head lad in his twenties and he fancied himself and always managed to get put in charge of the good horses when they came along. Not only that he was a real dictator and thought he could tell Higgins what to do. As one or two have discovered since, I have a natural resistance to dictators! I decided to straighten him out on a couple of things one rainy night in the courtyard. They had to pull us apart!

I could see there was no hope of getting rich quick as a stable lad. The wages were awful – 35 shillings a week. Most of that would disappear at Ted's betting shop, a little wooden hut across the road from the pub. I was the one kid in the stables who could recite timeform within two or three points and make up my own handicaps.

Hours I'd spend studying form when I should have been mucking out. Somehow I didn't relate those streamlined beasts on the race-course to the mountains of manure all around me! Not to put too fine a point on it, I was a shirker and a dreamer. My mind was elsewhere, taking me past the winning post at Ascot; and the flesh, I'm afraid was weak. Reavey gave us a hard time, but he'd every right to. He dismissed me four times in one day for being in the bookies when I should have been at work, but as usual, I managed to talk myself back into a job. I was very sharp at knowing when people were at their most susceptible and at playing on their guilt complexes. They took me back each time.

There were a few brownie points in my account with the Reaveys after I returned a purse full of money belonging to their six-year-old daughter. She'd left it in the orchard where she'd been playing. I handed it back to Jocelyn, Reavey's wife and said: 'Tell her to be more careful in future.' That went in my favour.

What didn't go in my favour was my weight. Any notion of becom-ing a jockey was sabotaged by Mrs Hillier's breakfasts. She was the cook at the stables and did she know the way to man's heart? Being up so early in the morning and breathing all that fresh air gave me a tremendous appetite. I used to spring up the hill as fast as my legs would carry me when it was dinner time. Mrs Hillier's breakfasts were her real forte though. The full works: egg, bacon, sausage, tomato and fried bread – food I never bothered with at home. When you've been used to a diet of Mars bars and Coke, it came as a big shock to the system. Within weeks, my weight had shot up to well over seven stone. After two years on the Hillier regime, I'd been meta-morphosed from a six stone ten pound weakling into a muscle-bound brute of nearly ten stone. Clearly I wasn't going to be another Piggott.

My mother would be on the phone regularly to see how I was progressing and whether I was eating properly. She wanted me to stick it out at the stable but there was no point. I realised that I could never deny myself the things a jockey has to deny himself. I didn't fancy breakfasting on a cigar like Piggott and taking tablets to make me urinate. What kind of a life is that? Funnily enough as it's turned out, food has interested me less and less. Since turning pro I reckon I've suffered from anorexia nervosa. Not exactly a hospital case, but frequently unable to swallow anything. Perhaps I should have per-severed on the horses!

It was good insight into the business for me. For one thing, I discovered what a hit and miss profession racing is. You can be an outstanding jockey, but if you don't know the right people, you'll never get the rides. Even a bad jockey can win on the best horses – and several of them do. There was a pal of mine in Ireland who was champion apprentice but still couldn't break through. He broke his heart for years trying to get the rides he deserved.

It would have been an exciting alternative to snooker if it had come off. To me there are few things more uplifting than a horse in full flight with a good jockey on board, in front of, say, twenty thousand people at York. To come out of the pack and head for the line with all those people cheering you on must be a great experience. To display your expertise for the world to see and appreciate is the most rewarding part of any sport I should think. A racecourse is a wonderful stage for that, better than a snooker table because the live audience is all around you.

That love of horses and racing has always been with me. At one time I was heavily into the stud book as well as the form book, learning all I could about breeding. Fascinating stuff, but there's much more to breeding and training than meets the eye. It's one of the longest apprenticeships you can serve. You hear of fellows being assistant trainers for fifteen years before they get a chance to set up on their own! You need a good brain to place your horses and you must know the racing calendar backwards. Very complicated business and I'm full of admiration for those who are successful at it. Recently, I've taken a half share in a couple of horses being trained in Ireland. They know how to treat them over there. Patience is the word, break them in gradually on the flat before they become jumpers. We'll have to wait and see.

So that was my racing career. I never did get a ride in public, though I still nurture the hope that I will one day. It would be nice to have a ride on an amateur licence in Ireland, perhaps even a tilt at the Corinthians flat race.

(Jocelyn Reavey: **My husband was from Northern Ireland as well, so he went out of his way to take on Belfast lads. We had Catholics and Protestants, it didn't matter. He used to say: 'Let's get them out of that dreadful place before they become gangsters.' I could see the same self-destruct instinct in Alex that I'd noticed in Eddie. Ulstermen seem to have a terrible death wish about them – it's the Celtic strain. Alex**

was a very nice lad underneath but every time you left him to do anything he'd be in the bookie's office. It wasn't legal in those days either!

He had ability as a horseman but no staying power. As a worker he was well nigh hopeless. He specialised in being a general pest. He was just a starved little rat from the slums.

After Eddie died he was very good to me. He made sure to send me flowers not a wreath. He wanted something more positive. He's been very supportive ever since – phoning from time to time and calling in to see me when he can.)

After the stables, I wasn't sure what to do with myself. I knew I didn't want to go back to Belfast. It had been a big decision to leave so there was no point running home after the first setback. In any case, I'd explored the job possibilities before joining Reaveys. The first job I landed immediately after leaving school was at the Irish Linen Company working for Sir Graham Lorimer. I was his messenger boy. He'd give me money for transort but I'd stick it in my back pocket to pay for snooker and run his messages on foot! I covered a few miles I can tell you ... all for the love of snooker. The trick was to hop the buses – jump aboard for 200 yards until the conductor spotted you, then leap off without paying. It was surprising how far you could travel that way! For months after I left the stables, my mother was phoning Jocelyn Reavey begging her to take me back because she couldn't keep me out of the snooker halls.

During those two years in Berkshire, I barely played a game of snooker. It wasn't deliberate, just the way things turned out. The effect was salutory. I missed the game like crazy and couldn't wait to get back to the tables. I headed for London. No particular reason but it was near and it seemed a waste not to sample the bright lights. Can you imagine a poor little Irish kid of seventeen alone in the big city? I was fortunate in one sense though – snooker was my guiding light. You're never alone with a cue! There was nothing else going for me. Only the love of the game, and the indestructible confidence in my ability. To play snooker I needed money and that meant taking a job in a London paper mill. Life was simple and straightforward, if exhausting. It consisted of work and practice. If I was on night shift, I'd get back to the flat in Leytonstone, catch four or five hours sleep, get up early afternoon and practise for the rest of the day until I was due back on duty.

I'd established a practice routine which kept me busy six hours a day. It was as though some outside influence was driving me on to a destination I couldn't foresee. Most people played for the fun of it, but there was a serious intent about my approach to the game which I didn't fully understand. If I'd been a George Best, I'd have set my sights on becoming a professional footballer, but professional snooker player! Who knew anything about that?

It was a lonely life in the East End but I met a host of lovely, warm people, true East-enders, not the spivs who hung around the Steve Davis camp years later. One friend was Derek Cox, a pianist with the London Philharmonic who used to play snooker down at the Windmill Street club with me. He was reckoned to be one of the best players in London at the time. I'd play him best of twenty-five frames for money. He was good, but I got the better of him as the weeks went on. One night, I pulverised Derek making six big breaks in succession. He looked at me with a hopelessly resigned expression and handed me his cue. 'That's it,' he said, 'I'm finished and you might as well keep this.' I'd made him give up the game!

Then there was a postcard dealer from Harringay who should have given up the game, but kept coming back for more punishment. I forget his name, but I remember what an oddball he was. Like a true masochist, he seemed to enjoy being beaten. The sort of bloke who would challenge Marvin Hagler to a punch up if he happened to walk into the room! He insisted on giving me seven points until he'd been thrashed so often that he increased the handicap to fourteen! A complete nutcase, but a valuable source of income. I'd collect £15 a time off him – more than I was getting at the paper mill.

Homesickness was taking its toll. I was thoroughly fed up with late night bus rides through dingy streets. There were a few weird characters in Belfast, but nothing like the deadbeats in the East End. It was no place for a teenager to be and the lure of home cooking and mum's waitress service became more and more appealing!

Inevitably, I was back in the bosom of the family a little over three years after embarking for England. I was tired after my adventures, and took a good long rest. My mother tried to persuade me to sign on the dole for about £4 a week, but I never believed in accepting charity. I was used to earning money the hard way, with my talent. Subsidising myself with other people's help you might say. For the time being, I was happy to stay in bed and wait for my breakfast. Little Lord Fauntleroy was probably born with a silver spoon in his mouth but I had better service I promise you!

Mum despaired of ever getting me up. She tried every trick in the book and one day it almost backfired. I'd been out playing snooker until 3 am and was virtually comatose in bed. She came upstairs in a panic to tell me the house was on fire. I mumbled: 'Mother, do me a favour. You can't get me like that'. Her voice became increasingly alarmed and eventually I thought; 'Maybe there's something in this.' The smoke hadn't got to me yet. After another half a dozen calls, I decided I'd better get up and investigate. Sure enough, the whole bottom part of the house was gone (we lived in a two-up, two-down terrace). The pictures were burned off the walls, the curtains were melting and the settee was ablaze. I'd been lying there with the smoke creeping up the stairs. I grabbed my new C&A suit out of the cupboard with my mother rushing around crying: 'My god, my house is burning down!' There must have been more than twenty neighbours queuing up with buckets of water. Mum said they'd filled every one twice while I was sleeping. Talk about Nero fiddling while Rome burned! Something had shot out of the open fire and set the place alight. Six or seven months later the house was completely refurbished at the council's expense.

(Isobel: **He didn't want to work. He was just a kid mucking about. I got him a job at the stitching factory where I worked but I was worried because he'd never stayed in a job more than a day or so. He left the same day. I didn't know what to say to the boss.)**

Things had changed for the worse in Northern Ireland while I'd been away. The streets had become distinctly less friendly. When I was a kid starting out at the Jampot, Belfast was a safe city. I used to roam the clubs looking for action with never a worry about personal safety. Many's the time I'd go off up the Falls or the Crumlin with that adventurous spirit of mine. It was a good place to be and snooker was a common denominator. Protestants and Catholics played against each other with only the occasional flare up, and then usually between a couple of hotheads.

We used to have these death-defying challenges whenever a couple of players who'd been gambling hard were at loggerheads. Instead of fighting a duel, the system was to race each other on the main road from the Jampot to the Windsor cinema, a distance of about 200 yards. The tough bit was crossing another main road without stopping. You could have been cleaned up any time, even though the races were usually run after midnight. I took part in it once or twice. Sometimes the two protagonists would argue about the photo finish, then it would degenerate into Catholics versus Protestants with a fair amount of animosity. Equally, I've seen battle royals between Kelvin School and Fane Street School which were both Protestant. Incredible affairs they were, about three hundred-a-side with the bars of park benches as weapons. You wouldn't see me for dust – I'd be off up the Shankhill!

When I returned from the stables, it was obvious that snooker players didn't mingle so freely any more. Before the troubles, both religions could walk into any billiard club in Northern Ireland and play what we called 'sticks'. You paid half a crown a time if you lost and it was like a running competition. The troubles spoiled all that. I saw the occasional flash of sectarian violence but fortunately missed most of it. I was aware of the friction though my mind was too young to comprehend. I was back to my hustling ways with a vengeance. When the Jampot got dull, I would repair to one of the other clubs in the city; the Crown, the Oxford or the Shaftesbury. Playing away from home was good training. Challenging better players on their home patch taught me a lot about adapting to different conditions. I guess I was hustled as much as I was hustling but that made me razor sharp. Eventually, at the age of seventeen and a half I joined the YMCA. It was a turning point.

Until then, I hadn't given much thought to league snooker. In the billiard halls, it never went on and I hadn't much contact with the YMCA and the constitutional clubs. I had, however done some marking for the best YMCA players like Campbell Martin, Billy Caughey, Tom McBride and the Leckey brothers, Ken and Danny. They were nice blokes once I was accepted about six months later. First I had to break down the class barriers, by which these fellows had made themselves impregnable from outside. In the meantime, I had to score for them each lunchtime. They weren't supposed to gamble, but they got away with it.

After six months of scoring, I got my break. One of the top players didn't show up one day and I asked to join in. They weren't keen to begin with, but I knew how to bend people. I said: 'Come on boys, play the white man, I've been scoring every day for six months.' I was in. What's more, I was better than they were. The photographic memory had been working overtime. They might have thought I was only scoring when in fact I was committing every match to memory and replaying it in my mind when I got home at night.

Before long, I was wiping the floor with them. I got so cocky I used to go around the table saying: 'Fares please' and collecting my winnings. One day I really excelled myself. There were five players, so you only had one shot in five. I started off on level terms and finished on minus 63. To do that at my age was unbelievable. After that, Higgins was *the* boy. Both snooker players and billiard players loved me because they'd never seen anyone do what I could do with the balls.

There was a sequel to the story of the pianist who gave up the game in despair. This time, it was an old boy called Charlie O'Hara, a 500-break billiard player. For a while, I didn't notice him, then I became aware that everywhere I went, Charlie was sure to follow. He started at the Oxford club, then moved over to the YMCA. Even when I was practising six or seven hours a day he'd be there. There's devotion for you. During matches while the opponent was at the table, I'd go and have a sit down and chat with him. He was a nice old boy and he had that lovely billiard bridge that characterises all good players. I appreciate what response you can extract from the balls by persuading your hands and fingers to adopt special positions. Move a finger and it can mean the difference between a sublime shot and a mundane one. Charlie appreciated it too. We were soulmates.

Charlie derived more pleasure and satisfaction watching my precocious young talent develop, than out of playing himself. That's the ultimate sacrifice. He was astonished to watch me play two tables during a session. It was billiards on one until I achieved the 100 or 200 break I was looking for, then over to the snooker table to try for a century break there. I had no intention of ever specialising in billiards, but I reasoned that keeping up the two disciplines could only benefit my play. Never a day went by without Charlie sitting alongside. In a curious way, he was a comfort and I was deeply flattered that someone should retire just to watch me.

A few of the top players at the YMCA like Campbell Martin had their certificates on the wall, commemorating the fact that they'd achieved the magical century break. The club was only too willing to pay five shillings for the framed tribute. I set my heart on joining Mr Martin and company on the wall. The trouble was that I'd go to pieces time after time in the nervous 90s. When the older chaps went back to work after lunch, I'd stay on all afternoon, practising alone.

I'd get to 96, 97, 98 then blow it. Eventually, I made my first bona fide century break at the age of seventeen and a half. Triumphantly, I marched the mandatory couple of witnesses to the club secretary's office and announced that I'd done it at last. The secretary said he'd see to it right away that I had a certificate on the wall. By the end of the week, I'd made 35 century breaks. They couldn't afford me. To this day, I've never managed to get that certificate I wanted so badly.

The floodgates were open now. Instead of an 80 or 90 start, I was conceding 100 and still beating all comers. They'll tell you how scrupulously fair I was too, calling foul shots against myself, which is more than can be said for some people I know. Predictably, I've never had any credit for being honest.

League snooker brought a new dimension to my play – and to the crowds who watched me at the Mountpottinger YMCA in Belfast. The 'Mount', as it was called was the mecca for snooker and billiards. Trying to get in there when I was performing, was like trying to get a seat for a Muhammed Ali fight. I'd pack the place. It was unheard of for someone that young in the Belfast and District League to be so good. I was re-writing the record books and they flocked from all over the place to see the new phenomenon. The buzz I got was unreal. That's when I first experienced the thrill of a large crowd routing for me. Before long, it was like a drug. I was hooked.

Two milestones along the way were the Northern Ireland Amateur Championship in which I defeated Maurice Gill 4–1 in the final, and the all-Ireland amateur title when Gerry Hanway from Dublin succumbed to the Higgins magic. Both titles were won in 1968 – my best year so far. The idea of turning pro still hadn't occurred to me. A pal of mine called Jacky Shannon used to take me over to the Carlton hotel where they'd installed a television set in the bar. Over a couple of half pints, we'd watch Pot Black for 25 minutes. The programme was in its infancy, and in black and white so the impact wasn't tremendous. The world of pro snooker didn't look that appealing to me. Despite the big crowds in Belfast, there was hardly any national media coverage of snooker. So what was I aiming at? The truth is I didn't really know. I was just making my way in life the best I could. A few part-time jobs around Christmas supplemented my snooker winnings. They weren't bad times.

In the background was another future world champion – Dennis Taylor. I first knew him when he was fifteen and covered in spots. We were never close from the start. I was a star long before he was.

When I won the all-Ireland title Dennis was an insignificant amateur. I travelled up and down Ireland for £20 a night getting through more work than pros like John Pulman. Dennis and I were chalk and cheese in temperament as well. I've always been happy-go-lucky; Dennis has always been dour. I was taken aback when he won the world title in 1985 but I guess every dog has its day.

I wasn't keen on Dennis but I *did* like his family and once took a shine to his sister, Molly. She was very attractive. As the golden boy I was booked to play at Dennis' home village of Coalisland. I stayed on to play in a little local tournament to be near Molly. It was tea and cucumber sandwiches in the parlour with Dennis doing his best to protect Molly from me. It was a crush which lasted only as long as the tournament. I thought I was in love and promised her we'd get engaged. But what did I know about love?

My drinking and high rolling days were still several years ahead. It was impossible to be up all night painting the town red, because nothing stayed open late enough in Belfast. I used to go around with a friend called David Wallace, something of a jetsetter who worked at a local boutique. David would frequent all the fashionable pubs and night spots. He loved pulling the birds too. After a match at the Mount, there'd be a short press conference with the *Belfast Telegraph*, then David and I would be off and running. Pretty innocent stuff though. We'd spend more on taxi fares than anything else – hopping from one Conservative club to another playing a few frames, swallowing a half of lager here and there.

They were the times when I kept the family in turkeys! I'd regularly win both the snooker and billiards handicaps at the YMCA and the prize was the traditional bird. I won enough turkeys to open a business and one Christmas I sold one of them to David for a fiver. Later in the day, we called around to his house for a festive drink, over which he told his mother he'd won the turkey playing snooker. She called me into the kitchen a few minutes afterwards and asked me to explain. Tucked inside the bird was a label – 'A. Higgins, winner'. Bad luck David!

(*Isobel:* **Sandy showed no signs of growing up. He was very childish at heart and a great prankster. He wanted to play around every day. You were never sure what he'd be up to next. When he came to see us in Australia, he used to pour vodka in the chicken's water just to see how they'd**

40

**react. We couldn't stop them bumping into each other and
falling over. Sandy thought it was a great laugh.)**

The meeting place for the beautiful people of Belfast was the Lido –
a sort of soda parlour which sold fish and chips. It consisted of a long
alley with about fifty booths and a dance studio next door. We'd all
congregate there for coffee and a spot of girl watching. I was still
untouched though I fell in love a few times. I remember a lovely girl
by the name of Hazel Chalkley. I was very fond of her, but after a
brief relationship, I was away on my adventures again. Some months
later, I discovered that the poor girl was pregnant by her boyfriend
who'd deserted her. To my horror, she was living in a girl's home. I
paid her one visit but never knew what became of her.

We had a few late nights, David and I, but I was dedicated to the
game. I suppose I was always a freak of nature in that I could get
home just before dawn, then get up a few hours later to produce
breathtaking snooker. Generally speaking, though I was taking good
care of myself. The name of the game was practice, from 11am to 9pm
every day. No one had to tell me to do it, I just did it. And ten hours
a day with two tables going (one for snooker, one for billiards) is not
a barrel of laughs. Few people in any sport are as dedicated as that.
Snooker was my natural idiom. All it needed was the practice to bring
it out.

1969 was a year of mixed fortunes, but it launched me on my
professional career. The setback was when Dessie Anderson from
Bangor, took the Irish amateur title from me. The most exciting thing
to happen that year was the Players Number Six UK team trophy.
The Belfast YM, under my captaincy reached the final, defeating,
among others, a very good team from Scotland on the way. This was
a new departure for us. It was one thing to play the best that Northern
Ireland could offer, something entirely different to face players from
other parts of the UK. You couldn't do your homework on opponents
like that. They were unknown quantities. To represent the whole of
Northern Ireland in a major final was a big thrill for everyone. Our
opponents were Penygraig Labour Club from South Wales and the
final venue was fixed for the Institute of Technology at Bolton.
Nostalgia came flooding back when we caught the ferry to Liverpool.
It was almost exactly four years earlier that I'd set off for the stables.

I elected myself captain again and decided to play number two. It
was a cunning ploy, or so I thought. The theory was that Billy

Caughey would, with a bit of luck, beat the Welsh number one in the first game, undermining their confidence; then I would demolish their number two before defeating their number one and putting us into an unassailable lead. Fine theory! Caughey was pulverised first game by Terry Parsons, the Welsh amateur champion. We had two or three officials from the YM for support, Penygraig Labour Club had brought 350 Welshmen down in coaches from the valleys. They were singing: 'We'll keep a welcome in the hillside' until I silenced the lot of them!

When I took over, we were 112 points behind, to be made up over the next two games. Twelve minutes later, we were 90 in front. You could have heard a pin drop! The match ended dramatically with my team 6 points ahead and everything on the final black. The ball was sitting nicely for Mel Jones, the Welsh player, only six inches from the pocket. He shouldn't have missed but somehow he overcut it and went in-off. We'd won. Poor Mel locked himself in his hotel room that night he was so distraught. After the celebrations, we challenged the Welsh lads to a race around the square next to the Packhorse pub, not far from Bolton Wanderers Football ground. John Shepherd was the only one who had a chance againse me, but I ran him into the ground. I was only twenty and built like a whippet.

There was an immediate spin-off from the Players victory. No sooner had John Pulman presented me with the team trophy and my picture appeared in the Belfast paper than a couple of far-sighted friends got in touch. One was Vince Laverty, who now runs the *Bolton Chronicle* and the other was a local promoter in that part of Lancashire called Jimmy Worsley who sadly died a few years ago.

Impressed with my performance against the Welsh lads, they booked me for a week to play the world professional champion, John Spencer. My fee was £30. Back I went to England to meet Spencer at the Bolton Institute of Technology and, do you know, I hadn't a care in the world. Some time earlier, I'd taken the opportunity of playing the Owen brothers, Gary and Marcus on one of the rare visits made by professionals to Belfast. The venue was the Royal Overseas Club and guess what? – I beat them comfortably. So comfortably they were reduced to complaining about the table. It wasn't the greatest in the world, but I'd had no difficulty compiling a couple of 70 breaks on it!

So Spencer was just another snooker player to me. He gave me 14, but I won with ease. Looking at the frame scores afterwards, the handicap hardly came into it. That win, as much as anything else, first persuaded me to give serious thought to turning professional. If I could beat the world champion, perhaps it was time I got my nose into the trough! Lancashire was a hot bed of snooker talent at the time. Most of the players I'd read about seemed to come from the Bolton–Blackburn–Accrington area, for instance John Virgo, Stan Haslam and Jimmy Heaton. There was no better place for an aspiring young player. At different times, I lived in all three towns – Oswaldtwistle as well – and snooker had progressed from being a passion to a positive obsession.

After making eight or nine century breaks at the Post Office club in Blackburn, or the Elite in Accrington, I'd have to take a breather for something to eat and drink, but like a kid enjoying his play, I didn't really want any intrusions. I remember once practising for ten hours before calling it a day and walking over to the White Bull in Blackburn for a half pint of beer. After a couple of swallows I was out of the pub and back in the snooker room to make another century break or two before dragging myself off to bed.

My game was improving all the time even though the living was rough. I had a series of pretty dilapidated flats and barely a decent shirt to put on my back. That's when I first met three guys who were to change my life. Their names were Dennis Broderick, a salesman who worked for a firm of Lancashire bar fitters, and two bingo tycoons, Jack Leeming and John McLaughlin. Just three guys who enjoyed a game of snooker in the Post Office club at lunchtime but realised fairly quickly what a diamond they had in their midst, and became my first agents. Money didn't come into it as far as they were concerned. It was sufficient just to see me develop – rather like someone who's come across an outstanding racehorse. Between them, they found me a more salubrious flat, bought me some new clothes and said: 'Right sunshine, here's your chance.' My fee would be £25 for an engagement.

I needed that impetus. It wasn't that I was unsure of my ability – far from it – just that there weren't any established guidelines for an amateur player turning pro. No one had made the transition for years. Today, you'd have to be amateur champion of one of the home countries before the World Professional Billiards and Snooker Association would entertain the idea. Because I had no idea what the life of a pro entailed, I suggested to the Association that I should serve a probationary period to see whether or not I could make a living at the game. They were only too happy to agree. In case the experiment proved a failure, I'd posted an entry for the English amateur championship.

It was a grinding, protracted affair over nine months or more, and my opponent in the first round was a chap called Reed. I couldn't tell you much about his game, because we never played. I withdrew from the competition once Messrs. McLaughlin, Leeming and Broderick helped me to see the light. I would probably have won the amateur title but what was the point in committing myself to a wasted year of playing nobodies? My sister, Isobel offered to give me £100 to enter the 1971 World Professional Championship, but I turned it down on two counts. First, I didn't like taking the money, and secondly, I wasn't quite ready to take on the world. Nearly, but not quite!

Happier times after I married Lynn in 1980.

(ABOVE LEFT) I take great pride in my appearance, bu it has occasionally landed me in hot water.

(BELOW LEFT) Come here, le me help you! Tony Meo ha a little trouble with his bow tie. I never had anything else!

(RIGHT) Lynn and I in my natural habitat – beside the bar!

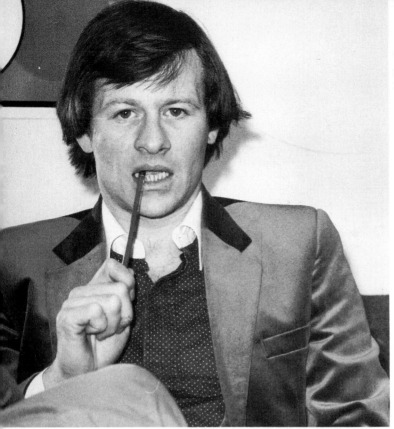

The Thinker – a few moments peace before the next big match.

(ABOVE) A chip off the old block. Lauren has the Higgins looks as well as temperament, poor girl!

(OPPOSITE) After snooker this is the sport I love. My handicap is 12.

(ABOVE) There's been a lot of pain between Lynn and me, but a lot of love too.

(OPPOSITE ABOVE) World Champion but the little girl who inspired me gets the wrong end of the stick!

(OPPOSITE) Lauren and Lynn spent hours in the dressing room watching play on television. (World Champion 1982)

(INSET) Lauren and Jordan. I wish I could have kept us together.

The picture seen by millions. Lynn and I after winning my second world title.

4

Positively Gale Force

Less than a year after turning pro, I'd blown open one of the cosiest monopolies in sport by winning the 1972 world championship. No qualifier had ever done it, and none has achieved it since. As an ingenuous youngster, I didn't realise the full impact of what I'd done until a few weeks later. At the time, beating the undisputed world number one, John Spencer in the best of 69 frames was enough to be going on with. The roar from 500 aficionados packed into the dingy British Legion club at Selly Park in Birmingham heralded my arrival on the world stage. They were sitting on radiators, bar tops, wooden boxes – anything they could commandeer to catch a glimpse of the new phenomenon. Britain was huddled together by candlelight trying to keep warm in one of the most miserable winters since the war. Ted Heath had taken on the miners and the country was in the grip of the three day week as the pitmen came out on strike and electricity was rationed. Alex Higgins, you might say, arose out of the darkness to become the guiding light for young snooker players everywhere.

With encouragement from Dennis Broderick and Jack Leeming, I turned pro because I desperately wanted to prove that I could make a living at the game which had taken over my youth. It wasn't an auspicious start. Dennis had to drag me out of bed for my first professional appointment. Eleven o'clock was a little early in the morning for me! No harm done though; we made it to Walsall with half an hour to spare. By the time we arrived, the sleep had left me and I knocked in a century break in less than four minutes against Graham Miles; the hurricane was brewing!

Having raked together the £100 entrance fee, I found myself in the qualifying stages of the 1972 World Championship. It started in the autumn of 1971 and dragged on for more than a year –

virtually overlapping the qualifying stages of the 1973 event! Unlike modern-day snooker, there were no fixed dates for the rounds – the two adversaries got together to find a mutually convenient time. That loose arrangement was to cause all sorts of problems later in the competition.

Progress through the qualifiers was achieved without alarm. I conceded only eight frames in the opening two rounds, beating Ronnie Goss 16–5 and Maurice Parkin 11–3. Next in line for the Higgins treatment was the Irish professional champion for the past two decades, Jack Rae. A lovely man, full of fun and a very attacking player. He used to love potting blues off the spot and knocking balls down the cushion. He was a bit of a father figure to me because right from my earliest days, Jack was the only Irishman I knew on the pro circuit. He used to tell me tales about Joe Davis and how he virtually ran the television programme, Pot Black as a private club. Many's the time Jack had to swallow his pride and play along with the ruling hierarchy. He didn't exactly throw games, but he knew that beating Joe was more or less a guarantee that you wouldn't be invited back onto 'his' show!

Old Jack wasn't very difficult to beat because he was past his best. To give him his due, he stayed with me for three of the four sessions, using all his craft against my rawness, but eventually succumbing 19–11. A few weeks after that, I beat him again to take the Irish title at Graignamanagh in County Kilkenny. It was January 1972 and the start of a momentous year. Jack made this assessment of me in one of the snooker magazines of the day: 'He's a fabulous player when he's going well. When he plays close around the black his cue action is marvellous but with the long ones he throws everything into it. He moves his head; his elbow juts out; he does everything wrong. And yet he knocks them in like nobody's business – amazing!'

Next stop was the world championship quarter-final but, silly as it might sound, I still had no awareness of what could lie ahead of me. It was all new and I daren't even look beyond the next round. I knew I was good in practice, but until you arrive at match situations, you don't know what you're really capable of. The quarter-final draw brought me up against one of the game's legends – John Pulman who'd been world champion for twelve years. I remembered the days in the Royal Arcade in Belfast when I used to go into the pub under age to watch Pulman on television. He was my first TV idol. I didn't see enough of him to know much about his game. What I did see I liked. His cue action was immaculate and his safety play was probably second to none.

Now here was the living legend, standing at the same table as me. It was a thrilling feeling, but I wasn't overawed because I had this supreme belief in myself. I'd already worked out my battle plan. These were percentage players and I figured the best way to beat them was to go for the jugular ... attack with brute force and frighten them to death! They weren't used to that. I overcame Pulman 31–23 and I guess you could say I blew him off the table!

We were staying at the Middleton Hotel in Morecambe and I'll never forget sitting down to have a drink with him the night after the match. I was only a fledgling, but I'd taken to drinking the occasional vodka. Pulman, as usual, was on whisky and water. I fell asleep at twenty past two in the hotel foyer, surrounded by half a dozen snooker buffs discussing the game. When I came to at half past five in the morning, Pulman was still there drinking his scotch and water. It was as if I'd been through a time warp and back! I felt quietly elated to have beaten such a great champion and managed somehow to get a message through to my parents who weren't on the phone.

John Pulman recalls:
Before the match, I'd had a three month lay-off with disc trouble and hadn't picked up a cue in all that time. That's not to take anything away from Alex. I first played him as an amateur when he came over to England with a team from Belfast. At the time, I was contracted to Player's Cigarettes – the first snooker player ever to be sponsored by a firm. I played Alex one frame; gave him a 21 start; made a break of 60-odd, and lost!

I remember seeing him practise once at Weybridge when he was potting balls from three inches past the middle pocket, off the cushion and into the top pocket. I couldn't believe it. The last time I potted one like that, a star appeared in the east! In 1972, he was playing better than he's played since. He came into fruition again in 1982, but the genuine Alex Higgins was to be found ten years earlier. He was a fantastic player, a genuis at the game. He could do things on a billiard table that no one else could. His cue power was something to behold and he had the quickest brain I've ever known, capable of sizing up any situation in an instant. The trouble was that he was too highly strung to be consistent. You could see it in those early days – brilliant one day and

47

awful the next. That, of course was part of his appeal, but also, I suspect part of his failure to capitalize fully on a God-given talent.

Rex Williams had narrowly beaten Ray Reardon in the quarter-finals, so there was no way I should have underestimated him as my semi-final opponent. We had to rearrange it three times to suit Rex. He gave us the dates to play at Bolton and we fitted in with his wishes. By the time he'd changed his mind for the third time, I was getting pretty fed up. Whether it was gamesmanship or not, I don't know, but it cost me money. I was beginning to get some recognition and a few engagements here and there. Several of them had to be cancelled while Rex reorganised his diary. In those days, we were on a percentage of the gate money and the crowds at Bolton Co-operative Hall were very good. All I made out of the semi-final of the world championship was £68 for the week! Dennis and Jack were not experienced agents in those days – they didn't even take a cut of my earnings. I should have earned far more. I've never been quite sure who was to blame. I swore it would never happen again.

I wasn't entirely happy about Rex Williams' antics, but not too worried about Rex Williams the player. I treated him more with disdain than anything else, and almost paid for it! I played ridiculous snooker for two days, showing off to the audience and losing nine frames in succession, but stubbornly refusing to alter my explosive tactics because I knew they would triumph in the end. I went hell for leather and tried to blast him into oblivion, but the table wouldn't take it.

Rex was playing the way he always plays. I don't think he could distinguish between billiards and snooker. As the reigning world billiards champion, his loyalties must have been divided. I've played both games too, and I know for certain that snooker's meant to be played much faster than that! My opponent had a fair record as a snooker player. It meant something to be ranked six in the world even if there were only half a dozen players on the circuit!

It took me three days and five sessions to get level. I'll give Rex some credit – he hung in well. In the end, his experience was no match for my flair and tenacity. If we'd played for another week, I'd probably have won eighty per cent of the frames. As it was, I was pleased to be 30–28 ahead in the final session. He pulled that back to 30–30. It was getting too close for comfort though there was no doubt in my mind who'd be the one to crack. It was a bit like Cassius Clay getting knocked down by Henry Cooper – a nasty surprise, but no real danger! In the deciding frame, Rex missed a vital blue that could have put him in the final, and left me a half a chance. The balls weren't very well set, but I made an important 30 break. I went for the gamble; potted a red, disturbed three others and finished on a colour. Fortune favours the brave! I took what was on and put him in a snooker where he couldn't connect. I left him directly behind a ball on the bottom cushion and that, effectively, was that.

(*Rex Williams:* It was no disappointment to be involved in such a marvellous match. I knew Alex was good, now I realised how good. As for rearranging the date, it was certainly not a case of an established player trying to put one over a newcomer. I was sponsored by Watney Mann at the time and my diary was packed with exhibitions on their behalf.)

Straight after the match I went to the practice table. It was no different from any other night when I'd leave the match arena at 10.30 or 11 pm and practise all the hours that God sent. I was in love with the game, possessed by it almost to the exclusion of everything else. Perhaps I didn't get the financial rewards I deserved, but there was no doubt about my share of the crowd support. When you go to John Spencer's home town and the locals are routing for you, you know you're the 'People's Champion'.

Sounds arrogant, I know, but I was confident that I could beat Spencer. A minor setback the week before the final failed to deter me. In fact, it turned out to be a positive advantage. As chance would have it, Spencer and I met in a sort of dress rehearsal. It was the Park Drive 2000 final played at Radcliffe Town Hall in Lancashire, and it began well enough for me. I was six frames ahead on the final morning when something happened to disturb my concentration. Ted Lowe invited me to appear on Pot Black for the first time, and asked me to meet him in the Piccadilly Hotel, Manchester for a chat. I felt like a salesman going for an interview. A 150-mile round trip from Radcliffe to Accrington (to change into suitable clothing), then to Manchester and back to Radcliffe was the last thing I needed during a snooker final. When Pot Black called, though, you had to go. It was to be my first experience of television and naturally I was pretty keyed up about the whole business. The Piccadilly cocktail bar provided the antidote to nervous tension, but also the seeds of my downfall to Spencer!

When I got back to Radcliffe Town Hall that afternoon, I couldn't pot a ball. From six frames up I went six behind. I was at a real low. Somehow I managed to square the match at 22-all with one frame to play. Spencer asked if I wanted to make the decider the best of three instead. It was a man talking to a boy, but being the headstrong lad, I said: 'One's enough for me, John,' The man was out of his socks, really twitching, but he went and fluked a red, got a 70 break and won the Park Drive final. It didn't matter. I'd learned a vital fact in that showdown – under pressure, the world number one would lose his bottle first. It was Spencer who'd wanted to hedge his bets, me who'd gone for the 'shit or bust' chance. I stored that information in the back of my mind. There was no doubt he was frightened of me. Frightened and trapped because a couple of days later, he'd have to tackle me all over again when the stakes were at their highest.

I wanted them to bill me as 'Alexander the Great' for the final, in the image of my sporting hero, Cassius Clay. That's how cocky I was. The idea of defeat never entered my head. Why should it have? It took Joe Davis nearly three decades to make 500 century breaks in public. I'd already made 580! My manager talked me out of the billing idea and I went up instead as 'Hurricane Higgins'. It didn't seem an impressive alternative. Alexander the Great was a figure in history. A hurricane was only a strong wind.

On the Monday we headed for the Selly Park British Legion just off the Bristol Road in Birmingham. Spencer stayed at the Strathallan Hotel on Hagley Road, one of the best in town in those days. You'd have expected nothing less of the world chanpion. By contrast, I dossed down at the Pebbles Guest House near to the venue. With me, my trusty valet and bodyguard, Bernard. I met him in Blackburn where he used to work as a chef. He was a snooker nut despite his 20 stone and loved nothing better than to watch me playing. (It was infinitely more pleasurable than watching Bernard stretch his ample girth over the baize – what a spectacle!)

Boy was it gloomy! Each day the power cuts plunged everything into blackness. The British Legion had made their contingency plans by setting up a generator in the hall. Before the final was over, we'd be playing in car battery lighting! A little different from today you might say. No television, no sumptuous dressing rooms and sponsors' lounges – just people packed into every corner and the sound of beer mugs jangling in the background. No place for the faint-hearted I can tell you. Tickets were 75p for the evening sessions and 50p for the afternoons.

They cheered for Spencer when he stepped out, but they cheered even louder for me and I knew I had them in the palm of my hand. It was the hustler from Belfast they'd come to see, not the world champion. Although he'd beaten me seven times out of eleven, I was as certain as anyone could be that this was the end of the road for him. During the build-up to the final, I'd bet more than £1,000 on myself to take the title. I wasn't going to slip at the last hurdle.

The opening couple of frames were a bit of a sparring session. by the third, I was potting the balls so fast the referee couldn't re-spot them quickly enough! Spencer could play quickly too and if anything, there was more urgency about his play than mine. I stayed with him without ever actually taking the lead. There was no rush. We finished the first day level but Spencer regained the lead on the second day, winning the first three frames. It was brilliant snooker. Spencer potting balls the length of the table, screwing back, hitting the bottom cushion and getting onto the blue, and me doing the same. It was Spencer at his best, graceful, positive, tactically perfect. He'd have beaten Reardon and Steve Davis at their best because he had all the shots. But he couldn't beat me.

At the end of the second day, I was 13–11 behind and that's the way it continued on the Wednesday. Nip and tuck. Spencer going two or three frames up with me closing the gap but being unable to nail him. I'd be in the practice room until the last moment before each of the sessions. Walking out of there to get changed, I'd hear the bell and the message in the dressing room: 'Five minutes Alex'. In the last frame of the day we had our little disagreement. I snookered Spencer on the last red which was sitting next to the pink. Spencer played an attacking shot and the referee, Jim Thorpe, called foul because the cue ball had hit the pink before striking the red. Spencer was outraged, protesting that he'd hit both simultaneously. I was given a free ball and squared the match at 18-all. Spencer hadn't finished. He went on protesting and complaining well after the frame was over – the sort of behaviour that would have incurred a heavy fine and newspaper headlines if Alex Higgins had been the culprit!

What happened next was unprecedented in snooker. Spencer asked the linesman to assist the referee for the rest of the match. I didn't object. I was a happy-go-lucky kid. I didn't want the linesman particularly, but thought 'What the hell?'. I was getting to Spencer by this time, and that little performance was all the confirmation I needed. He was playing really well, but he was up against this bloke who wouldn't die. Even the best players make mistakes, and that was one of his. If you keep on applying pressure it gets to everyone. (I remembered that lesson from the Park Drive.)

The upshot was that on the Thursday, the breeze grew into a gale and Hurricane Higgins blew his opponent off the table. I started with a 60–52 win in the first frame which gave me the lead at last. That was a major psychological moment. Although Spencer managed to draw level again, I replied with frame scores of 75–29 and 75–11 to go two clear. Still the guy hung on and going into the evening session, we were all square at 21–21. It was the eighth session of the match on that Thursday night before I turned the screw. I won all six frames, knocking in pots from all angles and going for my shots with the confidence of a man who knows his adversary's falling into his web ready for the kill. Yet, if it hadn't been for Bernard, I might not have been in the proper frame of mind for the day's play. As usual, the two of us had been out until 4 o'clock that morning, having a few drinks and losing a few bob in the casino. It didn't bother me. I was young and hyperactive and sleep was well down the list of priorities. Back we came to that miserable little room we shared at the Pebbles – no carpets, no central heating and just about as uncomfortable as you could get. The great advantage was that it was cheap.

At 9 am I was dead to the world and might have carried on slumbering all day. That's where Bernard came in. If you've ever had a 20-stone slap around the face, you'll know it's more effective than any alarm call! I protested that play didn't start until later that day so there was no need to get up yet. Like a faithful servant, Bernard wouldn't take no for an answer, insisting that I get up to practise before the first session of the afternoon. He dragged me down for breakfast. Now when you've been out drinking until the early hours, the sight of bacon, eggs and sausage doesn't exactly inspire you! I pushed the stuff around the edge of my plate and Bernard noticed my lack of appetite. 'If you don't want it, I'll have it,' he said and with that, two helpings of fried breakfast disappeared down his throat like a red scurrying into the top pocket! Revolting. I still managed to be at Selly Park practising for four hours before battle recommenced.

Winning those six frames gave me the foundation for victory. In case I needed any further incentive, a power cut the next morning came right on cue. Poor old John Spencer was trapped in the hotel lift with his wife for half an hour while I was making another century break in the practice room. We'd been plagued with power cuts all week, but this one was to prove especially beneficial. No sooner did Spencer get out from between floors than he pranged his car trying to dash through the streets of Birmingham with all the traffic lights out of order. Visibility in the hall was very poor. I reckon the generator must have been winding down and you had to screw your eyes up to see the balls. I didn't mind the power cuts. I could see better than Spencer!

I proved it by taking the first frame 90–15 on the Friday morning, for a 28–21 lead. If I thought it was over bar the shouting, I had another think coming. Like a great champion, Spencer showed that he was at his most dangerous when his back was against the wall. By the end of the day, my six frame lead was down to four at 32–28 and Spencer was playing out of his skull. This time, the pressure was on me. That night I told Bernard I thought we deserved better surroundings, so we moved out of the Pebbles and into the Strathallan. What a pleasure to have a carpet on the floor and some warmth in the room (when the electricity wasn't cut off!). I was determined to be in the best possible condition for the sixth and final day on the Saturday. Some of the experts had written me off now that Spencer had apparently weathered the storm. But they didn't know me.

Snooker's one of those games in which you can confine your opponent to his seat for long periods and play against yourself. That's virtually what Spencer did after I'd won the first frame of the day. For the following three frames, I hardly got a look in. Spencer took the second with a 123–0 whitewash; the third 76–21, and the fourth 85–42. Suddenly, he was only two frames behind at 33–31. I knew I had to keep my head or perish. In the next two frames, Spencer had good chances to close the gap even further, but I saw a chink of light and it was all I wanted.

The balls weren't in great positions – a couple of colours and a red on the cushions made the job that much more difficult. But I snatched my chance. Bang, bang, bang and it was nearly all over. I took the frames 96–16 and 88–14 to restore my four frame margin. Spencer was broken. As John Pulman pointed out when he presented the trophy; 'You've got to give the lad his due. He didn't see the table for three frames. Spencer had him by the Henrys, but one slight error and

Higgins was in.' Spencer was capable of doing the same. He could punish mistakes in the severest fashion. It's an ability you don't see so much today.

In the final frame, I made my biggest break of the match, 94 and followed it up with 46 to win 140–0. What a way to win the world title! My stomach was churning and I wanted to do a Cassius Clay and shout from the rooftops: 'I'm the greatest'. For once in my life, I bit my lip. When I went to collect the trophy I whispered under my breath: 'You've done it, Alex, you've done it!' The inner satisfaction was enough. Actions had spoken louder than words ever could. 1972 belonged to Hurricane Higgins.

Ten years later, it was wonderful to be able to do it all again, but that victory will always be the sweetest memory. I was the youngest ever world champion and I'd done it at the first time of trying with no traditional apprenticeship. I'd come up the hard way and triumphed. In one fell swoop I'd taken away the 'misspent youth' image because here was the youth and if its years had been misspent, why was it beating the establishment?

I only wish television audiences could have seen the match because it was surely one of the best finals of all time. Viewers would have been spellbound. It was all action, liberally sprinkled with big breaks and played between two men who were going for everything. The control of the cue ball was uncanny by both of us. When it stopped I was waiting for it, just like a bus driver waiting to pick up his passenger. People were amazed that someone as young as me could do these things on a snooker table. Don't forget we were playing with the old style of ball as well. It was as heavy as a rock! Spencer's cue tip was like a knitting needle which proves how good his cue action was. He played with a six-and-a-half millimetre tip as opposed to the ten millimetres of today. Imagine sticking that into a ball and not miscuing!

John Spencer's view:
Alex is right, it was remarkable snooker. Century breaks and quickfire potting all the way. In the evening session, despite the generator going on and off a few times, we played six frames in an hour and a half – and that included the interval. It was so fast the session was over by 9.30 pm and no-one knew what to do with themselves for the rest of the evening. Alex was the same then as he is today,

tremendous ability but lacking the consistency to win as many tournaments as he should have done. He was so unpredictable and the crowds loved him for it. Snooker was very fortunate that he came along when he did. Five years earlier and he might have come and gone without anyone noticing. Thankfully, he arrived just as the game was taking off. He was exactly what it needed.

What pleased me almost as much as the personal victory, was that I had broken into snooker's self-preservation society. There was this elite band of pros who tried to keep the game a closed shop. That's why they imposed the £100 entrance subscription for the world championships – to deter intruders. Fred Davis, Rex Williams, John Pulman, Ray Reardon, John Spencer, Sidney Smith and a few others had had it good for a long time. They were more than happy to go along with the system provided they were on top of it.

The feeling was 'I'm all right, Jack, bugger the others!' Just think how the game could have progressed if they hadn't held it back. I know a lot of players in Ireland who were suppressed when they might have made a good living out of the game. Selly Park British Legion was the beginning of the end of that.

I realised that there was a lot of money to be made at this game, even though my winner's cheque was only £480. It had all happened so fast. I hadn't been a pro for a year, in fact I was still within my trial period when I won the title. It's possible that someone soon will repeat my achievement of reaching the final from the qualifying rounds. Boris Becker did it at Wimbledon and one day the 'Higgins kids' will come along, the seven and eight year olds who took their inspiration from me. Just wait until they blossom.

There was a bit of a celebration with the press after the final but all the hustle and bustle in the British Legion ballroom didn't appeal to me. I spent the rest of the evening tucked away in the phone booth with £5 worth of coins telling the folks back home what I'd done. It was all very low key. When the press did get hold of me, I told them exactly what I believed: 'I want to make history by achieving things I've never done before; I shall be world champion for five or six years then when I'm thirty I'll retire. I'm very good at this game and am going to make a lot of money playing it. That's a fact.' As we know, it didn't work out quite the way I predicted.

5

After the Lord Mayor's Show

When you reach the top, there's only one way to go – down again. That's what happened to the twenty-three year old wonder boy. No management guidance you see: the family hundreds of miles away and, to cap it all, my cherished Burwat Champion cue irreparably broken in the panic stations over a trip to Australia.

Within three months of beating Spencer, I was due back at the British Legion to play a challenge match against John Pulman. Pully had fixed up the month in Australia. He's a shrewd old fox. He knew that getting the world champion there would get him there as well. Fair enough – the money was more than I'd ever earned and for a wide-eyed young chap who'd come out of virtual obscurity, it was a dream come true. Australia – I hadn't set foot outside Britain before!

I was scheduled to play Pulman at 2.30 in Birmingham, but got delayed sorting out my passport for Australia as I clean forgot about it until the last minute. I was naïve and never gave a thought to things like that. I got the passport but I was too late for the train. My old mate Mick Keogh from Accrington came to the rescue by agreeing to drive me to Birmingham in his bashed up Morris Oxford. A lovely fellah, Mick; he lived in a terraced house with four brothers and would do anything for me. My snooker cue travelled in one of those black tin cases – you know, the sort that members of Conservative or Liberal clubs hang on the wall. The locks were broken on my best blue leather case, so the tin was a makeshift solution.

Mick's car broke down on the M6 south of Manchester. I told him to get it fixed and that I'd get to Birmingham somehow. I set off down the motorway on foot hitching a lift. This guy in a juggernaut pulled up. It must have been one of the first on the road in those days. A few miles on I asked him to stop at the service station because he wasn't going fast enough. I said: 'Thanks a lot, pal, but I've got a tight schedule. I'll have to find something with a bit of kick in it.' I walked over to the petrol pumps where a French couple were filling up their Opel Kadet. I told them I'd pay for the petrol if they could just get me to Birmingham. They were nonplussed. I mumbled 'Snooker, you know, billiards' which left them even more confused. Before they knew what had happened, I'd commandeered the car. Twenty miles further on, the heavens opened. You couldn't see 30 yards in front of you, but I was in the back like a charioteer urging the Frenchies on ever faster. We got to Birmingham an hour late for the match. I put the couple up at the Strathallan Hotel at my expense and invited them to come and watch. While I fixed it up, I left my cue at the porter's lodge in its stupid tin case. Pulman sent his friend around in a big Vanden Plas to collect me from the hotel. I sent the cue on ahead and travelled to the Legion with the French couple.

When I took the cue out of the Vanden Plas, the end was hanging off! It was bent two and half inches from the tip. The priceless weapon had fallen down the seat of the car and been caught in the door. The tin case had offered no protection. Every time I hit the ball the cue broke a bit more. I'd had it since I was seventeen at the YMCA. It felt so natural that I couldn't imagine being without it. In those days, I wasn't up to the finer points of carpentery which have enabled me to improvise all sorts of cues. I still managed to beat Pulman with my French chauffeurs looking on, but the cue was finished and I was finished with it. It was like losing an arm or a leg.

I looked everywhere for a replacement cue but ended up with one that was too short and held together with a couple of nails and some plastic padding. That was the world champion for you! Is it any wonder I didn't capitalise on my new status?

Winning the title not only provided me with a passport to Australia but it was my passport to carnal pleasure too! My first coup was before my twenty-fourth birthday when a lovely young thing in a tight tee-shirt literally picked me up. I'd always thought there were two good reasons for a girl to wear a tee-shirt, and Margo was a perfect example! You might not believe this but I was at the airport in Belfast minding my own business when this vision of loveliness ran up and smothered me in kisses. Not being the sort to look a gift horse in the mouth, I welcomed her advances, and when she asked if she could come with me, I offered to pay for her ticket to England. I was heading for a tournament in Birmingham. Margo not only stayed with me for a couple of days – she practically devoured me! Apparently she'd followed my progress from a distance and always wanted to meet me: I was glad she did! I realised that snooker had made me a sex symbol and that I could cash in on my new-found popularity. Women were easy from that day onwards. I was only a skinny little bloke, but I could pull the ladies. It went to my head, but then I'd have had to be a saint not to let it. Snooker had always put a wad of notes in my back pocket and when you're single and twenty-three, what else is there to do but spend it? Card schools, casinos, the horses, champagne – you name it, I was in there. Gambling was in the blood. If I couldn't gamble with money, anything would do.

Kalooki is my favourite card game. Once on a flight to Canada with Del Simmons, my manager, I practically had to twist his arm off to play me. I offered him 50 dollars a game but he didn't want to play for money. I came down to 20 dollars, 10 dollars, still he wasn't biting, so, in desperation, I suggested we played for a pair of shoes. By the time we got off in Toronto, I owed him fifty pairs! I'd have gone out and bought them as well, but Del persuaded me that one would be enough.

It was wine, women and wagers all the time. One night in Portsmouth, I managed to combine all three. After playing a tournament there, I went to the Playboy Club and ordered champagne all round to celebrate my twenty-fifth birthday the next day. The drink was delivered by a Bunny girl called Kim who immediately took my fancy. I slipped a note into her bra top telling her my hotel and room number, hoping that she'd come up and see me some time! She did. I'd been back in my room precisely five minutes when Kim knocked at the door. Another bottle of bubbly and the night was ours.

We got on so well that she packed a bag and came with me to Exeter where I had an exhibition. When I got there, the organisers presented me with a fabulous birthday cake in the shape of a snooker table and lit up by twenty-five candles. Kim watched the play but neither she nor I could wait to get back to the bedroom! We took the cake with us and put it in the wardrobe while we celebrated my birthday in the best way I know! In the heat of the love making, I made the near-fatal mistake of forgetting to ask for an early morning call (I had to be in Manchester the next day).

I was in deep and blissful slumber when my own alarm mechanism went off. I woke up in a blind panic and discovered I had fifteen minutes to make the train. I flung my clothes into a case, dashed

dashed down to pay the bill and flew to the station while Kim was still fast asleep. I had two minutes before the train pulled in so I telephoned the hotel and asked the porter if he would take a message to my room saying: 'Thanks for a lovely time, Kim. Don't forget the cake in the wardrobe. Love, Alex.'

By then, I'd become a regular visitor to Australia. On that first trip with Pulman, we made a three-day stop-over in Singapore to play an exhibition of hexapool. It was played on a six-sided teak table with three pockets and three baulk areas in the remaining corners. Pulman and I played this peculiar game in front of 3,000 excited spectators in the People's Palace – a sort of Harrods Department Store arranged in tiers up to the roof. There were two commentaries going on simultaneously – one in English and one in Mandarin. That was my introduction to the Far East.

Australia became a real playground for me because my hell-raising reputation hadn't caught up with me then. They were good days. Sydney in the seventies was similar to London in the sixties ... a bit behind, but a swinging city full of women, money and massive gamblers. Australians are second only to the Chinese as a nation of gamblers. That suited me down to the ground. I was the boyo out there. In double quick time, I got to know Sydney better than the locals. I used to stand on William Street in the notorious Kings Cross area and hail the yellow cabs – then tell the driver he was going the long way round. 'Listen to me boss, I'm Alex Higgins and I know all the back-doubles.' Most of the drivers were Greek or Italian or Yugoslav and didn't know what time of day it was!

It was like Chicago in the days of prohibition. The discos were the speak-easies if you like. Every other establishment was a casino with its flashing neon sign. They were illegal, but the protection bills had been paid so they operated quite brazenly. It was a corrupt city; the police could be bought off easily. The Australian Godfather was a smartly dressed bloke called Joe Taylor. He'd made his money out of the Yanks who populated Sydney in the fifties when there was a lot of unrest in the Pacific and Japan. We became close friends, but not before I had to crawl on my knees and apologise to him. I used to go to a place of his called Carlisle House, an illegal casino with a snooker table on the top floor. One night I got into a fight with some of the regulars over the handicapping. I called one of the veteran pros a no-hoper and pandemonium broke out. I was screaming and shouting when suddenly a big hand landed on my shoulder and a

59

broad Aussie accent drawled: 'Stop shouting at my boys, sport'. I turned round and snapped: 'Shut up you old bugger!' whereupon I was lifted off my feet by a couple of bouncers built like barndoors, and deposited in the street with a warning never to darken their door again. I asked one of the bouncers who on earth the fellah with the big hand was. 'Don't you know?' came the reply, 'Why, that's Joe Taylor.' I'd heard about him, but didn't realise who it was. I took out a piece of tattered notepaper and sat in the gutter on a balmy Australian evening, writing an apology and requesting one more chance. Fortunately, Joe was magnanimous enough to grant it and we got on like a house on fire after that.

He loved his snooker and regularly came to watch me and have a few dollars on a Higgins victory. One of our favourite haunts was City Tattersall's – a bookmaker's club in Pitt Street. When Joe died in 1980 they put a big sign over his favourite card table. It read: 'This one flew over this cuckoo's nest.' Then, underneath a picture of Joe, it continued: '. . . and they all stared!' I got myself banned from City Tatts in 1985 for causing an affray. If Joe knew that, he'd turn in his grave. Considering the hours of pleasure I've given there, they ought to make me a life member!

I had a few flings out there. One I remember especially well was a gorgeous model called Chanelle who lived in the salubrious Double Bay area of Sydney. Aussie women like to give the impression they're hard and tough, but underneath, they're very sweet. Chanelle was a charmer. You could say I taught her all there was to know. My womanising horns were drawn in however when my pal, Phil Wilson from the *Morning Sun* newspaper arranged a blind date for me with the daughter of a racehorse owner. We arranged to meet in an Italian restaurant. As soon as I saw her, my head was turned. She was very glamorous with an irresistible personality. I bowled the lady with the help of a few Irish coffees after the meal. She also came from Double Bay and gave the impression that the family was fairly well moneyed. They were of German descent and had emigrated in the 1920s. That blind date led to me walking down the aisle at Darling Point Church in Sydney a couple of years later!

Her name was Cara and she was four years older than me. We had some marvellous times together at the clubs and at the races. As in most of my relationships, there were plenty of ups and downs. One of the downs was rather expensive. I'd won over twenty thousand dollars at the races – my biggest ever scoop mentioned earlier in the book. I kept six thousand dollars in my pocket for spending money, gave Cara two thousand for an air ticket to England and told her to look after the rest for me. We had a blazing row and she kept the money. I didn't pursue it.

I'd spend up to six months at a time in Australia then go back to England where Cara and I shared a flat that used to belong to the Manchester United goalkeeper, Alex Stepney. It was a long-distance international affair and I was quite happy to swing along. Eventually, I was back in Australia for a tournament in 1974 and Cara talked me into marriage. It was *all* she talked about that trip. She was forever wanting to make the arrangements and asking me if she should go ahead. I got carried along with it all and finally relented. I hadn't got the heart to 'do a runner' so the wild man of snooker had to admit that he was well and truly tamed. Cara's family arranged a big white wedding and a dozen or so Aussie jockeys came along to form an arcade when we came out of the church. Ray Reardon was there too. I think he came to gloat! My best man was Peter Wake, 'the mathematician' as we used to call him. He was the brains behind the betting syndicate called the Legal Eagles – a group of lawyers who would net hundreds of thousands of dollars on a regular basis.

The wedding night was hilarious. After the reception, we were due to go on honeymoon to the Barrier Reef, but I suggested to Cara that we call in at the Sebel Town House hotel near Rushcutters Bay where The Who pop group were having a reception for the launch of their musical, 'Tommy'. Roger Daltrey and all the boys were there; the champagne was flowing and the hotel was decked out in pinball machines. It was going to be a quick drink, but by the early hours, Cara and I were still going strong, she in her wedding dress still, and me in my tuxedo! The honeymoon had to wait until the following day.

We didn't have a very successful marriage, but we've stayed close friends to this day. The simple truth is that I wasn't ready for settling down and having a family. Cara tried to domesticate me, but found, like a few others since that it's a pretty hopeless task! We were always travelling backwards and forwards across the globe which led to the inevitable rows and tears. The marriage dragged on for three years, but I brought it to a swift conclusion when I met Lynn. It had been a mistake, but no one got hurt.

Controversy seemed to stalk me in Australia. I was having a great time with another of my Aussie girlfriends, Susan Bessell-Brown a top hotel receptionist. She was with me in Perth where I'd been playing a money match. Peter Wake had made the two thousand mile journey from Sydney just to watch me play, and the little group was completed by an Australian jockey friend called J. J. Miller. Now he was a tough nut! He was the sort of rider who'd do anything to win or stop anyone else winning. Old J.J. would virtually put another jockey over the rails as soon a look at him. We'd gathered at the Sheraston Hotel after the match and were enjoying a floor show. I wasn't the drink connoisseur then that I am today, so I plumped for Mateus Rosé. I didn't get beyond pouring myself a glass. As I was about to take a sip, all hell was let loose on the adjoining table.

It was occupied by an Aussie rules football team. They'd had a few cans of whatever and were getting a little boisterous. Suddenly one of their blokes – about the size of a double decker bus – leapt onto the table and started dancing. He wasn't too light on his feet this monster. Before his dance routine had progressed very far, the bloke went spinning off the table into ours with bottles, glasses and chairs flying all directions. It was as if a cyclone had hit us! I knew when to keep quiet and the size of those blokes told me this was one of them! Poor J.J. had less self-control. He's only knee-high to a grasshopper but he pointed at the football team and bellowed: 'Step over here you lot!' I wish he hadn't!

I'd never seen one bloke take on a rugby team before and I'm not certain I ever want to see it again. J.J. was virtually torn limb from limb by those jerks. The entire floor degenerated into a pitched battle – the sort you see in those bad western movies. For once in my life, I kept right out of it and swore there and then that I'd be meticulous in future about choosing my fight opponents! The only thing which stopped us being thrown out was J.J. himself. He was vice president of the football club!

Next stop on my pretty way home from Sydney to England was India. I was scheduled to appear in the Bombay gymkhana. After the experience which awaited me, let me say I don't care if I never set foot on Indian soil again. If they had a five million pound tournament in Bombay and invited me, I'd insist they send Bombay to England! It was the most disgusting hole it's ever been my privilege to fall into.

At the airport, I was met by four blokes in a weird contraption called an Ambassador. It was the only car they had out there apparently and looked like a Mini with an enlarged roof. It was five o'clock in the morning and there I was crushed in the back of this less-than-fragrant vehicle. The journey was like something out of 'Popeye' – we chugged down dusty roads at twenty miles an hour with tumbleweeds blowing past the windows until we arrived at the Nataraj Hotel. A splendid establishment the Nataraj! Cripples and beggars sleeping in the foyer; cockroaches crawling up the wall of my bedroom! The room looked as comfortable as a hospital ward. One of the kids who did the portering hung around in the room so I gave him one of my shirts. The little brat was in my room every five minutes after that, offering to fetch this and that.

Wilson Jones, the world amateur billiards champion was there and I invited him into my room to witness the biggest cockroach I'd ever seen. It was as big as your fist. I said: 'Will you just look at that Wilson!' The size of the thing must have slowed it down. It must have been the most pedestrian cockroach in the world. If I'd have been one, I wouldn't have wanted people stamping all over me! It was no contest. The Indian lads jumped on it from a great height. One dead – how many more to come? I took all the precautions and I whipped off the bed cover – I couldn't stand anything near my face which might act as a climbing frame for insects. What a night! I woke up every few minutes just to check there wasn't some other insidious creature creeping up on me! That was my preparation for an exhibition match the next day. It was to be the first day of a short tour of the sub-continent. It turned out to be the last as well.

I'd agreed to do the organisers a favour by appearing on an expenses-only deal. I was told it was a poor country, so not to expect a fat purse. The attraction was that the Indians were partial to offering presents instead of cash. Sounded okay. I played the Indian champion on a dreadful table. With my first hit I made a 109 break which, under the circumstances, wasn't bad going. One bright spark then offered several thousand rupees for a hundred break. I said: 'But I've just made one! What's the point of me coming all the way out here gratis for you to offer prizes after the event?' That did it for me. The temperature in there was way over a hundred so I stripped off my shirt, knowing it would upset them. They were beside themselves with indignation. It seems that if you display a little flesh over there, you're not one of the good boys. They'd rather you melt instead. I haven't much of a chest at the best of times, so I don't know what they were worried about!

I'd played five frames before I saw the colour of anyone's money. I was knackered, with sweat dripping out of every pore when this millionaire called R. K. Fasanjay walked across and offered me the night's star prize. It was a little tin cup! The bloke had made a fortune out of a local flourmill. I told him where he could stick his sanctimonious offering. I admit I'd had a few drinks, but the official version that I 'offended members by drinking, insulting the organisers and taking off my shirt' has to be put into perspective. According to reports, the Indian authorities 'put me on the next plane'. The truth was that I made my own way to the airport and was more than happy to get out.

I got to Bombay airport just in time to meet a girlfriend who thought she was coming to spend a few days with me. The girl was a well-known equestrian at one time and worked at a very famous London nightclub called Churchills. I'd arranged for a pal to get her an airline ticket to fly to India and meet me. I met her all right – on the tarmac. I said: 'Babe it's good to see you. We're leaving on the next flight!' It cost me £350 for the privilege of getting back onto the plane with her.

My dress sense upset a few other people too. Namely, the WPBSA who fined me £100 for wearing that green suit. Maybe it was a bit over the top. It annoys me when I get criticised for my dress sense. I think I've got more of that than most but down the years, the Association has complained about braces; open waistcoats; a fedora hat I once used; and last but not least, an open-necked shirt. They want me to look like a tailor's dummy, but I've got more flair than that. I think I have the best clothes in the game. I get them from Lewis Copeland, a top class Dublin tailors which has been established for 110 years. I love dressing up for the right occasion. Shoes are my particular pride and joy. I have more than sixty pairs at home. I believe that it's my business what I wear, no one else's. I must have freedom of movement to play my shots. I'm a sportsman, not a male model.

The business of the open-necked shirts was eventually resolved, but not without a lot of huffing and puffing. Right from the early seventies I'd been troubled by a rash under the chin. The lights seemed to make it worse. I mentioned it to my family GP, a Dr Burgess. He was sympathetic and diagnosed it as *psychosis barbae*, an irritation usually suffered by violinists and by no means an uncommon ailment. He gave me a doctor's note to say that I should be excused from wearing a tie or bow tie. That was okay with the WPBSA for a while until the kids began copying my practice of removing the bow tie. When I say kids, I mean the youngsters just joining the professional ranks. For a time I obeyed the powers that be and reinstated the bow tie for the sake of the sponsors. It was causing me endless discomfort but the Association decided that my doctor's certificate was no longer sufficient to excuse me. They insisted I went to see an independent GP to be nominated by them.

I had to waste a day catching a train from Manchester to West Bromwich where the WPBSA chairman, Rex Williams had arranged for me to see his man. Before going in, I looked up at the plaque on the wall and did a double-take. It said 'Dr Burgess'. He agreed with his namesake. Just for devilment, I handed in the original note from my own Dr Burgess and it was accepted. Don't get me wrong, I think a three-piece suit and bow tie is very smart, but I'd like to see the style more casual now. Still smart, but more comfortable, in line with contemporary fashion.

The Association got to hear a lot about me in those days. I was reported for demanding a stop to an exhibition match with John Spencer at a club in Hartlepool. There was no light over the table and you had to fumble your way around with the help of four arc lights aimed at the centre of the room from the four corners; hopeless. The shadows on the cushions were several inches deep. If I'd wanted a game of blind man's buff it would have been ideal. I complained several times to the promoter but he did nothing to improve matters so I conceded and walked out after being fouled in the eighth frame.

Spencer told me not to be a prima donna. He said the show must go on. I told him he must be mad to play in those conditions and we had a blazing row in front of everyone. If they hadn't held us apart, we'd have come to blows. I turned to the promoter and said: 'You're an arsehole to put on a thing like this.' I apologised the next day, but the damage had been done.

The spectators were hissing and booing because I refused to carry on. Then I remembered the world championship in the power cuts at Selly Park. It had been Spencer doing all the moaning there and I went on to beat him. Eventually, I came around to his view that the show should go on if the audience wanted it. It went on. I beat Spencer virtually with a white stick!

My short fuse landed me in hot water yet again at Ilfracombe. It was a testing time for me because I'd stopped smoking six months before. I'd become a chainsmoker and decided it had to stop. It was the Errol Flynn syndrome. I'd be playing like an idiot, lighting up; having three or four puffs then throwing it away and stamping on it saying to myself; 'Come on Higgins, that's not the answer.' I was uptight about one thing and another when this bloke in the audience thought he could impress his mates by baiting Higgins. I turned the other cheek once, twice, three times but the fool kept on taunting me about my wild man reputation and boasting that he'd take me on anywhere. If I'd had any sense I'd have given him enough rope and let him hang himself. Instead I rose to the bait and flung my cue at the bloke. It was a stupid thing to do because it could have damaged the cue! He'd achieved what he set to achieve and must have been rubbing his hands with glee when they frogmarched me out of the room.

Soon after that, I forgot the lesson I'd learned seeing J. J. Miller dismembered in that Australian hotel. I was in Montreal this time, enjoying myself in a downtown disco when this buck negro who stood nearly seven feet tall was giving me some hassle. He was trying to move in on the girl I was dancing with so I warned him to back off or I'd give him a knuckle sandwich, as big as he was. Lucky for me, Del Simmons was watching developments. He intervened and probably saved my life. 'Leave off Alex' said Del. When the black guy heard that, a big grin split his face. He said: 'Alex? Is his name Alex? Well whadayaknow, so's mine. Put it there, pal.' He held out his hand, I shook it and the next thing we had our arms around each other. Del nearly fainted with relief. He thought it was a miracle because a moment later the fellah would have pulverised me.

I must be a magnet for nutcases. One night I was playing in a northern club when another fracas broke out. This bloke walked up as cool as you like and walloped me right in the eye. I should have seen it coming, but I guess if I'm guilty of anything it's not always sensing how angry people can get when I insult them. It developed into a full-scale contest, feet, fists, they were all going in. I was in bad shape, but you should have seen the other fellah. Fighting with one eye shut isn't easy and I took more punishment than was good for me. It put me into hospital overnight when I should have been practising to meet Ray Reardon at the City Hall, Sheffield next day.

True to my reputation, I refused to cancel the match. The astonished gathering saw me appear wearing an eye patch with a hole cut in it! I've never been afraid to face the music, whatever I look like. Trouble was I couldn't get rid of the double vision. One Reardon is enough to handle, but two of them ...! I'd put in a few hours practice that morning after been discharged from hospital, but however I adjusted the eye patch, it did no good. I thought of strapping one of my arms across my chest and being introduced as Horatio Higgins! Then I'd have gone over to the ex-policeman and said: 'Kiss me, Reardon!' In the middle of the match, I dispensed with the patch altogether but still managed to give Ray a good tanning. Perhaps there's a moral there somewhere.

One way or another, I wasn't in the best of shape to defend my world title in 1973. I'd burned the candle at both ends and in the middle; I'd discovered the demon drink and I'd had my nerve ends shattered by a hundred-mile-an-hour lifestyle. Call it stress if you like, but I'd even succumbed in my battle against the weed. I was back on them before the championships came around. My second round match was against Pat Houliban at the Manchester Exhibition Hall, but it got off to a terrible start. I was twenty minutes late for the evening session after getting stuck in traffic. I didn't drive of course, so I was never master of my own destiny and had to rely on the kindness of friends, or the fickleness of taxi drivers to get me from one end of the city to another. On top of that, I enraged the organisers by turning out in white Oxford bags which were strictly taboo. It was evening dress or nothing. The delay and the bags cost another £100 fine by the WPBSA and a ticking off from the tournament organiser. Earlier in the day, I'd wound myself up into a frenzy because the championship programme showed my face plastered all over a cigarette advert. If they'd known the nerve-shattering campaign I'd been waging against nicotine, they'd have understood that it was a sore point.

So, once again, Higgins had to perform with the crowd jeering and several 'headmasters' wagging their fingers at him. I thought the best way to stuff them all was on the table. I made a quickfire 70 break in one of the early frames of the session and the audience was back on my side. They were eating out of my hand by the finish with Houlihan thrashed 16–3.

That took me into the quarter-final where the sexagenarian, Fred Davis gave me a hell of a contest. He could still play a bit could Fred and I was happy to shade him 16–14. There was some very good snooker, but the only thing people will remember that match for is the type of interruption you usually find only on a cricket field: 'Rain stopped play'! What happened was the roof at the exhibition hall sprung a leak and the rainwater plopped onto Fred's specs then bounced onto the green baize!

Steady Eddie Charlton stopped me going all the way to the final for the second successive year, beating me 23–9 in the semi. I was a shambles in that match. Eddie is an unexciting player, but he keeps coming at you. With my patched up cue I was no match for the Australian champion and my title defence fizzled out. During that period, I got to learn quite a bit about Charlton from my visits to his homeland.

The fact that the Aussies had hardly heard of me was down to Eddie. He'd brainwashed them all. They thought *he* was world champion. In fact he's never won a major title outside Australia. If you read his book you'd be excused for thinking he was king of the world! The Australian Snooker Association *was* Eddie Charlton. He held the Australian national title for about a hundred years until John Campbell got a look in last year. And he was thirty-two when he finally displaced Charlton. Warren King is almost the same age. There aren't any young ones coming through. It's a great shame because the scene was set in the mid-seventies for a revolution in Australian snooker. The facilities were out of this world; big clubs like Merrickville Sydney Suburbs and many others with all the modern equipment and money rolling in from the gaming machines. Audiences were big and enthusiastic. Tournaments weren't as well organised as in Britain, but at least you were out there in front of living, breathing spectators who gave the place bags of atmosphere. I enjoyed it. Two or three years later, they spoiled it by moving the big tournaments into televison studios with a studio audience of two to three hundred and prompted applause – like Pot Black all over again. That didn't work. It was organised by your man Charlton who seemed to miss the whole point. Snooker would have taken off if he'd had the foresight. The only tournament that I think was of any note for young pros was the South Pacific sponsored by the Japanese. The winner received a thousand dollars and two airline tickets to Europe for six months. They did the sightseeing bit, but the highlight was the visit to Sheffield to see the world championships. Most of those guys could only stand and stare.

I was upset by a remark of John Pulman's after my semi-final defeat by Charlton. He said he was glad I lost because I'd dragged the game down. Dragged it down? It was me who turned snooker into a craze. Its full potential wasn't to be realised for a further three years. Pully and I have an on-off relationship. I surprised him once when we were playing at a centenary celebration for the Conservative

Club at York. I played Charlton the first night and Pulman was due to meet Cliff Thorburn the next night. I found out that it was his birthday the following day and ordered a cake for him with the message: 'Happy Birthday, John, love Alex.' I said nothing but made sure he received it before his match. He was amazed that I even knew.

I made up for that gesture by chipping a bone in his knuckle! We were at the Ship Inn in Weybridge when I accepted Pulman's challenge to a game of spoof. Now Pully has quite a reputation at spoof. I don't think anyone's got the better of him. Being unable to resist a challenge, I took him on. The old dodger was taking tenner after tenner off me. I became a little agitated. Pulman pointed a finger at me and warned me to behave or stop playing. I grabbed his finger but wrenched it too hard, chipping the bone. A few days later, he was playing for England against the Rest of the World in a tournament sponsored by Ladbrokes. He had to perform with two fingers strapped together but it didn't seem to hamper him. On the contrary, he made the biggest break of the contest, won the man of the match award and was the only player not to lose a frame. I must stop doing him favours.

It was twenty months after failing to retain my world title that I next won a major tournament. The prize money for the Watneys Open was only £1,000 but I was happy enough to have another success under my belt after so much failure. For two years I'd had the feeling everything was turning against me. It was reassuring to say the least to get back on top. My victims on the way were Williams, Reardon and Fred Davis. I was re-emerging from the ashes.

Before that came the shambles of the 1974 world championships when I reached the quarter-finals by beating Bernard Bennett 15–4. Fred Davis was my opponent in the last eight. He won 15–4 but it was a sour-tempered match because of a piece of dreadful refereeing. Having been 13–9 up, I was pulled back to 13–11 by Davis who, at sixty-one was recovering from his second heart attack. In the twenty-fifth frame, Thorpe called me for a push stroke in the middle of what promised to be a frame-winning break. I was on a simple blue next and decided against using the rest. I have a pretty good reach so I hit the cue ball with plenty of side and watched it finish exactly where I wanted, neatly bisecting the yellow and the brown and landing perfectly for the last five reds. The referee ruled that the white had been too close to the blue in the first place. In his view the gap between them was no more than a sixteenth of an inch. To me, and to most people in a position to judge, it was more like an inch and a half. If

I'd potted the blue which I could have done, I don't suppose the referee would have uttered a murmur of protest. As it was he called foul and awarded Fred five points.

Fred knew he was wrong. He pulled away from the table and stood his ground for a long time implying that the referee had made a mistake. Needless to say, I was less diplomatic and protested long and hard, appealing to the referee to change his mind. He wouldn't, I suppose the thought of backing down in front of all those people was too much for him.

Every other player I spoke to after the match agreed that it was a fair stroke and I'd been robbed of a possible place in the semi-finals. I allowed that incident to disrupt my concentration and although I got back to lead 14–12, my mind had gone and Davis sensed it. He took the next three frames to go through. Once more the whizz-kid had been blown out through no fault of his own. The sad thing from my point of view was that I'd fallen over backwards to mend my ways and lose the wild man image for this championship. I might as well not have bothered.

The next year, 1975 was little better. That was the year the WPBSA decided to hold the world championships in Australia. The venue was Canberra Working Men's Club – another of Charlton's ideas. He said he was promoting the event to boost Australian snooker. It boosted him. He was in the easy half of the draw with the world's top three players, Spencer, Reardon and myself all in the other. I made it as far as the semi-finals again with victories over David Taylor and Rex Williams, but Reardon stopped me getting to the final – Reardon and my confounded tips. During the match I cracked five of them. You can't overcome bad luck like that. Charlton was denied his big moment when Reardon beat him in the final in front of his fellow countrymen.

That was no consolation to me though. Three years had gone by and I'd slipped further and further down. I didn't have any doubts about my ability. The problem was getting myself into so many scrapes because of my erratic temperament. I couldn't give snooker the attention it demanded. By my very nature I would never achieve a great level of consistency. It's my appeal and my downfall rolled into one.

6
Come the Revolution

Pot Black is dead and buried and that's the best thing that could happen to it! I had a running battle with the BBC programme. It was the forerunner of the television revolution in snooker, but it was always a second rate affair, controlled by a select group who didn't want their peace disturbed. You can imagine how suited I was to a cosy arrangement like that! I was the one who peed in the changing room sink at Pebble Mill because the toilets were too far away. It's all the respect the show deserved.

As a youngster I was overawed by Pot Black because it was the only place you got to see the stars. As soon as I became involved in the early seventies I thought: 'Jesus Christ what is this thing?' Each year at the most inconvenient time between Christmas and the New Year, they rounded us up like cattle and drove us down to the Birmingham studios. It was the worst thing you could put a player through. For one thing, his mind was on other things during that week; and for another, he was treated unbelievably shabbily. After lunch they stuck us in the studio for seven hours to play one frame. It was like playing in a greenhouse. I felt sorry for the studio audience trying to stay awake in that heat. Did I say studio audience? I got the impression that half of them had been exhumed to fill the seats. There was more atmosphere on the moon!

I could perhaps have put up with that if they'd given us a half-decent table to play on. Instead they imported this contraption which might have fetched a few bob at an antique auction. I'd have felt more comfortable playing on the floor! When I first played Pot Black, the pay was £300 for three boring days work. Even at the end, it hadn't risen above £1,500. Diabolical. There was no cash prize for the winner. In its death throes, they instituted a round-robin with a silver salver

71

for the champion. It failed to give the show the kiss of life they were hoping for. With so much real snooker on television, Pot Black had become an anachronism. The mystery was how it managed to hang on for so long. Viewing figures were dreadful. Yet before the revolution the show enjoyed a reputation it didn't deserve because it was the sum total of snooker on the box. People were deceived by it. They used to think the winner of Pot Black was the world champion.

It's been a good little earner for whispering Ted Lowe. I don't think he ever liked me much. Perhaps I wasn't establishment enough. At any rate I got the cold shoulder treatment in 1977 when I was left off the guest list for both the Pot Black and the Pontins Open. Coming after my first round knockout at the hands of Doug Mountjoy in the world championships that year, it was bad news. My form was good, but the luck wasn't with me. It looked like a long hot summer of discontent in store until my new girlfriend, Lynn suggested I enter the Open as a non-invited professional. She was no fool Lynn. The drawback was that I would have to battle through from the qualifying stages with 863 other hopefuls. *Infra dignitatem* for a former world champion you might think, but a perfect chance for me to cock a snook at Ted and the boys.

Down there in Group 14, buried among the also-rans was Higgins (A.) It wasn't an easy passage through to the final stages. I had real scares against three amateurs: Billy Kelly, Murdo McLeod and Doug French. I'd have liked to see Joe Davis or John Pulman forced to take on all-comers. Once Pontins let me downstairs onto the good tables, I was unstoppable. I thrashed Reardon and Fred Davis 4–0 to reach the final. I was spitting fire – determined to prove the organisers wrong not to invite me. Terry Griffiths was my final opponent – a shy young lad from the valleys who won the first two frames. He perished 7–5 and what do you know, the uninvited Higgins (A.) was Pontins Open champion. What I could have said when they presented the awards! Discretion got the better of me. I'd spoken volumes with my cue.

The crowd started chanting: 'What about Pot Black?' Lo and behold, I was soon back in the fold. They must have dreaded my return to Pebble Mill studios. I was always complaining about the poor facilities and threatening to walk out. Once I failed to turn up for the prize giving and had another temporary ban slapped on me. Their problem was that by banning me, they reduced their hopes of getting anyone to watch.

I could never understand why the producers of Pot Black allowed themselves to be upstaged by Nick Hunter, the network snooker producer for the BBC. The epitaph for the programme should be: 'It never moved with the times.' While Ted Lowe, Jim Dumighan and Reg Perrin sat back and relaxed, Nick saw the massive potential and moved in; I was very pleased for him. The game is purpose-built for colour television – it's the only sport which is. Mind you, Ted seemed to think colour had arrived in everyone's home long before it did. I remember his classic faux pas. 'For those of you watching in black and white, the brown is on the green spot!' Nick Hunter quickly showed that he had a deep love of snooker in the same way that he does with cricket. He loves the characters in it and he's enhanced the game by showing the emotion and the strain on the individuals that no one else had thought to capture.

I don't particularly want eight million people watching me bite my fingers. I've done it for years and I'm not proud of it. It's one of the concessions we have to make to television. It intrudes everywhere, exposing the snooker player's innermost emotions, and his unpleasant habits. I've been accused of being a bad influence on kids because of the cigarettes I smoke and the lager I drink. I'm also moaned at for continually hopping around in my seat. I've got news for the viewers – I'm not hopping about, I'm trying to see around the referee's backside. I never take my eyes off the game. I play every shot with the guy at the table, waiting for my turn to pounce.

Snooker, for all the production expertise, would not have made it on television if it hadn't been for me. Without Hurricane excitement, the game would have gone its own mundane way. That's not bombast or big-headedness. It happens to be true. No one would have queued to see Reardon or Spencer. I don't get enough credit for putting snooker on the map but it doesn't bother me now. If people had given less prominence to my off-the-table antics and realised what an ambassador I've been for the game, they'd have had things in proportion. I've been a passport for the uninitiated. They've grown to love my style and grown to love snooker through me. I don't know any other sport which has cast off its dowdy image and opened up to the youngsters in quite the same way. Golf is the only possible comparison.

Perversely, the revolution came a little late for me. I'd love to be a twenty-two year old again in the middle of the boom period in front of all those cameras. I can't think of a better way for anyone to show their worth than performing in front of millions of viewers and receiving mass acknowledgement of their talent. In 1978, when the BBC started giving big coverage to the sport, I was already thirty. An old thirty as well. My hustling days had seen to that. If it had fallen for me the way it fell for Steve Davis and the rest, life would have been far more manageable. There are so many tournaments now that exhibitions aren't so vital. My livelihood, as I've said before, depended on the one night stands. In a sense, playing on television has robbed me of a lot of those exhibitions. Because of the economic climate, the working classes can't afford big admission prices. When they can see the stars on the box why should they? Television has benefited most players with its bigger purses, but for someone like me whose world revolved around the working men's clubs, it's had its drawbacks. On balance, TV has widened peoples' horizons. It might raise the odd titter, but I genuinely want snooker to lose its misspent youth image and become as honourable as golf or cricket.

In the late seventies, when television was new, I was very conscious of the cameramen. They seemed to be sitting on top of you. There was some initial stage fright but I soon conquered that. Others haven't been so fortunate. Poor old Murdo McLeod for instance has never won a televised match. Until this year, Joe Johnson had problems with cameras. Now he's cracked it, I wonder how many more will come out of the woodwork? I have never deliberately played up to the TV audience, because I'm not really aware of it. I'm aware of the live audience in the hall. I don't give a thought to six or seven millions sitting in their armchairs. I play to the living not the dead! It's surprising what a comfort the cue is. In any other circumstances I'd be overawed in front of so many people. With a cue in my hand, I don't care how many millions are following my moves. It's a weapon and a crutch to me.

The stage was set for the 1978 world championships. We didn't know how popular it would be on screen but we had a pretty good idea. There was a new venue, the Crucible in Sheffield where the event's been ever since, and daily coverage right up to the final with its £10,000 first prize. What did Higgins do? Lose in the first round that's what! My vanquisher was none other than Patsy Fagan who did me 13–12 only a few days after I'd murdered him while defending my Irish Professional title. It was unaccountable that I should lose to Patsy but I think I must have fallen into the old trap of underestimating an opponent. The tension at the end of that match would have been enough to power a small town! I led 12–10 but Patsy battled back and the crowd were chewing their fingers down to the elbows. They made a deafening noise. Once or twice the referee had to calm them down. When I lost, a young fan of mine called Tony Metcalf who suffered from a serious illness actually fainted with the shock of seeing his hero beaten. The disappointing thing is that I'd been in good form that season. I'd beaten Dennis Taylor 21–7 in my first defence of the Irish title, and collected £3,000 for winning the Benson and Hedges championship with a 7–5 win over Cliff Thorburn. My first chance of reaching a truly national audience at Sheffield and I blew it!

My dear old pal Eddie Charlton(!) saw fit to arrange the World Matchplay championships in Melbourne that year, I was the only one of the thirteen top ranking players not invited. I've made my feelings about Steady Eddie plain. I had lots of very good friends in Australia who thought it was diabolical that I was effectively banned from the place. I don't deny that some of my behaviour over there has been a little rowdy at times, but how many Australians do you know who are shrinking violets? Because I told some club official to 'bugger off' when he tried to force me to wear a necktie, I was now paying the penalty. My fellow pros on the WPBSA stayed deadly quiet when I hoped they might speak out in my defence, so I had no choice but to sit it out. The event was a catastrophe anyway. It couldn't have happened to a nicer fellah!

The fights continued. One of the best was against my old mate Graham Miles who beat me to the £500 winner's prize at a tournament at the Double Diamond Club in Caerphilly. He'd had the run of the balls and I couldn't resist baiting him as the cheque was presented. I said: 'Graham, you're a jammy bald bugger!' He took a swing at me and sent me tumbling into the crowd. He missed but I'd overbalanced. I got my revenge in the dressing room. They had to send a couple of bouncers to pull us apart. Each of us was fined £200. It didn't stop there though. There must have been something about the Welsh air because we were in Pwllheli this time. I can't remember what started it but Graham and I were knocking the shangri la out of each other at this seedy hotel we were staying in. Later that night, I burst into the room which he was sharing with Dennis Taylor. I must have been a fearsome sight standing there in my underpants! I warned Graham that if he stepped out of line again, I'd have him. He must have been sh-- scared because as I left the room, he dragged a big old wardrobe across the door and tried to bribe Dennis to switch beds. Dennis told him to go forth and multiply. Next day, Dennis came out of the dressing room for his match with a towel wrapped around him like a boxer entering the ring. The crowd loved it.

I got into some fierce drinking sessions too, but nothing could beat my night at Oliver Reed's. Ollie and I had a mutual friend in Dessie Cavanagh, a former jump jockey who ran a taxi business in Dorking. Ollie wanted to meet the Hurricane probably to see which of us could drink the other under the table. He sent Dessie to pick me up. Ollie looked a bit the worse for wear. I think he was into the fifth day of a binge. I stood there like a lemon. Hands by my side not knowing what to expect. He focused his bleary eyes on me and said: 'Hurricane you're a pig!' That was a good start. I was shitting myself and thinking what an insulting bastard he was when he disappeared briefly and came back brandishing a bottle of whisky. 'If you're going to play,' he said, 'You'll need a drink.' With that he hurled the bottle at me. He strode over with a pint pot and told me to half fill it with whisky. Then he bellowed: 'Drink, Hurricane!' Well, I may be a bit of a high roller myself but half a pint of whisky was pushing it a wee bit. Then the games began. First it was table tennis for £20. I won. Next we had the tour of the baronial mansion. It was like a mediaeval castle. Only a handful of the rooms had been decorated.

In the middle of the snooker room stood an oak tree! He told me he couldn't get it moved when he had the extension done, so he built the snooker room around it. I won the snooker competition too. The drink carried on flowing as we made our way upstairs to the attic disco. It was decked out like the real thing with little alcoves and concealed lighting. Ollie ordered Dessie and his wife Sue to be the judges while we embarked on the next stage of the Pentathlon – disco dancing! I told Sue that whatever happened, I was to get ten out of ten. They did me proud. I wondered what was next. I might have known – arm wrestling. The Hurricane had no chance. He's a big strong fellah Ollie and he did me in seconds. It was a bit like that famous fight scene from 'Women in Love' except we were both fully dressed. Ollie seemed to be thoroughly enjoying his evening's entertainment.

He took me to a musty little room hung with hundreds of cobwebs and thick with grime and rubbish. It stank. He pointed to a skeleton on the wall and said: 'See that, Hurricane, you pig? – that's my grandmother. I dug her up!' I didn't know whether to take him seriously or not. While I was still reeling from that, he produced the filthiest glass you've ever seen and plonked it in the middle of a rickety old table. It had blue mould up to half way. 'All my friends have a drink out of this,' he explained, 'so here goes, pig.' I don't know what the hell he poured into it, I think it might have been gin though I wasn't in a fit state to tell. The glass obviously hadn't been cleaned for years. I could see that much. Thankfully, he changed his mind and offered it to Sue saying: 'Ladies first.' Poor girl was having kittens but Ollie's not a chap to argue with so down the hatch it went. I saw her face screw up and closed my eyes when my turn came. It was like dishwater but with a hell of a kick!

By now it was six o'clock in the morning and Ollie decided it was time to end the party. Somehow, I don't know how, he drove us the mile and a half down his private road in Dessie's taxi. We all got out and the next thing I knew, Ollie had tucked his feet under the top rung of a five-bar gate so he wouldn't fall over and he was saluting us with a bottle of light ale in each hand! Dessie said: 'He does this for all his friends. You're very privileged.' I've met the man a couple of times since and his new teenage bride. She's a lovely lady. I bet he doesn't put her through that ordeal!

Taxis and taxi drivers were my constant companions. So were British Rail guards. Travelling from pillar to post to fill engagements taught me the train timetables by heart. Ask me any of the connections and times for virtually any major town in Britain and I could have told you. I hated the travel. I've stood many times on a dingy railway station in the middle of nowhere, cold, wet, tired and hungry wondering what the hell I was doing. People may think it's a glamorous life being a top snooker pro, but it isn't. What's glamorous about arranging a journey from one end of the country to the other, planning to arrive at two or three o'clock in the morning, and trying to organise a takeaway curry and a couple of cans of beer for the train? I'll tell you – nothing. Unlike people with an entourage, I was forced to be a lone traveller at the mercy of the rest of the passengers. When I was younger I used to travel second class because I'd go at odd times when the trains were almost empty. As I got older the interruptions drove me insane. It didn't matter whether I booked first or second, people didn't respect my privacy. Being a television face in the late seventies didn't help. I developed a phobia about being recognised. Some people are polite but others see it as their moment of glory if I sit down in the same carriage. I'd get some bruiser walking up to my seat and trying to engage me in conversation. If I didn't reply, I'd be called a bastard then all hell would break loose. Often I've had to get up and leave a compartment because of verbal intimidation. You can't tell the guard when he's the other end of the train. You feel like an exhibit, a zoo animal. Being pointed at is all very well, but let anyone try it for six months and tell me he doesn't lose his patience. Sometimes it was like schooldays. I'd be reading the paper and minding my own business when some bright spark would shout: 'Higgins, come here!' My blood turned cold. You couldn't ignore the idiot. Everyone else in the carriage would stop what they were doing and wait for a response from me.

I've got quick eyes so I can spot the gawpers early. They think you don't realise you're being stared at or whispered about behind your back, but it's obvious when you're used to it. Even the well-intentioned ones get you down; asking how you got on in such and such a tournament and what happened in the match against Steve Davis etc. What they don't understand is that you've told it a million times and you just want to be left alone. Lynn used to say I should make a cassette so passengers could take it away and listen to it. She used to come with me on some of those train journeys and found out for herself what it was like. No wonder I get tense and wound up. From that it's a short trip to aggression. I was never sure whether the person walking up to me wanted my autograph or to smack me in the face. It has happened. No other professional sportsman has had to come into contact with the public as much as I did in those days. You wouldn't catch Davis on a train. I always tried to find a train with separate compartments. Then at least I was spared the horror of people walking past every few minutes.

The station I liked least of all was Stafford. I was always on the wrong platform waiting for a connection. The coffee bar was across that footbridge. When you're a nervous guy like me, travelling with your bag and snooker cue that have been on the road for a couple of weeks, you're looking for someone to spring out of the shadows at you. I daren't leave my cue behind either, so Stafford was always the place I didn't dare risk a drink or a sandwich.

Trains can get you into some terrible fixes. I remember in 1978 doing a trip from Manchester to Southampton. It meant going into London to change stations. I couldn't have been much past Crewe when the train stopped dead – for three hours! I couldn't phone anyone at the venue in Southampton; I couldn't leap out and hail a taxi. I couldn't do anything except sit there, becalmed. There was no information to the passengers of course. I couldn't tell whether I'd be able to fulfil my commitment or not. I'd caught the train at 12.20 and finally arrived at Euston at 17.10. I made a quick telephone call from the station to alert the organisers, then grabbed a cab to Waterloo, arriving in Southampton at 21.50. I'd already done a ten hour day. My opponent, Geoff Thompson from Leicester was awarded victory because I was late. Then they had the audacity to ask me to play an exhibition match against him. I did and beat Thompson 5–0. It was no good though. He went through to the next round of the tournament. Is it any wonder my blood boils?

My manager, Del didn't realise the problems I had. He expected me to travel from Redruth to Portsmouth in time for a tournament match against Doug Mountjoy. It was a Sunday – the day British Rail are always out repairing the track. I was such a regular customer, they sometimes asked me to get out and stick in a rivet or two! I said to Del: 'This is ridiculous, what do you think I am, an aeroplane?' I got up at five o'clock in the morning to keep faith with the organisers, but it was hopeless. I reached Portsmouth four hours late after endless stoppages. The organiser refused to allow me to play. Even then I played an exhibition so as not to disappoint the audience. If I hadn't cared about snooker so much, I'd have stayed in bed in the first place. I might have been entitled to sue BR for loss of earnings but I didn't think about it at the time.

At one time, I bought myself a portable television to help while away the hours on board train. I watched the Manchester United–Arsenal Cup Final that way. I had £800 on my team, United to win. I just managed to get the bet on before catching the train from Manchester. I should have been at Wembley, but pressure of work stopped me. I sat in the buffet car surrounded by stewards trying to follow the match. They brought me everything I could want – drinks, food, cigarettes. Talk about preferential treatment! At half time I switched off to save the battery but I couldn't get the damn thing to come on again! After ten minutes I gave up. With that the VIP service disappeared as well! A group of us finished up huddled around a radio which had to be pinned to the window because it had no aerial. To complete a miserable afternoon, Alan Sunderland scored the winner for Arsenal in the dying minutes and I lost my £800.

That was bad enough, but not as bad as a return journey I once made from London to Manchester when I was supposed to be going one way only! I'd fallen onto the train at Euston shattered after several days on the road. I'd had a few lagers and a bit of fun, so sleep soon invaded me. It was a deep one. I travelled all the way to Manchester and woke up back in London. Nobody had bothered to wake me! Then I had to travel all the way home again.

On the snooker table, I went from the sublime to the ridiculous. The Irish title had become an embarrassment. Not for me but for the two guys who thought they could take it off me – Patsy Fagan and Dennis Taylor. I defended it for the third time at the Ulster Hall Belfast, beating Fagan easily 21–12. There wasn't much point defending the crown again while I was so far in front of the nearest challenger. It meant a lot to me that title, but so did the world championships. It was seven years since I won it and 1979 offered no respite from the continual disappointment. Not long after my Irish triumph, I stumbled out of the championship at the quarter-final stage. Crazy really, I was 6–2 up against Terry Griffiths and going for a third consecutive century break which would have been a record for the championships. I got as far as 45 but allowed Terry back into the match to compile a winning break. We stood at 10–10, then 11–11 and I had a great chance to go ahead. I was 55–0 up when I fluffed a simple black. At 12–12 and in the deciding frame I went for a long red in the top pocket and got a kick. The ball stayed out and I watched distraught as Terry made a 107 break to beat me. As we know he won the world title that year at his first attempt and he's been a thorn in my side ever since.

Referees continued to bug me. They always have and they always will. I particularly remember an incident against Dennis Taylor at the Tolly Cobbold Classic in Ipswich. In the final, Dennis snookered me and I had to swerve the cue ball to hit one of the reds which was next to the black. I was convinced I hit the red as clear as day, but the ref called foul shot for striking the black. Later in the match he awarded a free ball against me for no reason that I could see. I didn't like Dennis's attitude and cursed him under my breath. It seemed to throw my old sparring partner and I went on to win the final. I was vindicated when the local television station replayed the so-called foul shot in slow motion. The ref and Dennis both reported me to the WPBSA for my remarks and got me a £200 fine. I dare say I was pent up at the time. I felt that the ref who'd annoyed me so much in the 1974 world championship quarter-final against Fred Davis, made another mess of it when I played John Spencer in the final of the Wilson Classic in Manchester in 1980. The yellow and the cue ball were very close, but I potted the colour at speed to bring the cue ball back up the table. The ref ruled that it had been a push stroke. I hit the ball with screw and left hand side which made it twist sideways before moving back up the table. There's no way you can play a push stroke with side. Every player knows that. I tried to explain the science of it, but the referee wouldn't reverse his decision.

John Williams is another ref who's caused me unnecessary anguish. I know he's only human but I'll never forget how he absent-mindedly picked up the cue ball instead of the pink once when I was playing Steve Davis and respotted it on the pink spot. Realising his error, he tried to put the white ball back where it had been but of course he couldn't remember and took a wild guess. A few years later I demanded that Williams be replaced when he penalised me for a foul shot. It was during my world championship quarter-final against Bill Werbeniuk. I rolled the cue ball up behind the pink ever so delicately and the ref judged that the balls hadn't made contact. I was convinced that he must have been the only person in the arena or watching on television who didn't see the contact and that the action replays proved that he was wrong. Werbeniuk won the frame but I wasn't going to let the matter rest there. I went over to see Mike Watterson who was promoting the championships and told him that unless the referee was replaced I'd walk out of the match.

There's no one who stands out as a competent referee in my view. Too many of them have gathered their knowledge from books. None of them can play. A professional player knows merely from the sound of a shot whether it's good or bad. You can hear a push shot if you've played snooker at a reasonable level. Our referees are prone to rash decisions and many are too stubborn to reverse them even when they know they're in the wrong. I've seen it too often. I don't begrudge a fellah a decent living as a referee, but I don't like amateurs messing about with my weekly wage.

Surely the answer could be to convert the lower pros on the circuit into referees. Some of them are finding it heavy weather down there. They're not getting any exhibitions and the nearest they get to the world championships is the qualifying stages. What's the point? They would serve themselves and the game better by turning to refereeing. They have the knowledge; they would do a much better job than the blokes in control now; and they could still make a good living. A referee can charge £100 a night for exhibitions. I'd feel happier if I knew the ref was a former player. I'd have more respect for him. So

81

come on, lads, stop clinging on by your fingertips to the lowest rung in the rankings – get out there and improve the standard.

I wouldn't like to do it myself. I'm a potter not a spotter but I had an excellent grounding in the Belfast YMCA. We all had to take our turn there. We knew the rules and we knew the secret of a good referee – being inconspicuous. When I was in charge of a game you wouldn't see me, I'd be out of the fellah's eye-line. I'd be playing with him, reading his moves and anticipating his positions. I wouldn't be trying to get my face on television. Nor would I make the fatal mistake of thinking I was as big a star as the players.

The 1980 season was my best since winning the world title. I reached two major finals. First was the Coral UK at Preston where I knocked out Willy Thorne, Fred Davis and Ray Reardon to reach the final. I was up against the twenty-three year old wonder kid Steve Davis (about whom more later). He'd only turned pro a couple of seasons before and was clearly going places. I was in terrible form when it mattered, though, to give Davis his due, he did play well. The upshot was he leapfrogged over me with a winning margin of 16–6 to win his first major title.

Five months later, my dream of recapturing the world crown slipped away because I played to the crowd. It was a magnificent final – one of the best on record. An armchair audience of more than fourteen thousand witnessed it and although Thorburn won 18–16 he warned that I shouldn't be dismissed lightly because I was still the greatest. I had a very tough ride to the final. Tony Meo had played out of his skin before going down 10–9 and Steve Davis made a 136 clearance in the first session. I was determined not to let him repeat his Coral whitewash and played some of my best snooker to win 13–9. It got harder and harder. Kirk Stevens was at his peak. Some of his long pots I'd have been proud of. He made me battle all the way. It was worth it in the end, a 16–13 victory sending me into the final after a four year absence.

Lynn had moved up a gear from being my long-time girlfriend to being my wife. We'd married at Wilmslow Reform Church in the January and the newly married man thought another Year of the Hurricane was nigh. Lynn watched most of the sessions, but she was unable to bring me that little slice of luck I needed to match my daring play. If I was to win the title again, I wanted to do it in style. I wanted people to remember the last time in 1972. If only television cameras had been around to see me then. They were here now and boy were the viewers in for a treat? I thought they were, but I reckoned without the old 'grinder' Thorburn. To begin with I played it cagey, leading 5–1, 6–2 and 9–5 before I threw caution to the wind. If the man upstairs had allowed me to forge ahead like that, I reckoned he'd be with me all the way. No fewer than four times I was fifty in front. Each time I let Thorburn back into the frame and left the colours neatly arranged for him to clean up. Inevitably he drew level at 9–9 but I still hadn't lost faith. Lynn couldn't bear to watch. She and Thorburn's wife, Barbara went outside for a coffee – it was that pressurised. I kept going for my shots hoping that fortune would be my guide. It wasn't. I held on at 12–12, but the 'grinder' wouldn't let me escape. I take my hat off to him for hanging in there, but no one will ever convince me that I didn't beat myself trying to win the stylish way.

7
Lynn

I fell head over heels in love with Lynn Robbins on our first date. We were sitting in Charlie Chan's Chinese restaurant in Manchester and she was the most stubborn person I'd met. Apart from failing to be impressed with the Higgins chat-up line, she made a mockery of my attempts to initiate her in the use of chopsticks! Initiate? – she was already an expert though she'd allowed me to go on thinking she was a novice. I knew I'd bitten off more than I could chew! Unlike other girls I'd ensnared, Lynn was fiercely independent and cynical about the world of showbiz. Everything I said she seemed to disagree with. I thought I knew something about pop music but she shot that down in flames. Her husband (she was separated) apparently played guitar in a Manchester group so she was clued up on that score too.

We met at George Best's winebar, Oscars, the day after I returned from Australia where things were getting tough with Cara. The first person I saw was an old flame of mine, Bernadette who used to do a spot of cleaning for me among other things. I couldn't help noticing the cool blonde sitting with her. If she noticed me, she didn't show it. In fact she was downright rude. Told me to fetch my own drink, and persisted in talking to George Best with her back to me. I guess it's the age old story – there's no bigger come-on than a girl who's not interested.

(*Lynn:* I remember my sister telling me she'd bumped into this wierdo in Oscars. Scruffy bloke by the name of Alex Higgins who walked in wearing one of those big Australian hats with corks dangling from it, an overcoat and a bow tie. Carol ignored him, so he chatted up one of our friends, Bernadette. Somehow Alex had persuaded this girl to clean his flat for him. She used to go in once a week and tell us how the place was littered with girl's things and bits of money lying everywhere. I didn't like him before I met him. He would ring Bernadette at home and expect her to drop everything to tidy his flat. He didn't pay her a penny. Never even took her out to dinner. I thought she must be mad. It was about a year after that when Bernadette and I were at the wine bar again. It was one of my rare nights out. Since my first marriage had failed, I spent most of the time indoors.

I thought snooker players were old men. Didn't follow it at all. So when Alex walked in, I was probably the only one who didn't recognise him. Bernadette said: 'Look, Lynn, there's Alex Higgins!' to which I replied: 'So what?' He had this dreadful raincoat on and came over to us as if he was God's gift to women. It was my round. When I asked Bernadette what she wanted, he dived in and said: 'Get me a large vodka and tonic.' I told him he could get his own drinks and left him standing there. He looked a bit shocked. He kept trying to chat me up, but I wouldn't have it. I didn't like the look of him. Chauvinists don't appeal to me. I'll give him one thing though, he was persistent. I told him I worked as a secretary at Manchester Airport. That wasn't precise enough. He needed to know where at Manchester Airport so I told him at the Serviceair desk. It was a foolish thing to have let out.

Bernadette and I were leaving to go to a disco, but Alex insisted on giving us a lift in his cab. Typically he sent Bernadette to phone for one and while she was away, asked me out to dinner. I said: 'No thank you.')

I was getting fed up with the girl. The cab had only gone a few yards when I thought: 'Why are you paying for their ride, Higgins? You're not getting anywhere.' When we stopped at the lights, I jumped out, giving it up as a bad job. There were plenty more fish in the sea.

(*Lynn:* I was furious. What kind of bloke offers you a lift then leaves you to pay the fare? I told Bernadette to get out of the taxi and we marched off for a drink. Alex wouldn't stop following us. He asked me for a dance. I told him to go away and leave us alone).

Luckily, she'd told me where she worked. I use Manchester Airport a lot, so I was bound to see her again. I couldn't wait that long. The girl intrigued me. Next day I phoned her at work and invited her out to dinner again. Higgins doesn't give in that easily. She resisted for a while, but eventually succumbed. They nearly always do.

(*Lynn:* He phoned for several days until I agreed. It was against my mum's advice. She warned me to stay away from him. She'd read about him in the papers – always drunk or fighting someone or chasing women. 'He's another George Best, he's no good,' she said. The more she went on, the more interested I became. It sounded like a bit of fun. I was twenty-one and had just finished an affair with an awfully nice but normal doctor. I was bored stiff. Here was my chance to do something different.

It was different all right. Alex literally whisked me off my feet. It was like a whistle-stop tour of all the nightlife Manchester had to offer. He said he'd take me to the best Chinese restaurant. He knew about Chinese food from being in Hong Kong. He said not to worry because he'd do the ordering. What he didn't know was that I was very well up on Chinese food myself. We had some good Chinese friends in town and had celebrated the Chinese New Year at a much better restaurant than the one Alex was talking about. I played along with it.

I asked him to pick me up at eight o'clock but he said he hadn't got a car and didn't drive. I thought he must be joking. He said he never had to make his own way anywhere and would send a taxi for me. I said I'd pick him up and we arranged the rendezvous for the Potters snooker club where he apparently had to practise. I got dressed up in a lovely evening gown expecting an elegant night out on the town. I was in for a nasty surprise.

At the Potters club, Alex was still playing snooker – in a pair of jeans three inches too short and a jumper with a hole in the arm. He waved me to sit down and proceeded to show off. After half an hour of this, he said: 'Right let's go.' I said: 'Go where? I'm not going out with you looking like that! Nobody takes me out dressed in old jeans and a jumper. Goodbye.' I went to walk out but he caught my arm and apologised. Said he didn't have time to get home and change and in any case this was all he'd got apart from the dinner suits he used for snooker. I had no choice. Off we went like the princess and pauper!

What a night! He took me to six clubs in an hour. I didn't

drink much, but he ordered me a vodka in each place. I must have had ten or so by the end of the evening and smoked twenty cigarettes. Normally I'd get through about three in one night. I wondered what was happening to me.

Finally we got to the restaurant. That was a real laugh. Alex said he'd teach me to use chopsticks and tried to show me how you could pick up one grain of rice when you'd mastered the technique. He couldn't manage it however hard he tried. I pretended to be an avid learner until the food arrived. Then I showed him I knew all about chopsticks. He wasn't too pleased. The conversation was more like a duel. I was contradictory about everything he tried to tell me. I'd sussed him out from talking to Bernadette and there was no way he could get one over on me despite the drink he kept plying me with.')

It was hard work, but I knew instantly there was something between us. That irresistible mixture of love and hate which was going to cause so many problems in the future. We talked a lot about our families. She told me her father was a keen snooker fan. That was good news. If I worked on him, I must stand a good chance.

(*Lynn:* He was so different from any one I'd ever been out with – doctors, teachers etc. My first husband was a computer programmer. All very staid. The evening finished at the Press Club at 7 am! I was worried what my mum and dad would say. They'd never believe I'd been out with Alex until that hour. They weren't used to things like that. I dropped Alex off at his flat. He invited me in to see some photographs of his family. At first I resisted because I had a bad experience with a dentist who wanted to show me his art collection. He finished up with his hands around my neck in the bedroom! Alex was a perfect gentleman. He made a coffee, showed me the photographs and I went home!)

Strike while the iron's hot I say. I didn't give Lynn a chance to settle. I was blinded by love. There's nothing like the direct approach. Next day I phoned her father and said: 'Mr Avison, I love your daughter.' Silence at the other end. Within a couple of months, I was lodging at their house. My flat was broken into so it seemed the sensible thing to move in with my girlfriend. No jiggery-pokery though. The family put me up in the spare room and I stayed there for two years.

It felt good to be part of a family again. I hadn't known that since I was fifteen.

I first turned up at the house that same afternoon. Lynn had gone out so I got Jim, her father to drive me to the nearest barber's shop for a shave and brush-up. I didn't want Lynn to see me unkempt. I hadn't exactly cut a dash in my jeans the night before. I asked her if she'd come with me to the shops and help me choose some casual clothes. Apart from snooker suits, I didn't have anything. When I got back from the barber's looking spick and span, I did the family bit. You know, playing snooker with Lynn's kid brother etc. I can be charming when I want to be.

(*Lynn:* **I could have died when I came home and saw the snooker cue in the hall. I whispered to my mum: 'It's not Alex is it?' She said: 'Yes, he's gone out with your dad for a shave.' We all had tea together and that's how it started. There was lots of affection between us. What I liked is that he never made a pass at me. I think that's why we stayed together. He knew I wasn't easy like his other girlfriends.'**)

The show had to go on. While I was busy trying to regain my world title, I had to travel a lot. Snooker was growing fast and during the season,there was hardly any let up. I had other girlfriends, but nothing important. Lynn was free to lead her own life while I was away, but I know she stayed faithful. She was that type of girl. We carried on like this for a year or so with me living at her parent's place and Lynn coming with me to tournaments and as many exhibitions as she could. It was good for her and for me. It gave her a taste of what a professional player's life is like. She found the schedule as exhausting as I did. Lynn was very naïve when it came to etiquette at snooker occasions. She came to watch me once with her cousin, another Bernadette and I had to have her ejected for laughing. I could hear this childish giggling coming from her direction. I thought it was great – one person disturbing my concentration and spoiling the show for everyone else, and it has to be my girl! The trouble was she wasn't interested in the game. Never has been. I put my cue down and marched over to her seat. 'Are you with me?' I asked. Still she wouldn't shut up so I sent for the doorman and said: 'Throw that woman out!' She told him she was quite capable of leaving under her own steam and got up and went. I realised I'd been a bit harsh, dropped my cue and ran to fetch her back. She never did that again.

It was useful having Lynn drive me to exhibitions although it almost cost us our lives on one occasion. It wasn't her driving at fault but the atrocious conditions. I was due to appear in the Yorkshire Dales which meant a long drive from London in foul weather – thick snow and fog. The car blew up on the way so we had to hire another. Now it was a race against time. We ended up where they make the series 'Emmerdale Farm', high up on a narrow road with a sheer drop on one side. Trouble was, it was my side and as everyone knows, I'm not the calmest of people, especially in a car. While Lynn twisted and turned through the snow, I was getting frantic. I could see the chasm underneath me. One false move and we'd have been a couple of corpses. We got there only half an hour late but were both badly shaken up. They couldn't believe we'd made it and handed each of us a large brandy to calm our nerves. Then they told us – the road was supposed to be closed because it was unfit for traffic!

(*Lynn:* Alex thought nothing of distances. He once bought me a Daimler. We hadn't owned it for more than a couple of hours when he said, out of the blue: 'Shall we go to Paris tonight?' He made it sound very romantic and suggested inviting our friends Geoff and Helen Lomas. I agreed but warned him I wasn't used to the new car yet. He said: 'Oh, you'll get used to it. You can drive me to Hull first and I'll play an exhibition!' I was game for anything. We left Hull at midnight; I drove all the way to Dover to catch the ferry at 6am, and continued from Calais to Paris non-stop. I was on the Champs Elysées and the rest were all asleep in the back of the car. I couldn't get off the roundabout, so I shouted to Alex: 'If you don't wake up we'll be dead!' Geoff and Helen woke up but Alex just mumbled: 'You're all right' and fell into a deep sleep again.

All the hotels were booked because there was a big conference on in Paris. Eventually I found this beautiful place right in the centre of the city. Alex said: 'Just give me another hour's sleep and I'll be with you.' It was 7 pm and I blew my top. *HE* wanted another hour and *I'D* been on the road for twelve hours! That ruined the weekend. I didn't speak to him the whole time we were there. He tried to win me over with a red rose bought from the hotel lobby. I told him what to do with it.

Helen, Geoff and Alex went out for the evening. I stayed on my own all night in this fabulous £150 suite. I wanted to go with them, but my principles wouldn't let me. It's a toss up which one of us is more stubborn!)

I did try to learn to drive. It cost me £500! Lynn gave me my first lesson in a new Renault I'd bought. I had all the business – the provisional licence, the 'L' plates and so on. All I lacked was the pedal control! We headed off towards Dewsbury down a nice quiet road and everything was going well. Steering okay; use of gears fine. Being the Hurricane, I wanted more adventure so we turned into the main road, completely forgetting that it was rush hour. Suddenly I was ambushed: a big bus on the left and a car pulling out on the right. Lynn grabbed the wheel and piloted us through the gap. I said: 'Right, that's enough, babe. I'm pulling off here,' and lit a cigarette to soothe my shattered nerves. I'm nothing if not resilient though. Tossing the half-smoked cigarette out of the window in a show of bravado, I set off again – straight into a lorry. Or rather it smacked straight into the side of the Renault. My fault – I hit the wrong pedal at the halt sign! I've never tried since. Don't suppose I will now.

(*Lynn:* Before we got married, Alex was quite a romantic. He used to take me to this lovely French restaurant called Elysées (memories of the all-night drive to Paris!). We'd have a candlelit supper then he would invariably buy me some item of antique jewellery which they displayed in a cabinet near the door. It was very crafty of them. Alex couldn't walk out without buying me something – not because I wanted it but because it gave him pleasure. That stopped once we were married! Then it was me trying to control the finances. He would squander money stupidly. I had to force him to put his winnings away in the Building Society. If I hadn't we'd never have bought a decent house.

It sounded romantic as well when he phoned me from Trinidad where he was on a snooker trip and said he'd arranged a ticket for me to join him. He said I'd love it; the weather was marvellous and we'd have a great time at a beautiful hotel once used by the Queen. When I got off the plane it was pouring with rain. Alex and three other men collected me in this tiny little car and we drove for ages until we arrived at a hotel straight out of Fawlty Towers! The swimming pool was empty. Alex said not to worry, they would be putting the water in any time. He showed me to the room which had newspaper stuffed in the windows

because there was no glass. I took one look and asked:
'Are you sure the Queen stayed here?' We both fell about
laughing.)

I couldn't tell her the truth over the phone could I? That it was the
rainy season when everything shuts up shop and that I was bored out
of my mind with nothing to do. It was a khazi. We were miles from
anywhere surrounded by dirt tracks which were turned into rivers by
the rains. I was playing exhibition matches for Shell. Lynn came with
me to the day's show, but she soon got fed up with that. The highlight
of my day was catching lizards for Spencer, the hotel cat! Lynn didn't
seem to think that was very funny. She threatened to go home unless
we moved into a decent hotel in Port of Spain. I had a word with the
sponsors, and they put us up at the Holiday Inn. She liked that – nice
swimming pool with a bar in the middle. We had five free days after
the exhibitions and spent them on the Robinson Crusoe island of
Tobago. I'm not really into beaches and sunshine but Lynn was. I had
to confess I couldn't swim which she seemed to think was very funny.
What kind of a fellah doesn't drive and can't swim? We were on the
beach right in front of the hotel so I had to do something. Lynn swam
out like a fish and beckoned me to join her. Then I had a brainwave.
I found an old piece of rope and tied one end around my waist and
the other round a convenient palm tree.

(*Lynn:* He looked so funny with his skinny white legs wading
out into the beautiful Caribbean sea with a rope tied to his
waist. Goodness knows what they must have thought on the
terrace where the guests were sipping their cocktails! I was
holding him up, trying to teach him to swim when the hotel
manager warned us not to stay out too long. The sun was in,
but only just behind the clouds. I was quite used to the sun,
but by the time I got Alex back to shore he was burned
scarlet. He was in agony for two days. On the third day we
went on a glass bottomed boat to take a look around the
island. We were in our swimwear admiring the coral but
the other chaps in the boat seemed more intent on admiring
me. In Tobago all the men were strong and masculine and
... well Alex didn't quite fit in somehow. Out at sea, they
invited us to put on snorkels and get out of the boat. Alex
wouldn't hear of it. How could he?
A couple of the coloured men were holding me in the
water to get a better look at the fish. Alex was sitting on his

91

own in the boat looking daggers. He shouted: 'So I'm just left in the boat am I while you get all the attention?' He was seething. I said to one of the he-men: 'Look, I'm all right on my own but my boyfriend over there in the boat could do with a hand.' He just went over to Alex; lifted him bodily out of the boat and carried him across the top of the water. It was so funny though I don't think he was too amused!

In a way I was getting my own back for some of the practical jokes he used to play on me. Always phoning up pretending to be someone else. Once I heard this Pakistani voice inviting Alex to play in a tournament in Karachi. He sounded such a nice man and very genuine. I was completely taken in until Alex could control himself no longer. It backfired on me when I took a call from a chap claiming to work for Prince somebody or other in the United Arab Emirates. He said the Prince really admired Mr Higgins and would like me to send some literature so they could book him for a few exhibitions. I told him to stop being such a bloody fool and come clean. When he said his name was Abdullah I nearly fell about laughing. There wasn't a sound at the other end and I realised he was who he said he was. I apologised profusely and gave him Alex's hotel number. Sure enough Alex took the call immediately and got himself some well-paid dates in Dubai. Those were the lighter moments, but it wasn't always like that.

We had plenty of rows. Alex took me to London one night to watch him play an exhibition. When I got there, it was a stag do full of wealthy businessmen. I was the only girl. I offered to go back to the hotel but Alex told me I could stay. They were drinking champagne like it was going out of fashion. The more they gave to Alex, the more he wanted to play for money. That's when the trouble started. John Virgo was there because Alex had got him the work, but he didn't want John getting involved in the money contests. He wanted it all for himself. They were shouting and arguing with each other so I went to the reception desk and called a taxi. I said to the driver: 'Take me to Manchester.' He almost fell through the floor. I told him I'd just had a flaming row with my boyfriend. We settled on £70 for the fare and off we went. Luckily Alex had asked me to look after a hundred pounds of his winnings so I wasn't short of cash. I left all my clothes and things at the hotel and travelled in my evening dress. On the way to Manchester I fell asleep and the driver got lost.

92

(TOP) Mum and Dad after my World Championship success at Sheffield. I didn't
have time to get back to Belfast.
Our luxury bungalow in Cheadle. Pretty soon it was a lonely refuge.

(ABOVE) Higgins in typica
pose: can of lager, fags
and the never ending fan
mail.

(LEFT) Adoring dad.
There's a special bond
between fathers and
daughters.

(OPPOSITE) Handshake
with the Ginger Magician
but notice the distinct lac
of warmth.

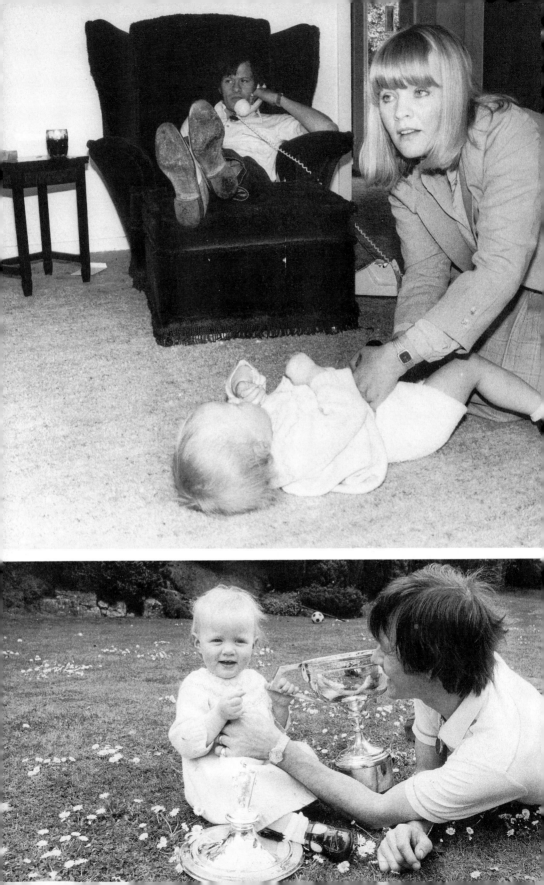

(ABOVE) In a thoughtful mood during a match.
(OPPOSITE ABOVE) I changed the nappies sometimes – honest!
(BELOW) Love among the daisies. Lauren meant the world to me.

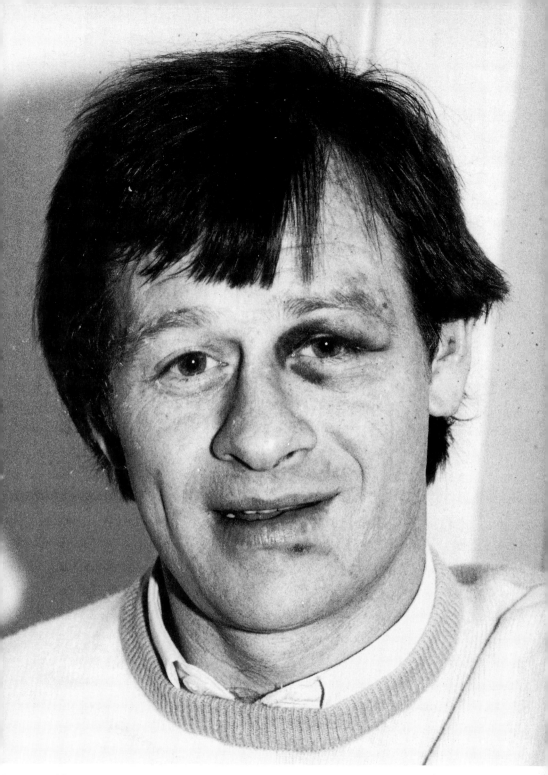

Not a pretty sight, but you should have seen the other guy! (after the fight with Paul Medati)

(OPPOSITE ABOVE) Del Simmons was very fair to me – but he would keep calling me 'son'!

(BELOW) Delveron House where Lynn and I planned to make a fresh start. It didn't quite work out.

Launch of Media Star Cards. *Left to right* Frank Bruno, Glenn Hoddle, Bruce Grobbelaar, Kenny Dalglish and Alex Higgins.

You won't see my style in the textbooks, but the cue action is spot-on.

We ended up in Rugby or some such place. Then a message came over the driver's radio: 'Have you got a woman by the name of Lynn Avison in the car? Alex Higgins has walked out of an exhibition match and is looking for her.' On my instructions, the driver said he'd dropped me off somewhere and I was on my way home by train. I wanted to throw Alex off the scent. I arrived at my mum's at 6 am to find that Alex had been phoning every ten minutes to see where I was. I disappeared for two days to keep out of his way while he staggered back to Manchester carrying both suitcases. He spent £50 in taxi fares looking for me all over Cheshire.

Alex tried to get me to give up my job at the airport, but I was keen to keep my independence. Then I went with him to Scotland where he was playing John Spencer. I'd had the flu and passed out in the middle of the match. They rushed me to hospital and found I was suffering from pleurisy. We had to stay up there for a week so Alex said I might as well hand in my notice because I was taking so much time off anyway.

After that I started travelling everywhere with him. In the early days, snooker wasn't that big. Most of the time he was playing at working men's clubs. Not the place for a woman really and I didn't enjoy it.

The relationship was going downhill. We constantly argued and I could see for myself the twilight world he lived in. It was all drink and groupies. Alex was so unpredictable it began to get on my nerves. He used to infuriate me with his outbursts. It reached the point where I didn't want to go out with him any more. I went on holiday to the South of France and left him behind. While I was there I met someone else. He was English and his parents had a big business in Cannes. They wanted to give me a flat to stay on through the summer. I wasn't in love with the fellow or anything, but it seemed a good way of breaking off with Alex. I came home to sort a few things out for the flat and told Alex what I was planning. He was terribly upset and begged me to change my mind. I realised I still loved him despite his moodiness so I stayed in England. Alex then started putting pressure on me to get a divorce.

As usual, I was carried along by it all. Alex has a way of doing that. Before I could give the matter much thought, he took me to see his solicitor. While he sorted out his own divorce, he did mine as well. It was over very quickly. Then we just drifted into marriage. It seemed the natural step. After two years at my mum's, we'd lived together for two years in our own house in Burnage. I insisted on that. My first experience with marriage had been such a bad one that I didn't want to rush into it again. Alex and I got on pretty well on our own. There were no children involved, no pressures on us and snooker wasn't as high powered as it is today. He had a big following of fans of course, but it hadn't become a big television thing then.

I coped with groupies quite well. Even though I was always with him there'd be one or two trying to get off with him. They'd chat to him over my head, but I put it down to being part of the job. The public paid his wages so I accepted it in the knowledge that he was mine. I felt secure. The problem of infidelity didn't come into it then.')

Lynn was a very dominant lady which was good for me. I can trample all over people if they let me, but not Lynn. She was straight-laced and sensible and wouldn't stand any nonsense from me. I had to toe the line for the first time in my life. That's what made it a good relationship. Sooner or later I was going to have to make a decent woman of her, so we decided to get married with all the works: big white wedding, four bridesmaids and a pageboy. Lynn's parents took charge of all of that. I didn't have much time. Marriage was what the doctor ordered for me. I'd had years of gallivanting. What I needed was a base, a home, a wife, and before long hopefully, some kids. I've always had a deep love of children. At the age of thirty-one I figured it was time to start thinking about my own. We didn't get the chance to have a honeymoon. I was booked for an exhibition.

(*Lynn:* I suppose everything in life is a gamble, but I didn't look at it as taking a risk by marrying one of the most eligible bachelors in the country. I just loved Alex. He'd calmed down a lot in his life. At the time I was happy. It began to get difficult once I got pregnant. Both pregnancies were bad ones. I couldn't travel so much with Alex. We had a nanny but I didn't want to leave Lauren with her all the time. That's not why you have children. Even when we went to Australia, I took the baby with me. It meant that Alex and I weren't as free as before. He couldn't adjust to that. You could say he was a doting father, but only when it suited him. He loved the idea of changing Lauren's nappy and giving her feeds, but by the time Jordan arrived, the novelty had worn off. He realised babies were hard work, not just playthings to be picked up and put down when you felt like it.

My parents had their differences with Alex. They liked him, but he was always likely to get into an argument. Compared to my relationship with Alex's family, it was mild. I sensed right from the start they didn't like me. My suspicions were confirmed when I went with him to a tournament in Dublin just before we were married. The Higgins clan came down from Belfast. The atmosphere was icy even though I helped Alex to win his match against Ray Reardon. I was sitting next to Reardon without realising who he was. He was ever so flustered. Without realising who I was either, he complained about the fan heaters in the hall and how warm he felt. He kept smacking his lips out of nervousness. When I found out it was Reardon I rushed over to tell Alex that his opponent was in a bad way and ready for the kill. Alex kept the pressure on Reardon and won easily.

A few minutes later I went to the ladies. While I was there, Alex's mother came in with one of his sisters. She didn't know I was there. I overheard her say: 'That f------ woman is taking my son away from me!' I couldn't believe my ears. I'd never heard that language from a woman. I broke down in tears and rushed out to tell Alex. He warned his mother never to do anything like that again. He said I'd done more for him than she'd ever realise.

They resented me because I was smart and good looking (well quite!) and didn't belong to their world. His mother and sisters used to usher him around at tournaments before I came along. They adored the limelight. Mrs Higgins loved to take the credit for him. It was always 'My son this and my son that'. Embarrassing really because wherever you went she had to make it known that she was Alex Higgins' mother. All mothers do that up to a point, but I don't know what she had to crow about. Alex left home at fifteen and virtually brought himself up. When he first took me to Belfast to meet them, his mother wouldn't even talk to me. When we were introduced, all she could say was: 'So you're another one of his floozies.'

It came to a head when Lauren was about four weeks old and Alex was on 'This is Your Life'. When Thames Television first asked me I was still pregnant and not too keen to get involved. In any case, Alex had often said that he wouldn't fancy it and if anyone asked, to say 'no'. I told his mother and sister Ann, about the approach and they were all for it. His mother thought Alex had a right to be on. She would. After Lauren was born I decided I'd give Alex the benefit of the doubt and go along with it. If he didn't want to do it in the finish, he only had to say 'no' to the man with the big red book.

Mrs Higgins and I had a heated disagreement at our house when Lauren was only five days old. I don't want to go into details but suffice it to say that we'd more or less barred her from the house. I swore I'd never speak to her again. The problem was: how to prepare for 'This is Your Life' when the two sides of the family weren't communicating? We went ahead with the Higgins family on one side and my family on the other, both keeping a safe distance. Alex's mum and dad and sisters didn't want to mix anyway. The night before the programme they gave us the script and we all had to go through it and make alterations where we saw fit. You could have cut the atmosphere with a knife. There we all were sitting around this big table. I objected to some of the silly bits they'd put in. I thought Alex would be really annoyed over stories about him collecting potato peelings and jumping up and down on his mum's bed when he was little.

I told Ann I didn't think there was any need to include stupid things like that. What had they got to do with the life of a world snooker champion? His sister turned on me and said: 'That's what happened so it's staying in. Who do you think you are interfering?' I could have insisted but I didn't. Alex said later he didn't know what they were talking about. It was very embarrassing. In fact the whole programme was embarrassing. It must have been obvious that something was wrong.

At the party afterwards, things became more heated. One of the family had a few drinks and slapped me across the face. I don't know what I was supposed to have done. They're a funny lot. I did my bit by inviting them over for the christening a few weeks later. And we paid nearly a thousand pounds to bring his sister Isobel and Alex's niece Julie over from Australia for Christmas.')

There's always been ill-feeling between Lynn and my mother. I wouldn't like to take sides although I will say that Lynn went out of her way to be pleasant. It must have been a clash of cultures. Both of them are very strong women in their own ways.

8
Lauren to Myself

The inspiration for my first world title had been Muhammed Ali. Ten years on my driving force was a lovely little blonde with shoulder-length hair and an irresistible twinkle in her eye. My daughter Lauren is a Higgins through and through. She has the same impish grin, the same restless nature, and the same knack of picking up vibrations.

I hadn't planned to call her down to the table after winning the trophy. It was pure instinct. I shall never forget picking her up and hugging her. A frightened little soul amid all that noise and all those lights, and yet the most important thing in my life at the time. I was in tears as several million television viewers will remember. Lauren couldn't understand why, but cried along just the same. All the anguish and the disappointment of recent years came gushing out of me. I wasn't ashamed or embarrassed. It was a moment to cherish and any-one who didn't think so couldn't have had an ounce of good in them.

I've re-lived that fortnight in Sheffield many times over and always come up with the same conclusion – that my victory was pre-ordained. My fate that year was inextricably wound up with Lauren and her growing awareness of things around her. At seventeen months she was beginning to realise who her father was. There was something between us which was almost impossible to define. Not mere telepathy, more an invisible force; the power of flesh and blood. I never believed in all that stuff before she came along. No one before or since has had the same effect on me. I loved her more deeply that I could have imagined.

I was aware of the bond almost from the moment I watched her come into the world. She was delivered by Caesarian section at St Mary's Hospital, Manchester and the birth took twenty-eight minutes instead of the estimated twelve. I don't mind admitting I was starting to panic. Being of a nervous disposition, I don't suppose I should really have been there in the first place. Looking back, I wouldn't have missed it for the world.

1982 had not been an outstanding year by any means. There was no reason to suppose that my ten years without a world title were about to end. Fatherhood you could say had a settling effect on me. For the first time in ages, my mental state was about right. It was all down to Lauren. Everybody mellows in time and Hurricane Higgins had become a big softie. I was the original doting father, following my daughter around the house to try to prevent those children's accidents. I couldn't bear the thought of her bumping her head or scratching her knee. Can you imagine the streetwise hustler fussing around like an old hen? If there'd been a roll of cotton wool large enough, I'd have wrapped her in it.

In that world championship year, she used to spend hours watching me clown around in the snooker room. I've studiously avoided trick shots during exhibitions because I reckon I do enough of them in tournament play, but Lauren was always asking me to perform, so I did. I'd do anything to entertain her. Practice took a back seat. It wasn't easy with a toddler crawling and walking about on the baize. She was fascinated by the cue and took great pleasure in smashing the balls about. A real chip off the old block. You have to give kids a grounding for a misspent youth!

During the championships, I took her with me into the players' room. There she'd take my cue apart and play with the chalk. In the breaks she came pottering in and sat on the table watching the television monitor while I poured myself a vodka and relaxed. Lynn would be hovering not far away, but Lauren never left my side. By the time the event was a few days old, she'd got to know most of the players.

As soon as I got to Sheffield I knew I was going to win. The circumstances were just right. It must be a bit like an Olympic athlete – if everything comes together on the day, he'll get his gold medal; if it doesn't he'll miss out and have to wait another four years for a second chance. I didn't get off to an auspicious start. The demon drink nearly finished me off in the second round against Doug Mountjoy. I got into a heavy session during a day off, and barely surfaced in time for the match. It was a case of getting into bed with the sun already over the yardarm and having to drag myself out again a couple of hours later.

I really had to dig deep to win because I was shattered. That's when I was first conscious of Lauren's influence. She watched the whole of the afternoon session when I was feeling at my worst. I couldn't possibly let her down. Against Willy Thorne in the quarter-final I made a couple of century breaks but didn't play anything special. What came next was one of the best matches ever seen in a world championship. Higgins versus Jimmy White; the Hurricane against the Whirlwind and Jimmy still a few weeks short of his twentieth birthday.

I first met Jimmy when he was fourteen and one of the dozen or so promising youngsters lined up to have a crack at me during an exhibition at an Irish working men's club in north London. I had to take on this group of local players as usual, and none of them struck me as anything other than enthusiastic amateurs until I came to a quiet fresh-faced kid. I knocked in a break of 88 and he replied with a 40 in double quick time. I was impressed. For a fourteen year old he already had a terrific talent and bags of confidence. What I liked was the speed with which he played. No messing about sizing up shots – a quick glance, an instant appraisal of the situation, then in went the pots. Because he was left handed I didn't immediately see myself in him. He favoured the right hand side whereas I favoured left, but in essence we were the same type of player. He was a very nice kid too – quiet and calm, not as boisterous as me. I didn't know then that he would soon stand between me and the world title or that I would almost certainly deny him the honour of becoming the youngest ever world champion.

Maybe he was overawed to come up against me in 1982. He'd come through against Cliff Thorburn, Perrie Mans and Kirk Stevens to reach the semi-final – and he'd beaten them all comfortably. News had been filtering through over the past couple of years that this young genius was on the warpath. He'd based his play on mine and that was the sincerest form of flattery. Jimmy and I are the only ones who play snooker for love. We each have a hundred shots in our armoury. No one else comes anywhere near that. What's more, we use them. Jimmy doesn't like hanging around any more than I do. He has the power game. It's great for the public and it makes such a change from the rest of the snails on the circuit. People watch snooker to see balls going down. The faster the better. Jimmy and I believed in potting as fast as possible and getting on with the next frame. I know for a fact that we both played for century breaks. We weren't interested in fifties.

Knock in a hundred, set 'em up again ref and let's go for another big clearance!

I felt sorry for him that day at the Crucible. When you see so much talent in such a young player and know that if hadn't been for one little slip, he'd have been on top of the world, then your heart goes out to him. Ever since that first day I played him, I've had a soft spot for Jimmy. If it isn't me winning a tournament, I'd wish it to be him.

He had me over a barrel at 15–14. It had been all I could do to hang on throughout the match, but now it was slipping away. I was dead. There's no question that if I hadn't been impetuous when backed into a corner, Jimmy would have gone through to meet Ray Reardon. He was applying the *coup de grace* with relentless efficiency in that thirtieth frame when he made his fatal error. He only needed one colour to win but left the red too close to the pink and missed it. I knew that was my chance, but that if I strayed a fraction out of line it was all over. There was so much pressure on me that I finished up in no man's land with the cue ball in a hopeless position. The temptation was to play safe, but with four or five reds on the table and Jimmy requiring only one of them, it would have been skating on thin ice every inch of the way. I decided to go for the main chance. I don't suppose there's any other player in the world who would have the nerve or the temerity to attempt a big clearance from that position.

The tension was crackling but I had that tunnel vision with the lamp of victory burning at the end of it. I was getting outside help – a combination of the man upstairs and Lauren. It wasn't me going for that long green, it was a force from without. I hit it beautifully and moved the red off the cushion. That was the vital shot. A shit or bust effort and I did it. The next half a dozen shots were sublime, out of this world and they broke poor Jimmy's heart. I had the bit between my teeth and went on to complete that magical break of 69 which people still speak of in hallowed terms. John Spencer described it as the best break under pressure he'd ever seen.

Julian Barnes of the *Observer* described me this way: 'Shambling and twitching, pockets distended by duck mascots, rabbits' feet and four-leaf clovers, Higgins lurched appealingly around the table like a doomed low-lifer.'

The pressure had been transferred back onto Jimmy. He was paralysed because he was so used to tightening the screw on others. I took everything he threw at me and came back with my second wind. The

Hurricane's never more dangerous than when it's caged in! There were a couple more big breaks, but at one point I did slip up and let Jimmy in with a reasonable chance. By then, though, he was dishevelled and broken. He rushed the shot and missed. I had beaten him.

Funny thing was that my cue that day was like a strip of rubber. I couldn't compete when it came to the long shots – a very heavy restriction. Fortunately I had such a varied game that I could adapt. I'll not forget the sight of Jimmy walking out of the arena. He'd played magnificent snooker, scented victory, tasted it even, and had it dashed from his lips at the last moment. He was stunned, but thank goodness, he's not the sort of chap to let things get on top of him for too long. Since then, we've become soul mates. He's my closest friend on the circuit though he's more introspective than me. He withdraws into himself a lot – a very private person – but there's a lot of understanding between us. We talk to each other about problems but rarely phone if we're in trouble. Both of us are too independent for that. Jimmy was a help to me during my traumas in 1986. More by being there than anything else. He came to stay at the house for a few days. We'd play snooker, have a beer, watch videos, listen to music, have a bite to eat then get back to the snooker table for another two hours. The conversation was more or less idle chatter.

As far as talent goes, Jimmy's just about on a par with me. He's won his first title, but hasn't really cracked the big time yet because his tactics aren't sharpened correctly. I felt sorry for him when he squandered that 7–0 lead against Thorburn in the Goya final. No one could have been happier when he eventually beat Cliff to take his first major title the same year. Jimmy's going to be around for a long time yet. He's still only twenty-three, it's all before him.

The WPBSA relieved me of £1,500 in another case of overkill. Kirk Stevens and I were playing for tenners in the practice room when I was caught short. A few lagers and lemonade had gone down during the session and you might say I was bursting. It was a long way from the room to the loo. I spotted a rubber plant and realised it was my only chance. It was midnight and there were only four people in the area. Three of them were blokes. I asked the woman if she'd mind moving around the corner while I had a wee-wee. It wasn't as if I aimed at the plant or anything. I shot straight into the soil. This over-zealous security man tried to feel my collar so I gave him a spot of the old Higgins treatment. The bloke could easily have forgotten it. Instead he reported me to the Association and was done for peeing in a potted plant! Fifteen hundred pounds thank you very much. It was the most expensive pee in the world. I often wonder how the rubber plant's doing. Perhaps it's learned to screw back!

I fancied beating Reardon. It was just a case of how long before I got around to it. It was poetic justice that I should do it in the world final because of that shambolic affair in 1976 when I conceded a frame too soon. Reardon would probably have won anyway, but I was distracted by my sister, Jean who was in a terrible state watching me lose. She was sitting at the table with me during the match, which wasn't unusual in those days, but would never be allowed now. Throughout those last frames she was crying and gnashing her teeth and I was more worried about her than the state of the game. She wanted me to win more than I did! The upshot was that in the confusion I handed the match to Reardon when I could still have won. I thought all the frames were finished. I got it into my head that he'd reached his winning total but he hadn't. I could have changed my mind and apologised for the mistake but I shook the fellow's hand and finito. Must have been the strangest victory on record. That was water under the bridge, but it was nice to extract my revenge six years later.

I'd perfected an ingenious routine at Sheffield that year. It's well known that I'm a night owl. During afternoon sessions I can be zombified. I look at my watch and wish it could be nine o'clock in the evening. It's only then I can feel any movement! I counteracted the problem by fooling my body into thinking the afternoon was really the evening. I had to get up at the crack of dawn. By 6 am I'd have taken a taxi to the Crucible and been ready to practise. A couple of times I was lucky enough to persuade some poor unsuspecting fellow to prop up the other end, but most mornings I was on my own. When everyone else surfaced around 10.30 I had four hours of solid practice under my belt. Then I drank a pint of milk to sustain me for the rest of the day. My mind knew it was a trick, but the body seemed convinced. I was much sharper during the afternoons though a little weary at the end of the night session.

It's a funny couple of weeks – trying to get yourself together and keep everything firing on all cylinders for that length of time. You can never tell what's going to happen. I've gone into the championships on top form only to be knocked out at the first stage. This time I was in the final and not playing that well. I've always said that the longer I'm in a tournament, the better I get, so reaching the final was proving a point. Funnily enough the actual match doesn't stick in my memory that much. The semi outshone it. I do remember losing three frames on the trot to put Reardon 15–12 up. All I had to do was give myself another dressing down backstage, talk to Lauren for a while, then take the next three frames to square the match. After that it was all downhill.

There was no singing and dancing in the streets. My main feeling was one of relief. I'd achieved something for someone. I suppose I could have given Lauren the cue and said: 'Go on, beat Reardon.' I don't recall any euphoria after that initial moment with my daughter. I'd won and that was it. I've become fairly hard-bitten over the years. Seen it all before. I got home to Manchester in the early hours of the morning. By lunchtime I was catching the train to Dyffed for an exhibition. Another day, another dollar! Snooker hadn't taken off then the way it has for Steve Davis. We poor mortals had to work for a living.

Within a few days of taking the title I heard Davis interviewed on Piccadilly Radio. He said something to the effect that he was the best player in the world. That was just before I beat him 5–0 at the Forum in Wythenshawe (the place where I conceded too early against Reardon). If Davis had won that encounter, I don't think he'd have got out alive. The crowd was very hostile towards him. They couldn't forgive him for coming into my patch and claiming he was a better player than the world champion. It was my first outing in Manchester since winning the title and I really enjoyed the evening. I stayed longer than usual signing autographs when John Spencer who was playing there as well took me aside and said: 'Come on Alex, you've signed enough.' It wasn't like John. He harrassed me out of the club and drove me to Portland Lodge in Manchester where 500 guests were waiting to celebrate my world title. Les Dawson was there; so was Willy Morgan and a host of other footballers; and so was my family flown over from Belfast. Lynn had arranged the party as a surprise – though of course it was me footing the bill! We were still going at 7 am next morning. I never did have an Irish homecoming like Dennis Taylor last year. My diary was too full to fit it in.

There's one chap I'd love to meet again if anyone can help me. He claims to be a bookmaker and is called Brian. He certainly had me fooled, and Del. The shyster took £900 in bets from us on Higgins to win the title. The price was 25–1. Neither Del nor I have clapped eyes on him since.

I might have been on top of the world, but I wasn't at all convinced I could stay there. I must have had a big heart to withstand ten years of late nights and hard drinking and still emerge as world champion. There was no question of physical frailty. My doubts centred on the dual role I was trying to play. Lynn couldn't grasp the importance of practice. She resented the time I spent away from home. She thought that if you were the best player in the world, that was it. Why practise? Even to this day I don't think she understands. She was more interested in Alex the husband and father. It was obvious we couldn't have it both ways. I was re-motivated. To be a modern day champion with all the extra pressures of television and increased competition was very satisfying. I'd justified my belief in myself. The question was where to from here?

(*Lynn:* Children had never really gone to tournaments at that time, but Alex wanted Lauren with him. She used to go into his room during the interval and say: 'Win Daddy' – and he did. It was incredible. If he felt a bit down during the match, he'd nip out to the toilet, give her a kiss then go back and win another frame. I had Lauren in my arms when he won the title. She was wide awake. The people behind me in the audience were pushing me forward and Alex was calling for me to go down. I didn't want to because I felt it was his five minutes of glory. Alex was pleading and the crowd nudged us forward. Suddenly there we were on television. People told me afterwards that I didn't look very happy. I suppose that was right. I remember standing there thinking: 'Well he's done it' and feeling absolutely nothing. I was pleased for Alex, but, at the same time, apprehensive about what lay ahead. I said to one of the players' wives backstage: 'Here we go. This is where my problems really begin.' And I was right.

I think on the whole I handled his success pretty well. It changed Alex completely. He started going to London more often, visiting the night spots and mixing with a different crowd. He seemed to draw away from his family. He was riding high and full of himself. His personality was transformed. Suddenly I didn't seem to matter to him. I was okay for him when things weren't going so well, but as soon as success came along, it was all forgotten. His attitude seemed to be: 'I'm the world champion and I can do anything.' There were times when I desperately wanted to leave him but he used to say: 'You can't walk out on me – I'm the world champion.' Like a fool I stayed.)

Lynn seduced me with talk about taking things easy now that I was world champion. She said I had nothing to prove any more, so why flog myself. I listened to that talk too much. Started to believe that I could stay at the top without practice instead of devoting myself to the game again.

(*Lynn:* I was the level headed one as usual. Alex got carried away with himself. I was used to long hours and lonely nights with him out of town, but it grew worse and worse. It got to the stage where I'd have to find out from friends what he was up to. He never told me anything. Perhaps it's just as well. I didn't much like the sound of what I heard. Alex claims that I nagged him about keeping late hours, but that's all in his imagination. It didn't bother me. I knew it was part of the job. I wanted him to make as much money as he could while he was in demand. The we could invest and he could ease off. I had plenty of help from a nanny while he was away. When he was fifty or sixty miles down the road I used to watch him. The only place I didn't go to was London. I'm not one for the spotlight. I never liked London. He had his separate collection of friends down there and spent more and more time with them. I knew there were other women. I could sense it when he came home. He must have thought I was born yesterday. When a husband disappears upstairs because he's supposedly tired, you know what he's been up to. I was disgusted by it. Not only that, I was genuinely afraid of catching something from him. How did I know what sort of girls he'd been with? There were other reasons for our split up. Reasons which I'd rather not go into.

It was inevitable that we would separate. It happened in late August 1983. I mention that date because it's significant. Practically all the flashpoints coincide with the start of a new season. I hadn't spotted the pattern then, but each of the subsequent break-ups happened at the same time of the year. It seems that something snaps inside him as the big tournaments draw near.)

9
Edge of Oblivion

Everything collapsed when Lynn walked out on me. It was the price I paid for winning the world title again. In the eighteen months since beating Ray Reardon at Sheffield, I'd gone from the peak of happiness to the depths of despair. As bad as things had been, I didn't expect it to come to a complete break. Somehow I couldn't believe that my wife would do the ultimate thing. She took out a court injunction to stop me seeing the children. When my solicitor explained the significance of that, I felt the blood run to my feet. Any attempt to see Lauren or Jordan would land me in prison. I couldn't bear the thought of that. How could I be a criminal for trying to see my own kids? I just dissolved in tears when I heard that news.

Thank God, I was able to challenge it in court, and the injunction was rescinded. I loved my wife very much and idolised the children. I still do. Lynn was probably right to be laying down the law. I did understand her problems. I never have been an easy bloke to live with but a leopard can't change its spots. The trouble was that my wife didn't understand my problems. My 'spots' arrived at fifteen when I left home. I was a cavalier, a man's man of a snooker player, if you like, the hustler's hustler. I'd been used to travelling all over the place hustling for a living since I was a kid. I didn't know any other life. It was all about machismo. The split with Lynn came because I couldn't conform completely to married life. Being a devoted husband and father was affecting my livelihood in the high pressure world of professional snooker. I tried desperately hard to combine the two roles.

Time and again, I caught the milk train home from some far-flung exhibition date to arrive, laden with presents for everyone, in time to see the milk delivered to the doorstep. I tried to spend as much time as I could with the kids doing the normal fatherly things. The result was that my snooker was suffering. Practice was down to an unacceptable minimum. If you don't keep your weapon sharpened, it goes blunt. What Lynn couldn't grasp was that I got a piece of paper from my manager each month which said 'go here on such and such a date' and 'there on another'. There was no room for manoeuvre. I was a slave to my schedule.

For the previous year or so there'd been loads of blazing rows. Lynn and I both have strong wills which contributes to the problem. Equally, there's been a lot of love both sides. Since the children came along, the marriage changed, Lynn couldn't come with me on the circuit like before. Left to my own devices, I was bound to wander from the straight and narrow. For heaven's sake, I'm not a monk! When the love and intimacy disappear at home what is a red-blooded male to do?

My wife seemed to turn to stone. For one thing, she used to have Lauren in bed with her from an early age. It started as a comfort thing when I was away, but pretty soon became a habit. Even to this day, Lauren still sleeps in Lynn's bed. It's wrong and it meant the end of our relationship as a normal husband and wife. That's where my late nights in front of the video began. Lynn would slope off to bed early in the evening, Lauren would be with her, so there'd be no room for me. To counteract it, I'd get a few cold lagers out of the fridge and settle down with my cigarettes and the television for company.

I would be three o'clock in the morning before I turned in, midday at the earliest before I surfaced, so I'd missed breakfast, missed mornings entirely with the kids and, more often than not, had to leave in a few hours for another appointment. Now that I was on my own in the house, I more or less gave up. The family unit had meant everything to me. Without it there didn't seem much point carrying on. What was it all for – the house, the money, if not for them? I tried to find the antidote by immersing myself in my game. I forced myself to go to Stockport and practise, but it was no good. I was playing out of my subconscious only. After a while, I'd have to put the cue away and come home.

Home. An empty house. Kids' toys strewn everywhere. Everything in the same place it was when I left it several hours earlier. That's when it hits you. I phoned Lynn at her mother's house and begged her to come back. The wires were red hot between Cheadle and Heald

Green – they're only a mile and a half apart. She wouldn't hear of it. It was the first time she'd made an independent stand like that and I didn't know how to handle it. If her parents hadn't lived so near, perhaps she'd have stuck it out at home. It was too easy just to run across the road at the first sign of trouble.

I lost count of the hours I sat at home and moped. I didn't want to do anything. With a superhuman effort, I once or twice got off my backside and walked a mile to the village pub at lunchtime. After the first pint I came home again feeling that everyone was looking at me. I had to get out, but didn't know where to go to hide. The press were hanging around my doorstep pestering me for the inside story. When you're public property, you can't even be depressed in private.

The last thing I wanted to do was play snooker, but I was booked for exhibitions. That survival instinct wasn't quite extinguished. My pride also wouldn't let me do what I'd never done – cry off an exhibition. I'd take a cab to Stockport station then sit on the train for another three hours feeling worse. I'd get to London, book into another dehumanised hotel and go through the motions. There was no one to share it with, no one to talk to except cab drivers. I tried to be as nice as I could with people but it wasn't easy.

As far as tournaments were concerned, I was fodder. All sorts of people were beating me including players I'd normally brush aside. Dave Martin beat me 5–2 at the Jameson International, but worse was to come. I lost to Mike Watterson in the first round at Bristol! I never liked Redwood Lodge as a venue anyway – it's got no atmosphere. Against Watterson I was just going to the table, hitting the ball and walking away again. My mind was shot to pieces. There was no way I could concentrate on anything except how to get the family back together.

In between matches, I became a recluse – locking myself away in the bungalow, drawing the curtains and living in a world of permanent darkness both mental and physical. Sometimes I sat all day and never spoke to anyone. Sometimes I didn't even bother to get dressed. There was no point, I wasn't going anywhere. Even though I was lazing around feeling sorry for myself, I wasn't relaxing. I started taking Mogadon tablets to help me sleep and got hooked on them. If two didn't knock me out, I'd try three and so on. Still I didn't sleep. Eating was out of the question. I tried takeaway Chinese meals or a curry but couldn't get past looking at them. There was a self-destruct element inside me battling it out with my time-honoured survival instinct. I had no idea which one would triumph. The thought of food became repulsive. It was anorexia nervosa. I'd got to eat, but couldn't force anything into my mouth. For a period of two months or so, I was only eating one meal a week. That's all I had to sustain me. I lived on lager, tea and fags. When those ran out I was in trouble. I've never been domesticated and the thought of shopping was too much. I didn't want to be seen in public anyway. My weight dropped from ten stone to nine. I had coughs and colds which lasted a week at a time. Not to put too fine a point on it, I was going downhill fast. If Lynn hadn't helped I would have wasted away.

To her credit, she didn't want to see me vegetate despite our problems. She was only a short distance away, and made sure that I didn't run out of supplies. She didn't ostracise me completely, but at the same time, made it clear the break was final. To lift my spirits, she arranged for the nanny to bring the children to the park so I could see them. I'd have about half an hour with them on the swings, but always with the nanny standing close by, then it was time for them to go back to Lynn and I disappeared into my hellhole again.

Even Lynn got tired of me forever begging her to come back, so her mother or father used to intercept the calls and refuse to let me talk to my wife. That was the last straw. In despair, I called my sister Isobel in Australia and asked her if she would intervene. I'd be sobbing down the phone, asking her to speak to Lynn. 'Tell her I love her and want her back, but don't say I put you up to it.' Isobel and I used to speak every day. She was so worried about me that she offered to send my niece, Julie over from Queensland to be with me.

As the weeks went by, Lynn softened. She eventually agreed to come away to Majorca with me to give the marriage one last try. We kept it a very close secret although she told her parents of course. They looked after Jordan while Lauren came with us. I think they tried to talk their daughter out of the reconciliation, but she told them she was going. It was a last desperate throw on my part – one that almost ended in disaster.

I had thought about suicide many times during that period. Until Majorca, I didn't think I'd ever have the courage to attempt it. The holiday went wrong on the first day. Because Lauren was so small, we didn't have the freedom to relax properly and enjoy ourselves at night. Being in a villa, we had no baby sitters. It all blew up that night after the three of us had been out for a meal. Lynn is a healthy eater, but I was still battling with anorexia. I couldn't face anything. The meal was ruined because of my neurosis about my daughter. I dreaded the thought of her having an accident, so while she was charging around the restaurant in true Higgins style getting up to all sorts of mischief, I was right behind fussing and fretting like an old mother hen, Lynn just kept on eating. She was in one of those moods of hers – refusing even to share a bottle of wine I'd ordered.

I said: 'Come on, let's get out of here', and we went to a pub. Again Lauren wouldn't relax. I asked for a beer but was so busy trying to look after my daughter that I didn't have a chance to drink it. When we got back to the villa, I sat down to unwind. I was all keyed up so I uncorked a bottle of champagne I'd bought to celebrate the reconciliation and settled down to read a book. It was about seven o'clock in the evening. We'd arranged to meet another couple at the harbour and go on to a nightclub. Lynn didn't want to go all of a sudden. She said we couldn't with a young child to look after. I said I'd go on my own then, and another almighty row started. She accused me of being unable to live without drink and said I wanted the best of both worlds – to have a family when it suited me and in between, lead the life of a single man. I told her not to be so stupid. All I wanted was for us to go out for the evening. It wasn't a lot to ask.

It reached screaming pitch and I could see there was no way out. Lynn didn't want the marriage patched up at all. That was obvious from her attitude. We were in Majorca under false pretences. My world was coming apart again. I shouted: 'For Christ's sake, Lynn, I'm a human being. I've got a personality as well you know!' Beside the bed was a bottle of nerve tablets I'd been on since the break-up. I grabbed a hold of them and said: 'Do you want me to take all of these, because I'm sick and tired of all this?' I swallowed the lot – 150 tablets shaped like smarties. With Lynn staring at me in disbelief I counted them as they went down. 'There's one, there's two, there's three, there's four.' Then I emptied the lot into my mouth. She just stood there with Lauren in her arms. Even that couldn't shake her. I took the remains of the bottle of champagne and swilled that down for good measure. I said to Lynn: 'There, I've done it. Now I'm going to the bar down the road. If you want to go and get a doctor, do so. If you don't, that's up to you – I don't care!' She didn't.

While she disappeared into the bedroom I made my last gesture before leaving – a suicide note in which I wrote: 'Now I've ended it all'. With that I went to the bar 60 yards away and ordered a bottle of San Miguel. Very soon I was getting drowsy. The stuff was working. I took another mouthful of Spanish beer and that's the last thing I remember. . . .

(*Lynn:* Alex was being completely unreasonable. How did he think we could go to a nightclub with Lauren to be looked after? He wanted to be a married man and live like a bachelor. I was so shocked when he swallowed the tablets, I couldn't believe what was happening. He said: 'This is how much I love you' and poured the lot down him. Even as I watched it, I thought he was shamming. A few moments later, I went out into the garden fully expecting him to have spit them up. He was gone! And I was in a foreign country with no idea how to contact a doctor.

To make it worse, Lauren had picked up a virus and was sick every few minutes. I bundled the baby into the car and set off to find our friends for help. We didn't know which bar he'd gone to. There was no way I could go looking for him. So while I tended to Lauren and her sickness, our friends searched for Alex. They found him slumped unconscious against a bar.

We rushed him to hospital where the doctors tried to ask me what it was he'd taken. I'd forgotten to bring the bottle with me so I tried to make them understand what transquillisers were. They took him straight into the emergency unit and gave him injections to stop him lapsing into a coma, but it was no good. They put him on a drip and a heart-support machine because he'd gone past the stage where they could pump out his stomach. It was touch-and-go. I phoned my father from the hospital and he said he'd catch the first available flight out to Majorca.

I stayed by Alex's bedside praying that he'd pull through. If he'd died, I'd have had it on my conscience for the rest of my life. I wondered how I could ever tell Lauren that her daddy killed himself while we were on holiday? The doctors didn't think they could save him and told me to prepare for the worst. Alex was in a coma for forty-eight hours but miraculously, started to recover. He must have the constitution of an ox. My father looked after Lauren while I kept a vigil at the bedside. The doctors were amazed at his recovery. They said he came within ten minutes of death. Feeling a little better myself, I went back to the villa and started to make arrangements to get Alex flown home where his own doctor could look after him. The next thing was that the hospital telephoned us and said he'd gone missing! The funny thing is he's never referred to the incident. It's as though he wanted to block it out of his mind and pretend it didn't happen.)

I remember waking up with something strapped to my private parts. It hurt. Then I realised I was on a drip and saw all this gadgetry above the bed. I decided I'd had enough of that and pulled the drip from my arm and the strapping from between my legs. I hate hospitals. I wasn't going to stay in there a minute longer than I needed. Still feeling dizzy and sick, I slipped out of bed and while no one was looking, escaped as best I could. Running was beyond me, but Hurricane still managed to evade his pursuers! They saw I'd gone and came after me. I had a head start on them. My mind was working well despite the coma. I figured that if I back-tracked, the last place they'd think of looking for me was in the hospital grounds. There I crouched until all the medical people had gone. I'd thrown them off the scent. First thing I did was light up a cigarette then find my way to a bank. I only had a few pesetas on me and I knew I had have to get another air ticket if I was to get home without going back to the villa first. The nausea was terrible. I must have looked like death, but I managed to get myself to the airport and flew back to Manchester without telling Lynn.

She'd find out soon enough. I wasn't over-impressed with her performance. You'd have thought she'd have asked my manager to come over and help out. Instead she ran to her father again.

I took the overdose to shock my wife into action. I wanted her to know that I was a real human being with feelings and a personality. A wife who cared would have done something to help instead of turning it into a national disaster. All she had to do was phone a doctor when I swallowed the tablets.

Who knows what goes through anyone's mind when they try to take their own life? I didn't really want to die but some part of me obviously did. I guess I couldn't take the shattering realisation that a holiday intended to patch up the marriage had been a total waste of time.

Lynn said that she would consider coming back to me only if I went to hospital for a complete check-up. She thought there was something seriously wrong with me. It wasn't just the mental breakdown, but the fact that I was losing so much weight. I agreed to go

112

into Cheadle Royal, a mental hospital nearby. As soon as I walked in I knew I'd made another mistake. I was surrounded by a bunch of headcases. They had these therapy sessions in which the inmates all sat around discussing their problems and playing silly games. I couldn't stand that. It was all bullshit. Okay if you had some of your marbles missing, but there was nothing wrong with me.

I gave it two days. On the second day, I walked into the session and they were all doing anagrams! I took one look and said to the doctors: 'I've had enough of this. I'm going home – ta-ta.' On the way out I added: 'By the way, the answer to the anagram is operation.' To this day I haven't paid the bill because one of the hospital staff tipped off the newspapers that I was having treatment. They apologised but I told them could stuff their £400. I didn't go into a private hospital to have my privacy invaded.

I put it all behind me when my wife came back. You could keep your mental hospitals – the only therapy I needed was to have my loved ones around me. Then I was back on the road with a vengeance. Only a month after lying in a coma I was beating Steve Davis in the final of the Coral United Kingdom Championships. I'll tell you all about that but for the moment, let's consider this man they call the Ginger Magician.

10

Ginger Magician

The hustler has little regard for his opponent. With Steve Davis it's different. He's the only player to have crawled under my skin. I don't like admitting it, but he bugs me. At the best of times I'm not a heavy sleeper, but before a match against the Ginger Magician I can get screwed up. Trying to beat him became an obsession. Not just for the personal kudos, but for the sake of the sport. Davis belongs to the cold, clinical school of snooker, dedicated to amassing trophies and money. My game is played for love.

Despite the bad publicity that has dogged me every step of the way and my own shortcomings which have landed me in hot water more times than I care to remember, the public love me. They warm to me because I'm human. I have all the frailties they recognise in themselves, but a divine gift they cannot equal. Davis sends them to sleep. Spectators have no point of contact. How can you relate to a robot? They like to sense what a player's feeling, put themselves into his shoes. That's a hopeless task with the Ginger Magician. You'd get more reaction from a stone! I suppose they need someone to boo as well as someone to applaud. Davis has the satisfaction of being the world number one, but there's only one People's Champion and that's much more important to me.

I've never been the sort of person to win at all costs. Defeat doesn't gnaw at my insides like it did with Davis when Dennis Taylor beat him on the black in the 1985 world championships. That's probably why I haven't won as much as my talent deserves. Losing to Davis nevertheless is a pain. I stand as a bridge between two generations of snooker players: Spencer and Reardon on one side, Stevens, Knowles and White on the other. I have a certain amount of respect for them all, but feel confident I can beat them. That goes for Taylor as well.

The hard fellow to beat is Davis. You have to admire the way he eliminates every ounce of emotion from his game and concentrates on one thing – grinding his opponent into the dust. But equally, he's boring; a slow-moving creature more likely to turn the kids away from the sport than fire their imaginations. Davis can't help it. It's in his nature.

I remember in the qualifying stages of the Coral UK in 1983, the year I went on to beat Davis in the final, we were playing on adjacent tables. He was up against a useful opponent and I was playing a complete unknown. At the most there were a couple of dozen spectators watching his match, but three hundred or so glued to mine. That says it all.

It was Davis who indirectly landed me back in the dock for swearing on camera. I'd beaten him in the Benson and Hedges Masters and out of relief to be on the winning trail again, I turned to my legion of fans and whispered the immortal words: 'We are f------ back!' It was no more than a whisper. Unfortunately, the BBC kept their cameras trained on me and the whole nation was able to lip read. If it hadn't been for the television director that night, hardly anyone would have known. It was typical of my luck; all I was doing was savouring the moment. Until then I always thought the BBC snooker producer, Nick Hunter was a pal!

A few moments after the victory I was caught off guard for the second time. Another television crew jumped on me for an interview before I had a chance to wind down. In the heat of the moment I said I hated Davis. The interview was shown the next morning and viewers must have got the impression it was a considered opinion. Of course it was nothing of the sort. I don't have an ounce of affection for Davis, but I don't hate him. What I do hate is the sinister bunch of hangers-on who follow him around.

I first met them down at Romford in the late seventies when Barry Hearn booked me for a series of money matches at a seedy little dive called the Matchroom. Little did I realise I was being used as fodder for Davis. Hearn was nurturing this talent and a troupe of East End desperados were growing fat gambling on his ability to take on all-comers. By getting me down there, Hearn was guaranteed a full house. In those days the Matchroom was part of the Lucania chain of clubs which Hearn later sold off to make his fortune. Don't get the idea Davis started off in some romantic little corner of London. The place was full of tin ashtrays ingrained with dirt. If you asked for another cup of tea, it came stale and cold in the same chipped cup you used the first time. You had to stand up because there was nowhere comfortable or clean enough to sit down. I detested being asked to play in those conditions. There was no love lost between the Hearn camp and me from that moment on.

Before those engagements at Romford, I knew very little about Davis. I'd seen him occasionally knocking about as an amateur but that's all. Now I watched him grow. He was obviously a very good player. A little rough at the edges but with geniune class. As a bloke though, he didn't have much about him. It was Hearn's ideas which made him grow. With his manager pulling the strings and calling the shots, the young Davis was happy to do as he was told.

Before he hit the heights there were fellows in the Matchroom making a fortune backing him as an amateur. The grudge matches were always Davis versus Higgins. The crowd was hostile towards me – something I'm not used to. They were a bunch of hoodlums; real tough East-enders who'd jumped on the Davis bandwagon the moment it started to roll. They came from all over dockland and that part of Essex to feed off the young wonder boy. When we played, they screamed and shouted like banshees. You could hear murder in their voices. I took a few followers with me from London (I lived there for two years) but they were *real* Eastenders; friendly, sincere types who'd go out of their way to do you a favour. Walking out of the Matchroom, I felt I was taking my life in my hands. There was a set of poky wooden stairs lit by a single bulb which led from the tables to the bar downstairs. Making my escape was a precarious business, especially if I'd won. I never lingered very long, just collected my winnings and got the hell out.

That's where the hate started. You couldn't feel hatred towards Davis as a human being, but you couldn't help despising the attitude of his fans. They were the dirty tricks brigade – not interested in fair play, only in winning at all costs. I took great delight in ramming their ill-gotten gains down their throats by beating Davis. He beat me plenty of times too. Overall I guess you could say he had the edge. There was one match when I was six frames behind going into the final session. I bet Hearn £1,000 that I'd win. He was laughing all over his face until I made it all square with one of my famous Houdini escapes. Hearn and his acolytes were worried sick. Unfortunately, I couldn't quite pull it off.

Although Davis was a good player, I would never have taken him to be a future world champion. He had no natural flair. It was all down to robotics and the unalterable laws of geometry. He's always been Borg-like; never betraying any emotion and concentrating so hard you could almost hear the machinery ticking over in his head. Even today I wouldn't rate him the best in the world. On a scale of 1 to 100 I'd award Davis 91 with Spencer and Reardon at their best scoring around 97. There's nothing outstanding about his play except for the discipline. It's only because of Hearn that he's been so far out in front of the rest.

It was my misfortune to have to dash all over the country playing one-night stands to supplement my tournament earnings. Davis, lucky fellow, was protected from that. Hearn's seen to it that he earns well outside the game. Consequently there's been no financial pressure. He's been free to concentrate on his game and free to practise until the cows come home. It's impossible to overestimate the importance of that. I'm not offering it as an excuse – it's a fact. Hearn has done a marvellous job selling the Davis image. There's more charisma in my little finger, but somehow the public have gone for it. His manager's kept him exclusive and that's made all the difference. You wouldn't find him catching the milk train to get home from some far-flung exhibition date. I wouldn't wish that on anyone.

Before the 1982 world championships, I decided it would be best for me to join the Hearn camp as well. I knew I'd virtually have to sell my soul but on the plus side, I knew this company would take charge of everything, even down to paying the electricity bills. Hearn's players don't sign a cheque without his permission! It's easier than keeping a little black book with all your expenses in. I was prepared to swallow the indignity of that for a slice of the action. Hearn had different ideas. He turned me down point blank, saying I was impossible to manage. He didn't like me, that was the truth. It hurt to be put down like that because to this day I believe I'm a better player than Davis. He's the clean-cut ambassador, but I could have done it too given half a chance. With the correct handling, I could have been a much bigger business proposition than Davis. It might have saved me from the troubles and pressures that have undermined my career, but it wasn't to be. Looking back now, I'm glad in a way that I didn't join the Hearn club. All that glistens isn't gold. Their life is about money. There's no passion for snooker. It's just a business. Let them get on with it.

It was a clever move by Barry Hearn to sign up the world champion,

Dennis Taylor and later Willy Thorne. That should help the Davis image considerably. Having Taylor there means that at least there's someone with personality. The other members of the Hearn establishment, Tony Meo and Terry Griffiths are pawns. I'm convinced they were taken on for Davis' benefit – just to perpetuate the myth of a snooker stable turning out players like racehorses.

The Ginger Magician came along at the perfect time. He walked into a goldmine that I'd helped to create and he had the youth to take full advantage of. I probably let down the fans by not winning everything in sight, but when I was Davis' age, the game was in a makeshift state. We were professionals but there was precious little professionalism about the way the game was run. By the time Davis came along, the big sponsors were getting involved. I was still very much the man, but there was no order of merit. He was organised and ready for the explosion, I wasn't. I'll get the romantic obituaries when I retire, Davis will have all the money.

Davis is not very complimentary about me, but I suspect he has a sneaking admiration. In his first year in the championship I beat him 13–9. In one of the middle frames he knocked in 130-odd but was dumbfounded when I went to the table and compiled a maximum clearance. Davis' eyes were nearly popping out of his head. It was a combination of bewilderment and admiration. The matches between us are heavily divided in his favour, but he knows that when I really get myself together, I have the armoury to beat him. He refuses a lot of the shots I'd play, but the ones he does play are practised and practised until they're in the groove. With all the time he's had to devote to his game, he must have gone over every shot dozens of times.

Davis plays the ball softly – much more softly than I ever did. It's a good idea because modern tables are suited to that. I've started to strike the cue ball more softly than I used. These days you can be missing the pot by quarter of an inch and find that you still go in at the right speed.

We've had a few confrontations across the green baize, Davis and I, culminating in that Coral UK final at Preston which you can read about in the next chapter. I've had the odd slice of good fortune, but on balance, he's had more than his fair share. I called him 'lucky' when he beat me 5–1 in the Jameson quarter-final at Newcastle and I meant it. Many in the game would agree with me that he has more than his fair share of luck. In that game at Newcastle, he had so many lucky breaks I wondered what the hell I had to do to beat the guy! It was infuriating because I felt good and was playing well, but still got hammered. It shows that a scoreline doesn't always tell the full story.

Earlier that year, his luck almost broke Jimmy White's heart in the final of the world championships. Jimmy was 13–11 behind going into the final session, having performed a miracle to get back into the match. I wasn't the only spectator willing Jimmy to win. In the first frame of that session he was in control. There were two reds on the cushion with White 34 in front. The blue was safe and so was the other colour. Suddenly (if that's possible with Davis), the world champion made what can only be described as a lunge at the balls. He got a cannon with one red flying into the middle pocket and the other bringing the blue off the cushion. The second red finished up over the other middle pocket and Davis was left with the easiest of clearances. It happened at a crucial time too. There's a big difference psychologically between 13–12 and 14–11. Jimmy was shattered by it, you could see. You had to fancy him to take the title for the first time until that stroke of luck. It's typical of what happens to Davis.

I remember playing him in the Irish Benson and Hedges and clawing my way back from 2–4 to 4–4. I looked like going ahead. All I had to do was pot the green off its spot. It was a half-ball and I was playing against the nap. That and a couple more colours and I'd have gone 5–4 ahead. As I hit the ball, I got a kick and the green stuck over the pocket. Davis went on to win 6–4. That was a nasty shock because I wasn't in the best form and I'd been digging very deep to stage the fightback.

It takes an awful lot to get to Davis. There are several thicknesses of ice to penetrate first. But he can be got at, make no mistake. A perfect example was the quarter-final of the Benson and Hedges Masters at Wembley in 1985. We played the best of nine frames as usual and I'd given up the conquest twice as a lost cause. I actually told myself 'Forget this one, babe, he's got you again.' At 4–4 he passed up yet another glorious chance to bury me and book his place in the semis. I'd constructed a useful break, but in trying to get position on the blue, left the cue ball too close to pot it. That would have won me the match. I had no alternative but to go for a safety shot. I misjudged it by three quarters of an inch and realised that I'd left it open for Davis to pot his blue and put me out of my misery.

For some reason, Mr Iceberg refused the shot. I thought to myself: 'Jesus Christ, this bloke's cracking up!' When someone offers you a lifeline, you grab it with both hands. Here was the world champ turning his back on the *coup de grace*. There wasn't even a decent safety shot on. After the blue, he could have got perfect position on the pink and that would have been curtains. Instead, he allowed me back into the match and I won 5–4. It was a packed arena and my fans went wild. I might have thought I was 'f------ back' but I had another think coming. Terry Griffiths went and spoiled it by knocking me out in the semi-final. If one of the Hearn lads doesn't sink you, another one will!

Without a shadow of doubt, the strain was beginning to tell on Davis that season. Dennis Taylor, Willy Thorne and Silvino Francisco all burst through to take their first major titles, making it clear that the rest of the world is catching up with the Magician. Thorne beat him in the Mercantile semi-final before winning the final and with his partner, Thorburn, knocked Davis and Meo out of the Hofmeister World Doubles. Perhaps the guy's only human after all! The fact is there's not much to choose any more between the best thirty players on the circuit. It's all down to bottle these days. It's a game where you've got to be able to soak up the pressure. Davis stood alone for a few golden years, but Thorburn is close on his heels and the rest aren't so very far behind. That fear of playing Davis which has paralysed so many players is subsiding.

The biggest humiliation I ever had at his hands was in 1983 when I went to Sheffield to defend my world title. He extracted full revenge for my Coral victory five months earlier by thrashing me 16–5 in one of the most one-sided semi-finals you're ever likely to witness. My followers have grown accustomed to my erratic form over the years, but they couldn't believe the change in me that day. Neither could several million television players. What they didn't know was that it wasn't Alex Higgins playing out there – it was a doped-up fool.

Six weeks before the competition, I put myself on a course of multi-vitamin tablets. I'd tried them the previous year when I made my comeback to win the world title, and they'd done me a power of good. I don't eat much at the best of times, so I need to get some goodness from somewhere. At that time, I was taking three to four tablets a day. I was getting the same problems again a year later – poor appetite, lack of sleep and tension, so Lynn encouraged me to try the vitamins again. A beautician friend of hers had been to the house and recommended some new tablets. I'd had a go at alfalfa and all sorts of things before hitting on these B-Complex tablets. They were okay, but I went over the top with them. A week before the Davis match, I doubled the dose from five to ten daily. I didn't have a care in the world. I was losing 9–2 to Davis and telling my manager, Del: 'Don't worry, I'll get him, there's plenty of time.' I felt terrific – more relaxed than I've ever been. It's no wonder, the vitamin tablets were acting as a tranquilliser. There was no adrenalin going around in my system, so no sense of danger. Before I realised what was happening it was all over and I'd surrendered my hard-won title in the most pathetic fashion.

Given the number of times we've met professionally, you might be excused for thinking that Davis and I have struck some kind of relationship. We haven't. We're like ships that pass in the night, usually on different oceans. He plays snooker his way, I have to try to counteract it. Our respective private lives don't come into it. His little clique stays very close and doesn't mix. Most players get together for a drink or a game of cards in the hotel or at the venue during a tournament but I can't ever remember seeing Davis there.

He hasn't changed a bit since those early days. Still the same computerised approach to the game, still the same lack of rapport with the public. According to his image he's Mr Clean. Only drinks water during a match, doesn't smoke, never gets into trouble, never runs off with wild women. You'd think butter wouldn't melt in his mouth. What the hell does he do for kicks? He can't spend *ALL* his time playing space invaders!

Davis can afford to be aloof from the rest of us. When he wants piano lessons, he goes to the extreme of having an instrument sent to his hotel. During the space invaders craze you wouldn't see him on the machine in the hotel foyer. Not Davis. He had one installed in his bedroom! It doesn't bother me. There's never been any warmth between us. I doubt we've exchanged more than a dozen words in ten years. Frankly, I'd rather have a drink with Idi Amin!

11
Houdini and the Magician

(Coral UK 1983)

It's often been said that I play better in adversity. I'm rarely too far removed from some personal crisis or other, so that could well be true. The survival instincts are very strong and they were never stronger than at Preston Guildhall in December 1983. More dispassionate judges than me have described my victory over Davis in the final of the Coral UK championsips as one of the most memorable of modern finals. Who am I to disagree? Leaving aside the quality of the play, it proved that I could climb two mountains at the same time. I conquered my domestic traumas and the world champion in one fell swoop.

As I've said, the tournament came around scarcely a month after my suicide attempt. I've dragged myself out of some abysses in the past, but never one as deep as that. The turning point was when Lynn took pity and moved back with me two weeks ahead of the qualifying stages. It was a family home once again and the dark clouds drifted away. I felt stimulated and re-energised. The tunnel vision of which I'd seldom been capable in recent years returned. My eyes were sharply focused on one thing – winning the UK title which I'd never managed before. Out there on the snooker table I could hopefully signal to the world that I was still in the land of the living.

(*Lynn:* Whether it was motherly instinct or not I don't know, but I couldn't bear to see what was happening to Alex. He was spending too much time alone. He'd withdrawn completely into himself and I was terrified he might try to take his own life again. He wasn't eating, he didn't sleep and he looked dreadful. Everyone said he was finished. In the end, I weakened. We just decided to get back together so I left my parents' house and moved back into the bungalow

**in Cheadle. The change in Alex was immediate. I cooked
him some of his favourite casseroles. He began to put on
weight and rediscovered his urge to practise.)**

I practised like I hadn't practised since I first turned pro. Ten hours
a day for eleven days! That's how badly I wanted the title. My schedule
of exhibitions and personal appearances usually left me only three or
four days off at a time. Thankfully that winter I had a longer lay-off
than expected. I wasn't about to waste it. I'd have loved a few rounds
of golf but I wouldn't permit myself the luxury.

It was a dreary business taking taxis each morning to play at the
Masters club in Stockport. Without an audience I'm only half the
man. Nevertheless, I stuck at it. For the first few days, I achieved
nothing. It was just a question of going through the motions; getting
my body into positions it hadn't been used to for some time. The
after-effects of Spain still lingered. The improvement didn't arrive
until day six or seven, then things started to buzz.

On the seventh day I was hitting the ball so sweetly it was a joy to
behold. Days eight and nine were even better. By day ten I was playing
out of this world. My partner was Warren King, the former Australian
amateur champion. To make life less dull, we played for stakes of a
fiver a time (I still needed that little incentive to keep me going). On
the tenth day of practice we played twenty-seven frames and I won
twenty-five of them. Included in that sequence were five successive
century breaks, two nineties and a couple more centuries with a 147
maximum thrown in for good measure. Even with form like that I still
didn't feel that eleven days were enough. I figured that somewhere
along the line I was going to have to beat Davis. I hadn't done that
since the quarter-final of the 1980 world championship three years
before. To be confident of repeating it I'd have preferred six weeks of
practice!

In the early rounds I wasn't exactly prolific. Murdo Macleod had
me 0–4 down and I had to slug it out to win 9–6. That was tough
going. Slowly my game improved. I walloped Paul Medati, one of my
sparring partners, 9–1, then beat Knowles and Griffiths without too
much bother to reach the final. Who should be waiting for me there
but the Ginger Magician himself! As the tournament wore on, I felt
myself beginning to acclimatise. The longer I'm involved, the more
dangerous I am. Familiarity breeds contentment as far as I'm
concerned. I must have a routine. My drink, my packet of fags and

my ashtray all have to be in the right place. A simple thing like seeing the same fellow bring my drinks to the table became a source of comfort.

For the first session of the final I was in a dream. Davis was perpetrating a few flukes again – three to be precise. It prevented my winning three of the opening seven frames which might easily have been mine. Something hadn't quite clicked with me. My legion of followers were kept very quiet by the Magician's relentless progress. Despite all the practice I'd put in at the Masters, I felt disorientated. My photographic memory was like some of those holiday snapshots you see – blurred and under-exposed. There were too many unforced errors but I knew I only needed to get into my stride and everything would be okay. At the end of the first session, the scoreboard told the grisly tale: Steve Davis 7 Alex Higgins 0. I was being blitzed.

(*Lynn:* I couldn't get to Preston because it was Lauren's birthday party that Saturday afternoon. While I was pushing the trolley around Sainsbury's buying knick-knacks for the party I overheard someone saying that Alex was 0–7 behind. I thought: 'Oh my God, what on earth will I say when he phones up to tell me?' I couldn't get home fast enough, dragging Lauren and the shopping bags to the car park and hurrying back to the house. I was dreading the phone call. The wife's the one who has to pick up the pieces. She worries herself sick while her husband's playing, knowing that she has no control of the situation. Then when he's losing, she has to find the right words of encouragement and try to gauge his mood. With Alex, that's never easy! When he called I told him not to worry – just to relax, enjoy himself and play his natural game. There was nothing to lose after all. His reaction astonished me: 'What are you talking about? I'm going to win!' I've never known him so confident. There was an unmistakable ring in his voice. Considering he was so far adrift it was quite a shock. I believed him. I put the phone down and tried to carry on with the kids while the press were knocking the door down trying to get a picture of the birthday celebrations. I suppose it did make quite a contrast to the gloom at the Guildhall. All I remember is getting the party games over with as fast I could to drive to Preston and be with Alex.)

I had a few visitors in my dressing room during the interval. First one in was the professional golfer, Andrew Chandler who's a good friend of mine. He walked in with his head in his hands. I was furious. I shouted at him: 'What's the game? If anyone should have their head down, it's me not you!' I told him that if he'd come to commiserate, he could clear off because I was going to win. Just then there was another knock at the door. In came a five foot spray of flowers, closely followed by a couple of fellows from Ma Baker's pool club in Derby. The owner, a lovely chap by the name of Wally had invited me there for a drink once when I was playing at the Assembly Rooms. The flowers were very impressive – there must have been £200 worth with a note which said: 'Come on, you can do it. Wally and all at Ma Baker's.' I couldn't possibly let them down.

My final visitors that day were Del and Rex Williams. Rex handed me a half-pint glass containing five vodkas with a topping-up of Coca Cola and ice. 'Come on, Alex, you have a sip before you go out again,' said Rex, 'it'll relax you.' They wanted me to beat Davis as much as I did. I told them I didn't need the vodka because I was on Mackeson. That was a deliberate change from lager because I thought the sugar content would be nutritional. I was too nervous to even look at food! The pair of them insisted, so I drank some just to please them. From that day on I've referred to them as Doctor Rex and Doctor Del!

Inexorably, I began to take charge. I got it back to 7–3 with a break of 76 and Davis was beginning to twitch. Still a long way to go but the Magician showed signs of faltering. He missed a couple of reds during that tenth frame. Like all predators, I could smell blood. We finished the day with Davis still ahead 8–7, but I was perfectly placed to strike on the Sabbath!

Inch by inch I worked my way into a position of control, levelling at 11–11 and going ahead for the first time at 12–11. Davis was sweating. He might appear outwardly to be Joe Cool but I could almost feel his heartbeat. The hustler can instinctively pinpoint the emotional state of his opponent. He knows when they're suffering and Davis was going through hell I promise you! I went 14–12 into the lead and the world champion was cracking. He started to applaud my shots: a little tap of acknowledgement on the table. I would never do that. It's bad enough sitting in your corner watching. You can admire from afar, but applauding isn't on. You're there to play snooker, not to praise the other fellow. Funnily enough I wasn't playing that well.

The only thing that could stop me now was bad luck. I live in mortal dread of that: a kick here, a fluke shot there. You can never tell when it's coming and it can scupper your best-laid plan. In the twenty-seventh frame it happened. Not a kick or a fluke – a cameraman!

There was a shot I had to tackle from the dodgy distance of about six feet. Dodgy because the cue I was playing with was too whippy by half. My world championship cue from the previous year had been smashed in the post remember. At that distance you have to punch the shot a bit. I got down to play it and was committed to the shot when I caught sight of the BBC cameraman moving over the corner pocket. The bloke was actually nodding! I missed the pot but didn't complain because it would have seemed like sour grapes. I had to carry the nodding cameraman all the way as Davis came back to lead 15–14. It was a joke. To have mounted a recovery like that, only to be baulked by a confounded cameraman. For a time I thought I was fated to lose after all. The words going through my head were: 'Davis, you lucky bugger, you're doing it again!' I remember thinking how lucky he'd been with his cues. After each of my world titles my trusty weapon had been snapped in half, yet the Magician even got himself into a car crash and his magic wand emerged unscathed. I wondered how he'd have coped with a makeshift cue for most of his career?

The rest of the match is a blur. I vaguely recall making a break of 77 in the final frame to win. I remember the din from my supporters and the stack of good luck cards and lucky omens all over my table, but the actual finish is lost somewhere in the emotion of that Sunday evening. The next thing I was aware of was Lynn falling into my arms as drunk as a skunk! While they got ready to make the presentation, It was all I could do to hold my dear wife up. She felt like a sack of potatoes. If I hadn't been there, she'd have collapsed on the floor.

Davis disappeared through the door and I was mobbed by my adoring fans from Yorkshire and Lancashire. I felt no great emotion. I'm not one to jump up and down. It was just another day. Snooker's such an enigma that no-one can ever master it. You can be in control for ninety-nine per cent of the time then one quirk of fate can finish you off. That's why it's such a beautiful game.

(*Lynn:* I don't drink as a rule, but I had to have a few that night to calm myself down. I remember standing at the bar with Rex Williams and he bought me a couple of glasses of white wine to steady my nerves. When Alex won I was so thrilled and so proud of him. The image of him lying so pathetic in that Spanish hospital bed flashed across my mind and my heart went out to him. I got more satisfaction out of that win than the world championship because it had been such a miraculous fightback. People behind were urging me to go on the floor to Alex but I kept crying 'No, no, no!' In the end, I was pushed and practically collapsed in his arms. I couldn't believe that he'd done it from 0–7 down that Saturday. I was so pleased that the critics who'd said he was washed up would have to eat their words. I'm certain that a lot of that victory was down to us – to Lauren, Jordan and myself. Alex was secure again after his nightmare and he was as happy as I've ever seen him.)

You had to admire Davis for consistently producing the goods. Everybody can do it for so long, but he's done it longer than most at a fiercely competitive time. The longer he goes on though, the more the certainty that someone will one day catch up with him. Without taking anything away from the man, he wasn't the same player even then. He'd suffered a few defeats (not at my hands necessarily), but it was the first time he'd been caught like that. I went back into the player's room and said: 'There you are, boys. There's the chink in his armour. There's your starter for ten! I've done him and I'm not even playing.' I beat him on four counts: discipline, safety play, potting the balls when they were there to be potted, and last but not least, sheer guts and courage. I've never been short of those.

I broke the habits of a lifetime by having one quick drink with Davis at the post-match reception. He looked more haunted than *I* normally do. If he hates losing to me as much as I hate losing to him, I can just imagine the agonies he was going through. I'm the first one to feel sympathy for my opponents when they're beaten, but how could I feel sorry for a millionaire. Unlike me, Davis didn't ever need to work again ... and he was only twenty-six.

Lynn and I celebrated at the Sandpipers Club in Fallowfield where my friend, Max Brown had arranged a party for twenty or so close friends. It had all been too much for my wife. She was asleep before we got there and I ended up dressed in a sweater and serving the drinks until well into the night. All I had were a few lagers. It was good to know that when all the dust had settled I had my wife and family to go home to. We'd saved our marriage and sealed it with a famous victory. Or so I thought.

Less than a year later, Lynn had gathered up the kids and fled to her mother's for a second time. I dreaded the thought of going through all that again. I tried everything to keep the family together ... even down to asking Helen Lomas, the wife of my former manager to intervene.

(*Lynn:* Even after we'd got back together there was no communication. We led separate lives: me and the children on one hand; Alex and his cronies on the other. The doting father we saw when Lauren was born had vanished. Jordan never got the same attention. Now kids were a drudgery; something he couldn't be bothered with. He'd go off and play his snooker and golf and leave me to bring them up single handed. That I could just about take. What I couldn't tackle was his increasingly bad temper. I couldn't discuss anything with him. He'd fly off the handle at the slightest excuse. Alcohol is one of his biggest problems. It distorts him. He knows it but falls into the same trap next time. He can't say no. That's why he spends so much of his life apologising to people for things he's done and said when drink got the better of him. You can take so much of that, then you've had enough. After one blazing row – drink induced of course – he was so sorry the following day that he bought me a Mercedes. That was his way. He sometimes surprised me by turning up unexpectedly on the milk train. He thinks that by apologising and buying gifts he can keep winning you round. He frightened me that summer after beating Davis though. There was so much pent up aggression in him.

He used to accuse me of spending all his money. He loves telling people that, suggesting that if it wasn't for me he'd be well off. It wasn't like that at all. To listen to him you'd have thought I had stacks of jewellery and Dior clothes. I haven't. He bought me a diamond for £8,000 once, but I didn't want it. It was too pretentious and I told him so. I told him to send it back and he did. Are those the actions of a greedy spendthrift?

After all these years, I still don't know what to make of Alex. He's so many people rolled into one. On the one hand he's sensitive and caring; then he can be quite vicious. Sometimes he's generous with money but when we fell out, he'd take it all off me. The Saturday I was leaving him for the second time, he confiscated a diamond watch he'd bought me in Australia.

He could have made things better for both of us by coming home from his exhibitions and tournaments like other players did. He'd have you believe that he was always on the road or working. That's not true. Between tournaments in recent years he's had a lot of time off. The fact that he chose to play golf instead of bringing up his kids isn't the fault of his profession. It's his fault even if he won't see it. I tried to reason with him. I told him that when you've got kids you've got to spend time with them and give them some stability. They don't ask to be born. A lot of players, when they've finished a show at 10.30 pm do the decent thing and go home. Not Alex. He'll stay and play a few more frames. If he'd come home and gone to bed and had a decent night's sleep, he could have got up and had breakfast with the children.)

What Lynn didn't understand is that you just can't switch off after a match. It's all about adrenalin. I'm on a sort of high. More so than most players because of my nature and the way I play. I could never just go to bed with a cup of hot chocolate like Lynn seemed to think.

With the help of friends, I managed to undermine Lynn's resistance after she'd left. We kept in touch most days. I figured that a house move and a fresh start could tilt the balance and bring us back together. One night Lynn and I and another couple went out for dinner and on the way we passed a house for sale in Prestbury. We'd seen the details and knew they were asking £235,000 for it. I'd tried to get Lynn interested but without much joy. When we drove by, I suggested we pulled into the drive. The house was empty so we looked into the windows. My eye was taken immediately by the oak-panelled snooker room. I astonished Lynn by asking her if she'd like it. I didn't give her much choice. We were still separated, but I turned on the charm and talked her around to my way of thinking. Before she knew it, we were back together.

(*Lynn:* He just swept me off my feet again. He fell in love with the snooker room and turned to me in the car on the way back and said: 'Shall we buy it?' I reminded him that we'd split up. He said: 'Oh go on, Lynn' and started the ball rolling just as he had when we first got married. From there I fell into his trap. To be fair, we'd been talking about getting back together. He thought that buying the house would bring me back. I liked Delveron House but once we'd split up again, he accused me of forcing him to buy it!

I thought it would work out at Delveron House. I hoped it would. We made promises to each other. I swore I'd lose weight and get back into shape; Alex vowed that he'd cut down his commitments and spend more time at his new home. Neither of us kept our word. Food was my escape from the loneliness. The more I ate the less I wanted to meet people and so it went on: a vicious circle. I joined Weightwatchers twice but gave up. I guess I was trying to hurt him the way he was hurting me by staying fat. I knew he hated it. I wanted to keep him at bay. I couldn't bear him to touch me. I developed this mortal dread of Aids.

He imagined I had a marvellous life in his magnificent house with its two acres of land. It was awful. The house was isolated so the children never saw anyone their age. I had no social life outside the place and because it was so huge, it took all day to clean, even with a helper. I didn't like his suggestion that I had it made and didn't know how lucky I was. He thought he had it tough in his profession, but he never gave a thought to my side of it. He didn't realise the pressure that builds up when you're the one left at home. It's the wife who has to pick up the pieces afterwards. She's the one who has to soothe the troubled brow and massage the ego. That's not easy. In any case, how could he say snooker was a hard life? What about the blokes who have to spend their lives underground? What about the ones with no job at all. That's what I call a hard life. It was *Alex* who didn't know he was born.)

It wasn't surprising that my form suffered badly towards the end of 1984 and the start of 1985. I was at rock bottom you might say. I cast my mind back to Muhammed Ali and the way he kept fighting back when they said he was finished. The difference was he wanted to do it all again. I wasn't so sure I did. When the time came for me to defend the Coral UK title I'd won against Davis, I felt like a heavyweight boxer coming out of retirement and not having the willpower to go through with it. I was thirty-five going on fifty and surrounded by enthusiastic braves fifteen years younger. They had the time and the love of the sport to practise. I felt washed up and lacking in any kind of motivation. Domestic problems had taken their toll. I played like a man in a dream when Davis beat me 5–1 in the Jameson tournament at Newcastle and even worse to lose to Mike Hallett in the qualifying rounds of the Rothmans. The eagerness to play just ebbed away. It happened the same after winning the world title, but I managed to raise myself to beat Davis and win the Coral UK. I wondered if that was my final fling.

One of the difficulties was the shorter nine frame matches. I knew that I could still take on anyone over the marathon course but with the game suddenly reduced to a five furlong sprint, I was open to attack from all sides, especially the young brigade. They say I encouraged them by banishing snooker's stuffed shirt image. It seems all I was doing was laying the seeds of my own destruction. The youngsters were desperate to get one over me and I can't blame them. When it's the best of five you can make a couple of mistakes and be out. Perhaps Davis was right when he said that I was no longer a force to be reckoned with over nine frames. He did say I was his biggest rival in the longer matches and so it proved at Preston. The Hurricane blew up again at one of his favourite venues, but not without some controversy.

I fought my way into the final for the second year running with a 9–7 win over Cliff Thorburn. He was leading 6–5 when he snookered himself and nominated the green ball to get out of it. When I say he nominated the green, I know that now but at the time I had no idea. That's where the trouble started. Neither I nor the referee, John Smyth heard Thorburn's call. When he struck the green, the ref penalised him a maximum seven points for not naming the colour. Thorburn was furious. He complained to the referee then stalked out of the hall. He appealed to me for help, but I hadn't heard a thing. The press took it out on me because the word was apparently audible on television. Unfortunately, the television mike over the centre of the table was of no use to me. I was sitting a fair way off and straining to see around the ref. He should have called not muttered. He hadn't lost the game, so I couldn't see what all the commotion was about. After that he did lose the game and it served him right. It took him three weeks to apologise. By then though it was too late. I'd already been condemned as the villain of the piece again.

So it was all set for a repeat of the previous year's final; Davis versus Higgins. The crowds who'd deserted the game during my poor run of form came flooding back to the Guildhall hoping for a repeat of my Houdini act. It wasn't to be. I came back well to 8–9 after being 5–9 behind overnight, but Davis played some of his best snooker to beat

131

me 16–8. I was only a shadow of the man from the year before. Even my daughter's fourth birthday couldn't inspire me to the heights of 1983. Afterwards, it was my turn to apologise for being childish. I'd accused Davis of being lucky when he beat me in the Jameson. He was but I shouldn't have said so.

12
Drugs

I never thought the day would come when professional snooker players had to cower in the corner of the gents' toilet peeing into plastic bottles! Compulsory drug testing was introduced for the 1985 world championships after the Kirk Stevens–Silvino Francisco affair.

Silvino had accused Kirk of being 'as high as a kite' during the Dulux British Open final that year and the game came in for a lot of unsavoury publicity. The WPBSA decided to clean up the image once and for all. Barry Hearn was the driving force behind the new drug-testing edict. I respect and understand his motives, but I think it was a massive over-reaction by the Association. We're not like a soccer or cricket team. We're individuals struggling to make a living. Athletes are only subjected to random tests but in snooker we ALL have to deliver into those plastic bottles. It's degrading and I think everyone resents it.

The players should be allowed more say into what goes on. The twelve-man committee issues its decrees and we all have to obey. Yet a good many of them have their own foibles. Rex Williams, the chairman makes no secret of his use of valium during tournaments. Still they sit in judgement on the rest of us and we have to suffer the slings and arrows without a whimper of protest. Whatever happened to camaraderie I wonder?

Drug testing held no particular fears for me. I never have and never would resort to drugs to improve my performance. I made a mistake once with the vitamin pills and it taught me a lesson. I like to be *compos mentis* when I'm playing. My game depends on detecting and reacting to subtle changes of mood in my opponent and the audience. You can't do that when you're stoned. I get my 'high' from having a fluctuating audience. I can make them laugh or make them cry. Tie them round my little finger. I agree with the game's administrators that drugs cannot improve performance. Kirk has found that out the hard way. On drugs you're a robot.

It's true I like a few drinks when I'm at the table, but not to improve my game. It helps remove that restless edge. While the game's underway drinking and smoking just become reflex actions. I might get through six or seven pints of lager and lemonade, but they have no effect on me. The alcohol's absorbed because of the nervous energy. I might as well be drinking water. Whatever people may think, I don't believe I have a drink problem. I've seen how the hard stuff can tear your insides out. There was a time when vodka was my favourite drink at the table, but not any more. A friend of mine from Belfast went down that road. He finished up under the surgeon's knife. That told me all I wanted to know about abuse.

I have smoked cannabis and occasionally sampled cocaine. That statement's not intended as a boast or an apology. It's a fact. There's no percentage trying to deny it.

The drugs scene of the sixties and seventies passed me by. It was the province of drop-outs, undergraduates and the middle class and I didn't fit into any of those categories. Until I reached the age of thirty I was naïve and uninitiated. The first time I came across cannabis was at a party. Someone offered me a smoke as naturally as you might hand the cigarettes round. Everyone seemed to be indulging so I saw no harm in it. Since then I've enjoyed smokes at social gatherings and in the privacy of my own environment. To me it's a pleasant way to relax, nothing more. Since relaxation is at a premium with me, it can bring much needed relief. In no way could my spasmodic use of drugs be classified as a craving, although, curiously, cannabis does trigger off a craving of its own – chocolates. After a few smokes I have this insatiable appetite for After Eights!

The strongest stuff I smoked was Colombian resin. I'm not sure how it came to be in the area. We called it rocket fuel because it sent you into orbit! Cannabis is so freely available these days that I'm not surprised so many youngsters get their hands on it. I've not come across pushers on the snooker circuit but I guess you can always get hold of the stuff if you want it badly enough.

I don't remember precisely when I was introduced to cocaine. It must have coincided with the stress and worries over recent years. Heaven knows, I've had enough excuses for seeking solace if I'd wanted them. I must point out that I have not used cocaine to any great degree. It has been a social thing, like cannabis. There've been countless parties where it's been in plentiful supply and inevitably, someone offers you some. Once or twice, I'll admit I've been led astray, but I was careful not to dig my grave too deep. I would never have got myself into the mess that Kirk did. I've watched him melt down the drug and mix it with soda in a glass. He really was in a state poor old Kirk. It made my stomach turn. Kirk's liking became an addiction as he's since confessed, I stayed with him for a couple of days to help him sort himself out, but it had gone too far. There was nothing I could do. When I heard he'd collapsed and been rushed to hospital, I was frantic to see him but the staff at St Stephen's wouldn't allow visitors. I was worried he'd gone over the top, but happily he was okay.

I've been offered cocaine by Kirk, but only on a casual basis. He wasn't a supplier or anything like that. The main supplier was a desperate character by the name of Smokey Joe Thickett, well known in the north of England. I've seen him so strung up on coke he's barely been alive. He was at the party Lynn threw for me after I won my second world title.

He had a collection of deadbeats around him, some of whom I knew but hadn't seen for years. They gave me the creeps, as thin as rakes and barely able to help themselves. One of the more ludicrous suggestions I read was that Smokey gave me coke to snort in the toilet after my victory. As usual, the man was talking nonsense. I was already high enough from beating Ray Reardon. Why did I need cocaine to lift me?

Over the years I bought the odd 'line' for £50 or so. I was experimenting to see what all the fuss was about. Nothing serious. To pretend that I was spending £1,000 a week is too silly for words. If I'd still been alive, my nose would have been burned to a cinder. That's the behaviour of a hopeless addict. I'd have been needing the drug every day and unable to hold a snooker cue. Apart from that, where was I supposed to have found the cash? My bank statements would have made interesting reading and I should think the tax inspector would have been pricking up his ears. It's inconceivable that I would spend that kind of money. I haven't had a big bet for three years, nor been to a casino for five. Money's too hard-earned to blow it.

Concocting some so-called revelations about me and cocaine would come very easily to Smokey. If it weren't so pitiful it would be funny. He's one of a little group of parasites who've been lured out of the woodwork to tell their cock and bull stories. They've made a meal ticket out of me. Thickett is a friend of my former manager and best man, Geoff Lomas whose wife has also jumped on the newspaper bandwagon. She's the one who came around to our house in tears one Christmas because Geoff had walked out on her. I gave her a few hundred pounds to buy the kids some presents. A fine friend she turned out to be!

Cocaine was present at parties during a break I took in Marbella towards the end of 1985. I tried some but reckoned without the shady characters on the Costa del Crime who are on the lookout for well-known celebrities and their off-the-field pursuits so they can sell their stories to the less scrupulous papers. To them I suppose I was manna from heaven. It was at the height of my domestic troubles and I was feeling pretty low. There was a girl who conned her way into a party we were having on a friend's yacht the day before I was due to fly back. I'd enjoyed a few days' golf with friends and some of us were getting nicely into the rosé champagne on the last afternoon. It was slipping down very nicely in the Spanish sunshine, considering it only cost a couple of quid a bottle from the local supermarket.

Afternoon turned to evening and, yes, there was some coke passing around. The girl was still hanging around at three o'clock the next morning. I had a plane to catch at six o'clock and needed some sleep. After the others had more or less dispersed, she made her move to get me into bed with her. She was one of those ladies who get a kick (and a few bob) out of boasting that they've made it with someone famous. I told her to get lost and said I was off to catch up on my beauty sleep. Obviously the woman was more offended than I thought. She invented a story about my being too stoned on coke to perform between the sheets. I'm telling you I'd have had to be stoned to go to bed with her. Blind as well! I wonder how much she made out of her miserable bit of gossip?

The same newspaper report claimed that I hid my drugs inside the trophies on the mantelpiece so that Lynn wouldn't find them. Someone with a vivid imagination dreamed that one up. For a start, I don't have many of the trophies on display. It's true I sometimes use the cups to store cue tips, razor blades, chalk, that sort of thing, but did anyone really believe there was a drugs haul under that lot? The Manchester police know exactly what goes on. They know who the pushers are. They've never raided me although they're welcome to. Perhaps if they dug up the garden they might find a body as well!

In spirit if nothing more, I'm behind the campaign against drugs. I'm not the type to jump on a bandwagon so you won't see me taking an active part. In any case, I couldn't swear that I would never touch drugs of any sort again. That doesn't mean I want kids to copy me. I'd like to take the opportunity of warning any of them who read this book not to dabble. The drug scene is a nightmare once you get into it. Look at Kirk. I'd beat the life out of Lauren and Jordan to get the message across to them. I've seen the rotten side of life and drugs are the bottom of the abyss.

13
Stop the World . . .

For no reason that I can think of, the start of the 1985–86 season was the signal for some of the fish-and-chip newspapers to launch their 'crucify Higgins' campaign. It began the moment I arrived at Derby Assembly Rooms to play in the qualifying rounds of the season's first tournament, the Goya Matchroom Trophy. The place was buzzing after a photograph of me with some young woman appeared in one of the Fleet Street rags accompanied by a so-called revelation about my tweaking her nipples. As usual, it was an old picture I don't even remember posing for – I get asked to do so many standing alongside this and that young lady – and the story was pure fiction. That's never bothered papers like the *Sun* and *Star*. They know that if I sue them, as I could have so many times, they'll get an even bigger splash out of the court case and sell enough extra papers to pay for the damages. I can't win. It's the last time I'll pose for photographs with young females.

What the papers never care about is the effect on the person they're pillorying. It never occurs to the bums who write that garbage that someone might actually suffer as a result. I couldn't concentrate on my snooker. I was more concerned with what Lynn would be thinking. I kept trying to phone her from the players' lounge but my home number was permanently engaged. Whether she'd left the phone off the hook because she didn't want to talk to me, or to thwart the press who were sure to be pestering her for a reaction, I had no way of knowing. Lynn has learned over the years not to believe half of what she reads but it's still not very nice.

So the pressure was on from day one of the season. I wasn't to know that it would intensify as the season wore on. When the Goya tournament proper came around, I was due to play the world champion in my first televised match of the season. Dennis Taylor didn't worry me at all. His being world champion made me even more determined to knock him off his pedestal. I knew he wasn't nearly as good as me and couldn't wait to prove it.

As everyone knows I played like a complete idiot and lost 5–1. In the first four frames, my aggregate points score was only 37! At the time, no one had any idea that I was playing under the heaviest strain imaginable. My marriage had just collapsed after the most appalling night of my life; I'd spent two hours the previous evening locked up in a cell at Macclesfield police station, and travelled to the match with a hairline fracture of the ribs.

It gives me no pleasure recalling the events of that night. I'd planned to have a quiet evening in watching the Barry McGuigan world title fight and enjoying a takeaway Chinese meal with a few friends. That part was all right, but Lynn went to bed early complaining that she was being abandoned again. I didn't feel like turning in. I went upstairs and told my wife that I was popping out to the pub down the road for a couple of nightcaps. It just so happened that Daniella, the Spanish au pair had gone there earlier with another Spanish girl who was au pairing at a neighbour's house. There was nothing sinister in that. I don't drive, and neither did Daniella, so the obvious place for us both to be was the pub two hundred yards away. There was no question of my taking her for a drink. I didn't even know she was there till I walked into the lounge. I had one drink and came home, Daniella was already back. I asked her to get me a coffee and bring it to me in the snooker room. I was going to show her some of my shots with the new cue butt I'd fitted together.

All of a sudden, my wife was shouting accusations at me from the dining room where she'd been spying on us. I thought she was asleep upstairs, but she'd been hiding on the landing. Lynn claimed I'd taken Daniella out for a drink and accused me of trying to have an affair with her. That wasn't the first time. The au pair had only been in the house a couple of days when she heard a couple of friends and me playing snooker late at night. The noise woke her and she came down to investigate. What was I supposed to do? I didn't know how to handle someone who'd only been in the house that short time. Anyway, she came in and watched us playing. I didn't invite her. It wasn't even my decision to have an au pair. Lynn hired her. I just paid the wages. Lynn never let up about that. She was convinced there was something going on between us. Although I have a reputation with women, I would never dream of 'playing' at home. I'd have been pretty stupid to try it under my own roof wouldn't I?

That night the lid blew off. It was the culmination of four years of pressure. The whole episode was so preposterous you'd hardly believe it. One thing I will not stand for is being accused of something when I'm fairly and squarely not guilty. I lost control. That's why the television set went out of the window. I had to vent my fury somehow. It was better than hitting Lynn. What is a fellow to do when his wife is behaving like this? I phoned her father and said: 'Your daughter's playing up. She's being ridiculous. All she wants to do is fight. You'd better come round – I've had enough.' I let my wife speak to her mother. That was a big mistake. The hysterical mother took it upon herself to call the police. If I hadn't made the one call in the first place, I'd never have been arrested. The complaint didn't come from my wife – it came from fourteen miles away!

(*Lynn:* I was in bed when I heard the au pair leave the house. Alex came upstairs and said he was going out for a drink. When I accused him of going to meet Daniella, he flew into a rage, and stormed out. She came back at about eleven o'clock and I decided to get up to see what was happening. When I heard Alex coming back, I hid on the stairs. He said: 'Make me a coffee Daniella' then whispered: 'Come into the snooker room, I've got something to show you.' She said: 'Are you sure your wife can't hear us?'

I nipped through the dining room to hear the conversation. The au pair said to Alex: 'I think someone is listening to us.' Alex came running through to where I was and blew his top. He said he'd been showing Daniella his cue. I said: 'Since when have you ever talked about snooker to au pairs or nannies?' Alex went berserk. It was the first time I'd caught him red-handed. I shouted that he was disgusting and ran back up to my room grabbing Lauren and locking both of us in the bedroom. We cowered behind the bed while he smashed the front door windows with one of his golf clubs.

It was terrifying. Alex came upstairs bellowing with rage and battering on the door saying he wanted to have it out with me once and for all. Lauren was screaming and clinging on to me. This went on for four hours and I heard him throw the television set through a bedroom window. He was wrecking the place.)

140

The police had it in for me. They roughed me up good and proper. It was completely unnecessary – my nine and a half stone against three burly coppers! They shouldn't have been there in the first place. I may have had a few drinks, but throwing a television through a window isn't exactly hurting anyone. The police don't normally take sides in domestic squabbles, but they did this time. I grabbed the kitchen knife and pretended I was going to end it all. I shouted at them: 'Do you want me to slit my throat or something? How can you believe this lot and not listen to me?' It was five against one. When they tried to restrain me there was a heck of a struggle. They damaged my ribs trying to slip the handcuffs on and one of them was supposed to have a twisted wrist. They can't take anything in the force these days!

Most of the rough stuff happened in the car on the way to the station. I shouldn't have tried mixing it with the 'Mounties'! When I got to Macclesfield one of the able-bodied officers saw fit to tell the press and the world: 'We've got Higgins locked up'. It was a big story for someone, but it didn't do me any favours. In fact the local constabulary haven't done me many favours since I moved to Prestbury. I've had a few of them in my house to sample my whisky and I've let them use my drive as a turn-in for their patrol cars. I know they have a job to do but you get some sour apples in every barrel and I found three of them in one night!

At the station, they tried to humiliate me like they always do when they get someone famous under lock and key. They clapped me in a cell and worked on my pride with that holier-than-thou smugness of theirs. I wouldn't say they were the Gestapo, but it was heading that way. Then they left me alone in the cell for two hours or more with just a packet of fags for company. They said they were charging me with breach of the peace then drove me back home. They could quite easily have forgotten the whole episode.

Damaging my own property hardly constitutes an offence. As for breach of the peace – my house is isolated. The neighbours didn't complain. They wouldn't have heard machine-gun fire! The police definitely overstepped the mark. They believed Lynn's father when it was obvious that most of the hysterics were coming from my dear wife. Instead of leaving me alone to watch the video, she kept stirring it until I could take no more. When I got back to Delveron House, Lynn and the children had gone. I was well and truly alone with a big match to play the following afternoon. I took a couple of sleeping pills and went to bed at about five in the morning.

(*Lynn:* It was the worst night of my life. While the struggle was going on with the police, Daniella sat sobbing on the front doorstep. Goodness knows why she was so upset. She was partly to blame. That first week she came to the house, she was in the snooker room until three o'clock in the morning in her dressing gown. That infuriated me. The next morning at ten o'clock, there was still no sign of the au pair. A fat lost of use she was to me fast asleep in bed. I was trying to get rid of her. It was sickening.)

When I got up on the Sunday, I could hardly move with the jabbing pains in my ribs. I sent for an osteopath who lives nearby, a chap called Dennis Brown. I got a report from him to say there was heavy bruising – a diagnosis which was confirmed a week later when I had a full check-up at Macclesfield Hospital. They said there was a suggestion of a hairline fracture as well. I wanted to get it on record that I'd been roughed up by the police.

I didn't have time to see a doctor to get any pain killers so on the way to Trentham Gardens, I stopped off in Stoke on Trent and bought one of those painkilling sprays that footballers use. I was forced to start a big match and a new season not only in physical pain but with the embarrassment of having been arrested and the torment of knowing that my marriage was over. I didn't feel too clever that day but it never occurred to me not to turn up.

Snooker is show business and the show had to go on. I even managed a humorous interview with Dickie Davis before the match and put on a pretty good act I think. That was the professional in me. Others might have thrown in the towel under that pressure, but the old survival instincts saw me through. At the time, no one apart from my wife's family, the Macclesfield police and some lucky freelance journalist had a clue what I'd been through the night before. There was no one I could talk to about it. My agent lived 250 miles away and my own family was across the water. I kept it all bottled up inside.

There are two sides to every story, but I for one always tried to keep my marriage alive. It was dead and buried now. That was the biggest burden to carry as I set out to face the world champion. The pain and the embarrassment were secondary. Apart from losing my wife, I'd lost my children again. That really hurt. It's hard to keep your mind on potting balls with all that floating about upstairs. Compared with those matters, snooker paled into insignificance. I absolutely hated the game at that moment. You could say my deep love of snooker went out of the window with the TV set! It was mainly because of the demands of the game that my family life was in tatters.

I was never going to beat Taylor. I tried but Dennis played quite well. I suppose he was buoyed up as the world champ out to prove himself again. My points total was ridiculously small in the first four frames, and I went on to be well and truly trounced. After the match I broke down in front of Del and told him everything that had happened. Looking back, I believe the earlier newspaper stories about my alleged philandering episodes were the straws which broke the camel's back. Lynn had taken those reports very badly. The wounds were too deep to mend; the gulf between Lynn and me was unbridgeable. At that stage I didn't even want us to get back together. I felt as though eight years of my life had been wasted – except for the children.

I wanted to erase that evening from my mind. It caused me too much heartache. Whatever else I'd been, I'd been a great provider and, hopefully, a good father.

Del suggested I went to Spain for a week to recuperate, but it wasn't possible. There were too many things to be sorted out. My wife was adamant that the parting of the ways had come.

I bought her a £65,000 house a stone's throw from her mum and dad. I thought they could tie a piece of string between door knockers! I wasn't shirking the issues. My wife could have had anything she wanted. Even so, the police found time a few weeks after the arrest to let her break into Delveron House. There seemed to be one rule for them and another for me. They watched as she broke the windows to unlock the front door. As far as I'm concerned, that's criminal damage. Obviously Lyn had to have access to get her things, but if this is a lawful society, what were the police doing supervising a break-in? They did it without informing me. Surely that's against the law?

(*Lynn:* Alex had locked the doors and left a set of keys in the back of the lock so that I couldn't get in. If I hadn't asked for police assistance, I'd have had nothing in my house. I took the washing machine, the spin drier, a bed for the children, the dining suite and a large picture we had in the hall of Alex being presented with the world trophy. I was afraid he might smash that in one of his rages and I wanted

to keep it for the children's sake. I didn't bother to collect
my diamond ring. I only wanted the essentials. By this time,
Alex had already got a new girlfriend living with him. I
didn't go near any of her stuff.)

I first met the girl in Manchester. I'd seen the face a year before, but
hadn't made contact. I invited her out and we got on very well together.
She was an absolute gem and seemed to understand my situation. She
had a place in Manchester, but moved in with me at Delveron House.
It was good to have someone to talk to and to get some genuine
affection. I have a very active mind and we sat for hours talking about
books, poetry, films, you name it.

It was a bit frightening getting used to the bachelor life again. In
public I was shy, stupid though it sounds. It would take a few drinks
to bring me out of my shell. My new girlfriend was a godsend. She
cooked for me, comforted me and came everywhere she could with
me on the snooker circuit. Our relationship was passionate. She used
to wake at seven in the morning feeling amorous. I'm not used to that.
I wondered if I could stand the pace. Usually it was me who frightened
people, but she terrified me. She was one of these energetic modern
young women who hold nothing back. Sometimes I think she forgot
I was an old man of thirty-seven, thirteen years her senior.

I fell foul of the law again receiving a court summons to appear
before Macclesfield magistrates. I couldn't go because Jimmy White
and I were defending our Hofmeister Doubles title in Birmingham.
The police were insistent, but I phoned the clerk of the court and was
under the impression that he was deferring it until sometime in the
New Year. I asked my girlfriend if she'd write confirming that everything was in order. She put her own address on the letter so the second
summons was sent to her house in Manchester when I was playing
another tournament in Nottingham. Consequently I had no idea I
was supposed to be in court on December 19th, the same day that I
was due to play Steve Davis in the Kit Kat Champion of Champions
event.

Next thing I heard was that the police had issued a warrant for
my arrest. Some reporter from one of the fish and chip journals told
me at the hotel when I got up that morning. When Higgins is playing
snooker everything has to stop – even the law! I turned up to a
photo call at Nottingham University with all the other former world
champions, but no one wanted to know anything about the tour-

nament. The Higgins warrant had overshadowed everything else. While the sponsors, players and pressmen were drinking champagne, I was in a little back room frantically trying the persuade the clerk of the court that I couldn't let the organisers down. Snooker had to come first. He said they were coming to arrest me. I said they couldn't do that because I was in the middle of a tournament. He wasn't the least bit sympathetic so I said: 'Go on, arrest me if that's what you want and I'll sue you for loss of earnings!' He tried to come the heavy but I told him the confusion was created because of a mistake by the police. They knew where I lived. They arrested me there for Christ sake! What was the point of sending the summons to an alien address? I told the clerk they were completely out of order. He had to accept it in the end. They should have sent the letter recorded delivery in any case. It was more pressure on me – just what I didn't want. It seemed that every time a tournament came around, there was another trauma. It's not surprising that I got hammered 6–1 by Davis that evening. My life just seemed to be filled with drama. It was all boiling up again. Already I was growing jaded with the game but decided that I had to keep on forcing myself. I couldn't just go out like a lame duck.

My snooker was going downhill. Jimmy and I were dumped out of the qualifying rounds of the Doubles. It didn't help that we were both up until four o'clock the morning of the match – or that we had a disagreement over money during a night of fairly heavy drinking. Then I lost my Kit Kat semi-final against Davis and to cap it all, Ray Reardon beat me in the final Pot Black series at Pebble Mill. I was easy meat.

The house became unmanageable with no one to clean it and no washing machine. I was surrounded by dirty dishes and washing and didn't even have a kettle to make myself a cup of coffee. I had to do that in the microwave. It didn't feel much like Christmas. My girlfriend put up a tree in the lounge and hung a few baubles on it and the mantelpiece was crammed with cards. To keep out the prying eyes of the photographers, though, I had all the curtains drawn in the house. The playroom below stairs was the most poignant. The kids' toys were all there, but no kids. I collected Jordan for a weekend and brought him back to the house but Lynn wasn't keen on his seeing me with another woman.

I had to miss Lauren's Christmas party at school, but I went a couple of days later armed with twenty-five bags of fudge. At first I didn't go into the class. I leant by a tree in the playground and just

145

watched her through the classroom window. It was like a scene from *Kramer v. Kramer*. There was my daughter at play while I could only watch with my nose pressed up against the window pane as it were. What made it worse was that when I did go over to the classroom to give away the fudge, Lauren refused to see me. What had happened to the little girl who'd helped me to win the world championship?

(*Lynn:* Alex was the only father who didn't show up for the school Christmas party. It was no wonder Lauren was frightened seeing him. She still remembered the night of the television set. When he came to collect Jordan for the weekend, she stayed in her bedroom screaming that she didn't want to see him. It was terribly sad. I didn't want it that way. I didn't like the idea however of Jordan being taken back to the family house with another woman. It was the first time he'd seen his father since that night and there was this strange woman in our house playing with him on the snooker table! It wasn't very subtle of Alex to turn up on the circuit with a new girl on his arm so soon after our break-up.

I was worried about the effect of all this on Lauren. One day, coming out of school, she turned to her friend and said: 'My daddy gets drunk and smashes windows. I wonder if he'll come here and break these windows too.' I was close to tears hearing that. She's at private school and as a rule the parents don't read the garbage papers. But she heard one of her classmates saying that Lauren's mummy didn't live with her daddy and that one day her mummy would marry another man and then she wouldn't want Lauren. Typical of the cruel things kids say to each other. I had to carry her into school because she didn't want to leave me.

Once the novelty of having a new girlfriend wore off, Alex started coming round to my house a lot and phoning me three times a day. Sometimes he'd arrive on the doorstep with a packet of bacon and say: 'Will you cook this for me?' When he stands there with that little-boy-lost look on his face you can almost forgive him everything.

Repeatedly I told myself I wasn't going to fall for it, but I couldn't resist him. There was still something very strong between us. It was strange how I enjoyed hearing from him even after that terrible night. As we know, he can charm the birds out of the trees when he wants something. When I feel that I'm forgiving him, I remember certain things that have happened and it brings it all back home.

Christmas was very sad. For the first time, Jordan was old enough to understand what it was about. He was asking when his daddy was coming round to see him. Alex came on Christmas Eve and spent a few hours with them, then he showed up unexpectedly on Christmas Day. His girlfriend had cooked them a turkey but I finished up making him tuna sandwiches in the afternoon. While he was fixing Jordan's train set on the carpet I thought what a shame we couldn't be like that all the time. We all got on so well together and the children were really happy with him. It made me very depressed to think they weren't getting the fatherly love that other kids were getting. Then I thought to myself that if they saw Alex twice a week they'd get more attention than if we were living together all the time. It was a lovely day. He stayed till quite late and we buried the hatchet. I think that's when it hit home that he didn't have us any more. It was the turning point for him. For the previous couple of months he'd been having a high old time enjoying the bachelor lifestyle and thinking that's what he'd been missing – the unattached male going to the clubs etc, getting up when he wanted to. I think he realised it wasn't everything.)

I would have loved to get the family together again and told Lynn so. We could have let her house and moved everyone back to Delveron House. Lynn wasn't sure what to do. Even when she said she couldn't come back, I got the feeling she wanted to all the time and was just waiting for some excuse to say 'yes'.

The Christmas festivities had hardly died down when I had to prepare for my next public appearance – and it wasn't on the snooker table. I never expected the world's press to be in attendance for a silly little court hearing about some domestic trivia which had been blown out of all proportion. You'd have thought 'News at One' would have had a few more pressing engagements!

Over the holiday, I'd run out of oil for the central heating system. Apart from freezing to death, I had to manage without hot water as well. On the day I was due at Macclesfield magistrates, I couldn't even wash my hair. Instead, I thought I'd have a bit of fun and try the old Frank Worthington look – slicked back hair, Elvis Presley style. The newspapers loved it. It made me look like a criminal but I thought 'What the hell, they think that's what I am anyway!' I put on my favourite double-breasted suit and my racing topcoat. The whole thing would be a bit of a gamble! I nearly had second thoughts about the hairstyle but decided to be brave and face the music without a hat.

When I got there, the place was swarming with reporters and cameras. I thought something important must be happening! Behind the courtroom, I signed a few autographs for the remand prisoners and then came my turn. It felt odd standing there in the dock though I guess I should be used to it by now. I've been accused and convicted of things all my life. I wanted to get the hearing over with as fast as possible. I knew there'd be a binding over, but can't say I was overjoyed to be sentenced at all. Having done no more than damage my own property, I don't think I should have been dragged up before the magistrate in the first place. If I'd have fought the evidence, I'd have come away clean but my brief advised me it would be too involved if I'd revealed that the police had done a bit of the hard stuff on my body.

I didn't like the things the woman prosecutor was saying about me, but for once I had to stand there and swallow it. It wouldn't have taken much to persuade me to challenge her remarks. I wanted everyone to know that the police were equally guilty. Discretion got the better of me. We decided to let sleeping dogs lie and cause less embarrassment. That slap on the wrist cost me £800 in legal fees.

14

... I Want to Get Off

Things were closing in on me. I felt I hadn't a friend in the world. I finished up under a psychologist and was as near to a mental break-down as you can get. The break-up of my family was tormenting me. I had to put it to the back of my mind somehow and prepare for the next big tournament, the Mercantile Credit Classic in Warrington. Living alone wasn't good for me, but my girlfriend went back to her flat because it seemed that I was jumping out of the frying pan into the fire – finishing one serious relationship and getting involved in another. I had to be free to breathe and couldn't do with people crowding me.

Needless to say, any thought of practice had gone out of the window again. I'd gone to the Potters Club in Stockport to try to get my eye in – but not literally! I had a few frames with Paul Medati, a long-time professional snooker player who's not quite good enough. I'd known him for years but there'd been always been plenty of niggle between us. He was a backbiter was Medati. I wanted to play for money and give him a 20-point start but he wouldn't have it. More than his pride could bear I guess. I was down in the dumps because Lynn had just refused yet again to come back to me. I'd been to her house earlier in the evening pleading with her for my sake and the kids' sake to give it another try but she wasn't interested. I couldn't get it off my mind.

Between frames with Medati I kept phoning my wife trying to make her see sense. I'm nothing if not persistent. When I came back to the table after the third or fourth call, Medati stuck his big nose in. He told me to stop flogging a dead horse and said there was no point trying to rescue the marriage because Lynn wasn't interested. I wasn't taking that from him. His girlfriend was goading him and he kept on digging at me until I couldn't take any more. If he thought I was going to scuttle out of there with my tail between my legs, he was sadly mistaken. Before I could move, someone grabbed me from behind. It was an ambush! He offered to fight me in the car park. Higgins in a car park? He had no sense of theatre. I said: 'Do me a favour, I'm not duelling in any car park.' I worked myself free, put my cue away and invited him into the matchroom.

He laid the first one on me then I knocked seven bells out of him. The punch which blackened my eye made me so angry that I just took him apart. Sometimes you have to be hit before you hit back. It only lasted a couple of minutes. I had him on the floor telling me he'd had enough and begging for mercy. I said I hadn't quite finished and gave him a little more of the Higgins treatment with the toe of my shoe. In the middle of it all, Medati's wig flew off. You could have knocked me down with a feather! I knew the fellow wore a hairpiece, but didn't realise it covered his entire head! Suddenly I had this boiled egg under my arm. He grabbed the wig and scampered off to the car park after one last kick from me. I didn't want to cause him undue pain, but regardless of who was right or wrong, no one would ever say Higgins was a chicken.

I looked around and the bouncers were coming after me. I said: 'Don't worry, chaps, it's been a nice fair fight behind closed doors. You'll find Medati in the car park. I'm going home.' A friend of mine, Shep, drove me home where we opened a bottle of champagne and he did a jig of delight.

(*Lynn:* **Alex turned up on my doorstep at 1 am nursing a badly swollen eye. He pointed to it and said: 'This was for you!' I told him he shouldn't bother to fight on my account. I didn't want it. He asked me if he could stay the night. I said 'no'.**)

I wanted to stay at Lynn's because I was due to play Dennis Taylor on television next day, and needed some care and attention, as well as someone to make sure I didn't oversleep. Once again I'd been involved in a brawl on the eve of a confrontation with the world champion. Lynn wouldn't play the Good Samaritan so I went home. Medati phoned to say he would keep quiet about the fight, but that his girlfriend had talked to one of the papers. I had no intention of discussing the matter in public because I wasn't especially proud of what I'd done. Equally I didn't want to embarrass Medati about the wig. What would the papers make of it?

(*Lynn:* I phoned Alex the next morning to make sure he didn't miss the match. A woman answered. A friend of Alex's had asked her to stay the night because he was in a bad way. It was 10 o'clock and I told her it was time to wake Alex up. I hung on until he came down and I heard him shouting to the girl: 'What are you doing in my house?')

I had to have an alibi for the eye which had turned twenty shades of black and blue overnight. I went riding with a solicitor friend of mine, and dreamed up the story about falling off one of his mounts and getting kicked in the eye. He agreed to go along with it. I had to act fast because several million viewers would be watching me that night. I thought I covered it up pretty well. I smeared the eye with make-up from the self-service kit I had. I often used to put eye shadow on before playing in front of the cameras. When I was 4–2 down to Taylor, it began to irritate like mad and I had to wipe the eye. The make-up came off and the whole world could see what was underneath. Then the press got hold of it!

Amazingly, I beat Taylor with some good snooker, but there was no hiding place now. After the press conference when I spun the line about the riding accident, I had to go on television to be interviewed by Dickie Davis. I should have had an oscar! Of course it couldn't go on. Already I'd let it slip about Medati and the wig and before long the Spectrum arena was buzzing with fanciful versions of what had really happened.

Why did I lie about the black eye? Well, as I eventually admitted on 'News at Ten' that night, it was simply to keep the pack of reporters off my back. I knew the story would have to come out because Medati's girl was about to 'sing'. I 'came clean' in the ITN interview and treated it all as a harmless bit of nonsense. My family didn't see it that way. After the match my mother and my sisters were on the phone wanting to know what had happened and if I was all right. The fun element soon subsided when I was badgered by the press that night and the whole of the following day.

I put out a statement explaining the situation, but still they wouldn't leave me alone. Reporters and photographers were crawling all over the house and hiding in the driveway where they thought I couldn't see them. What was it all about? If two grown men couldn't have a fight behind closed doors, what was the world coming to? No sooner did I turn one reporter away than another arrived. I agreed to let a photographer in to take a picture of the black eye then, next afternoon, the same bloke wheeled his way through the half-open door while my attention was taken by something else, and sat taking pictures in the snooker room for the next twenty minutes. It's an impossible situation. You can't be rude to them because it gets reported and if you're pleasant, they take advantage.

I ended up locking myself in the house and pulling all the curtains shut. It was the only way. The newspapers wanted a victim. Since snooker had become big-time, even outstripping televised soccer, there was a media mafia which wanted to discredit the game. They thought they could to it at my expense and they damned near succeeded.

Rex Williams was my next opponent for a place in the semi-finals. Now Rex hadn't reached a semi-final for about a hundred years! It looked a good draw for me but the confidence I'd built up since knocking out the world champion was all eroded by the time we came to the match. Seeing yourself labelled a liar across the front page of the papers isn't exactly guaranteed to lift your morale. I'd had very little sleep for three days and I was worried about the bad publicity over Medati. In fact, it was all I could do to step out of the house. I didn't want to be seen in public. I'd have sooner laid down and died. I was hemmed in from all sides. Uncharacteristically I gave in to defeatism. Beaten before I lifted the cue. I told myself the only way was to cut out the fancy play and just try to win. It was no good. After the first frame against Rex I lost interest. All I wanted to do was get away.

The WPBSA wouldn't let me. I was crying in the dressing room after losing the match and told Paul Hatherall, the Association secretary, that whatever happened, I didn't want any interviews. He said I had to but there shouldn't have been any compulsion about it. The only thing I *had* to do was turn up and play snooker. The Association is supposed to protect me from difficult and unpleasant situations, not force me into them. There are times when I don't want to talk, and that obviously was one of them. However I had no choice. They shoved me into a corner with predictable consequences – I exploded. It was the climax of a sustained period of stress. Having to answer banal questions about my black eye was too much on top of all the other problems. Frustration got the better of me. I threatened to blow the game inside out to the highest bidder. It didn't need a psychiatrist to see through that surely? It was my way of saying: 'Can't you see I've had enough? Why don't you leave me alone.'

It was bad enough trying to cope with three days of unbroken harrassment from the press, now I'd gone and lost to Rex Williams, an opponent I'd expect to beat ninety-nine times out of a hundred. No wonder I was upset and depressed. The reporters and officials didn't care. I wasn't supposed to have feelings like anyone else. I was fair game. The vultures kept pecking at me just like they do every time a new tournament's about to start. You can guarantee they'll be sniffing around trying to unearth some scandal or other. Why me every time?

As soon as I'd shot my mouth off, I knew there'd be repercussions. In future, if the Association insists that I give a press conference against my wishes, I'll give the newspapers three sentences and leave. They could have avoided it all by taking me away before I erupted. Del, my manager and Paul Hatherall could see the danger signs but chose to ignore them. And I'm the one who suffers.

On the way out of the hall, I called into the WPBSA room and asked for my wages – the sponsor's cheque for the losing quarter finalist. They refused to give it to me. I might have said some nasty things in reply, but they were being unreasonable and in any case it happened behind closed doors. They could have handled the incident privately without going to the trouble of setting up an independent tribunal. They seemed to want a whipping boy which was unfair considering all the business I'd whipped up for them over the years. I tried to reason with them. I said: 'Come on, fellahs, you don't have to put me through all this. Give me the money and let me get out of here.' The next thing I knew, they'd called for the tribunal to consider charges against me of bringing the game into disrepute.

Not only that but they invited John Pulman to be one of the independent judges. How could I stand for that? I couldn't accept having a former colleague sitting in judgement. I remember one night John was so 'tired' his head fell into his dinner plate. John, the man I served with breakfast in his hotel room in Canada because he'd had a skinful of whisky the night before? We've all had a drink and John would be the first to admit it. Fortunately, he had the good sense to turn down the invitation.

That night at Warrington was the beginning of the end of Del Simmons and me. We'd been drifting further and further apart. I could see I was becoming an embarrassment to him. After the business of the cheque at Warrington, there was no way we could work together for much longer. I was annoyed with him for not taking my side and he thought he'd be better off without me.

Just then, the first ever European tournament took place in Belgium. It gave me a respite. Getting away from Britain and the gutter press was precisely what I needed. Their attitude was turning me against the game I loved. At that moment I hated snooker. Pure, undiluted hate! In contrast, Belgium was a delight. The fans adored me there just as much as they did in Britain. They can pick up television coverage of the major tournaments, so they felt as if they knew me. I got the love without the aggravation. In that atmosphere I prospered for a while, beating Dennis Taylor yet again, though losing to Kirk Stevens in the semis. The relief didn't last long. When I got back to London and picked up the papers, the nightmare returned. Now it was stories about drug addiction, suicide attempts and any other muck they could rake up. It seemed that everyone I'd considered a friend was selling his or her salacious story. On top of that, the prospect of the tribunal hearing hung over me. I was warned that it might have the power to suspend me for life. All because I'd threatened in one idle moment to blow the game inside out. How could they suspend me for that when, by their own admission, there was nothing to 'blow'?

Two people stood by me during that crisis. One was Jimmy White who phoned to remind me that at least I had one good and reliable ally. The other was Ian Botham who seemed to understand what I was going through and offered me the services of his chauffeur and minder, Andy to help keep the press off my back. It was a kind gesture and much appreciated. I wish I could have helped him when it all blew up in his face. I'd met Both at the Old Trafford Test match against Australia. He invited me over for the day.

I was in a trough of despair. My wife wouldn't have me back; my private life was being stripped to the bone, and my colleagues were ganging up on me. I'm not mentally ill but I was unbalanced for a time. The worries drove me to the edge of a breakdown. Perhaps I went over the edge, I don't know. Luckily I had the fortitude and sense to seek professional advice.

Several people had told me about the value of hypnotism. I met a chap in Scotland some years back who said he could help me. I was interested but said I preferred to do it off my own bat. This was the time. I went to see a doctor in Manchester who specialised in hypnotherapy. I should have known it would be a failure. My mind was so active that he had to inject me with a sedative. That was the hard part. I hated needles and can't stand the sight of blood. Poor chap tried for half an hour to send me into a trance but even with an injection he couldn't do it! In the end, he had to give it up as a bad job. I knew there wasn't a man in the world who could hypnotise Alex Higgins!

Next I went to see a psychologist at a Manchester Hospital. He's an expert in stress. I had two exploratory sessions with him and he said there was nothing physically or chemically wrong with me except that I was prone to bouts of hyper-tension. The danger was not having any escape valve – no one to talk to about my problems. Even if Lynn had still been with me, I doubt it would have helped. She didn't really understand.

The specialist began teaching me to identify potential crisis points and control them. I started a course of anti-stress exercises which entailed lying flat out on the floor and letting my mind wander up and down my body, tensing it up and relaxing it again. It meant putting physical pressure on various joints like my little finger or toe and making them hurt. Once stress can be related to pain, it's much easier to relieve. When I get anxious, my shoulders get hunched. The doctor taught me to cope with that by giving myself a light massage of the neck and temples and removing the tension. It certainly helped though I wasn't sure I'd be able to keep it up.

My first appearance after those scandalous newspaper stories was against Terry Griffiths in the Benson and Hedges Masters. I should have won. The fact that I could go out there and play in front of all those people showed that my resolve was still there. I could see a small light in the darkness. They'd backed the untamed one into a corner and he didn't like it. The only solution was to come out fighting. I took the defeat graciously that night. My fans were there and that was a great comfort. They'll never leave me. When the British sporting public sees something it likes, it stays with it. Before I went out to play Terry, I phoned Lynn and asked to speak to Lauren and Jordan. Lauren came to the phone and said: 'Hello, Daddy. We were going to send you a telegram today, but we couldn't because it takes three days to get to you. Don't worry though, Daddy, and don't let the men bother you. They've been following me and Mummy around but don't let them get you down. We love you, Jordan loves you, so win this time.' I didn't win, but the message gave me the strength to go out there with millions of eyes riveted on my every move.

155

(*Lynn:* I was very worried about Alex while the newspaper stories were piling up. After speaking to him though, I felt that he had weathered the storm. I thought he could only build himself up from there – he certainly couldn't go any further down. Even Terry Griffiths said that he couldn't have played that match under those circumstances. It proves that Alex has a strong character. He couldn't have known who his friends were during that period. It was terrible at my end of it as well. Reporters sat outside all day in their cars and some of them sat outside my parents' house as well. We daren't go out. With Lauren starting to read, I had to hide the papers from her. She kept seeing her father's picture and asking me what it was about this time. Thank goodness it happened when they were too young to understand.)

15
On the Mend

The wounds started to heal when I took myself off to Dubai for a fortnight. Most of what the newspapers had been writing about me was gibberish, but after such a traumatic few months, I needed time to take stock; time to think about myself and where I was going. It was a sort of self-imposed rehabilitation exercise. A lot of nasty things had been said. My image had taken a bigger battering than usual. The position with the WPBSA was the most serious it had ever been. Having seen what they did to Silvino Francisco, I knew that they could put the boot in for me very easily. There were many who'd be only too glad to wipe me off the face of snooker. Yet I felt some security in the knowledge that a life ban on Higgins would do the game no good. They need sponsors; they need big television ratings there was only one person who could guarantee a packed house every time. Modesty forbids me going any further.

I rang an Arab friend of mine, Khaled, who arranged for me to spend two weeks in the Middle East, all expenses paid. In return I'd play a few exhibitions at his house. That was good enough for me. I planned to reset my body clock; to get to bed in reasonable time; to get up in the morning and have breakfast like everyone else; even to spend a little time sunbathing by the pool. Basically to try to act conventionally.

I asked Lynn to come with me, but she refused. I was sure she'd come back if she could guarantee that things would be different. Although she wouldn't go to Dubai, I kept in touch with her on a regular basis. She was as interested in my convalescence as I was. You don't spend all those years together and not have any feeling for each other.

It was cloudy in Dubai so the sunbathing took a nosedive. My diet improved however. Khaled had me installed in the Hyatt Regency Hotel. I had them bring me up my breakfast at 10 am each day as the new regime got under way. 'In for a penny, in for a pound' as they say. I went through the card from hash browns to eggs Benedict. I finally plucked up courage to have a stab at 'Hot Congee'. It was described as rice and chicken with a few spices thrown in. I managed to extricate some little pieces of chicken as I tried to come to terms with this new dish. All of a sudden, lying at the bottom of the plate I unearthed a fried egg. It stared up at me with a fat yellow face. It was too much at that time of day! Bang went my exotic breakfast experiment. I settled for something simpler after that.

The ordered existence was doing me good. I cut down on the drink intake mainly because the house where I played was dry. I got into the habit of having a couple of vodkas before playing, then nothing until after the game. It worked wonders – relaxing my nerves and stopping me from having to dash to the toilet every few minutes like I do when I'm on lager and lemonade.

While I was there I made one maximum break which got into the local papers, and followed it up with a 140. I missed the last black! More astounding were my antics with one hand! Someone laid down the challenge so, for a laugh, I showed them what I could do with the left arm behind my back. The break built up slowly, 15, 20 and so on until I reached 50 and was still going strong. There was one shot down the length of the table where I really needed the left arm to steady me. I had a go and in it went. The break finished at 85! I think the Arabs were suitably impressed.

Black eyes and tribunals seemed a million miles away. I was mixing with a decent set of Arabs and ex-pats with no tension in the air. Everyone was very good to me for a change. The only snag was that I was missing one important creature comfort. In the second week I rang a girlfriend and invited her to join me. She was the 'mystery blonde' the papers referred to. Before she came I met a fascinating English actress who used to be in a science fiction television series. She was appearing in a Noel Coward play which I went to see. I must have been relaxed to go to the theatre! She looked ravishing on stage – about forty years old and not unlike Alexis in 'Dynasty', from a distance anyway.

I had a few drinks with the cast after the show. This actress seemed well disposed towards me so I invited her out to the 2001 club later that night. She said: 'Come on, let's go' and practically towed me out of the room! I just followed in her wake. We emptied a bottle of champagne then I suggested we finished the second one in my room. Up she came, dazzling in black satin with a tantalising cleavage. In the room I excused myself while I went to the loo and when I came back, she'd disappeared into thin air. I didn't even hear the door. I called the porter and said there was a woman in black wandering around the hotel with 250 dhirams of my money about her person! It was a ruse to get my own back.

Next thing I knew, they pulled her out of her cab for questioning before realising there was no substance to the allegation. The telephone wires between my hotel and hers were hot that night. I couldn't sleep so I put in the first call. 'You're not a nice girl,' I said, 'just disappearing like that without saying thank you for a pleasant evening.' I invited her for an early breakfast – I was well into those! She agreed but asked me over to her hotel. Before going, I put on Arab robes and the sunshades and went incognito. In the foyer I stopped to buy her a beautiful desert orchid. She seemed to appreciate that. I asked her what was for breakfast and she boasted that she had an electric toaster in the room. Big deal. Anyway, there I was eating hot buttered toast at about 7 am and trying to fathom out this strange woman.

I watched her painstakingly putting on her make-up and invited her out to lunch on one of the harbour boats where they did great lobster. She was telling me what good value the music cassettes were in Dubai so I said 'Let's go and see.' We walked out of the hotel and I said: 'Wait there while I pop into the bank and get a refill.' When I came out she'd done another bunk! Later I phoned to leave my parting message: 'Congratulations on being a will o' the wisp. Your next part will be in "The Lady Vanishes!"'

The most invigorating part of the trip was a twelve-hour rally across the sand dunes. Not really Higgins, but I figured a change was as good as a rest. We climbed aboard these souped-up Range Rovers with me in my helmet and patent leather shoes, firmly strapped into the passenger seat. There were six vehicles in a line going lickety-split across the desert like a scene from 'Whacky Races'. Seventy five miles an hour on the sand was shifting. Pretty soon I got used to it and was so blasé by the finish that I was on the car telephone arranging the rest of my social calendar!

I came back from Dubai with my batteries recharged. I hadn't had a holiday like that for a long long time. That Sunday I took

Lynn and the children out to lunch in Prestbury and we had a nice time. I was loaded up with presents for them, so I couldn't go wrong. Lauren was so pleased to see me that she wanted to come to Derby to watch my first round match in the Dulux British Open. I invited Lynn to come as well but she thought it would create too much publicity.

I learned a few valuable lessons about myself. Not least that I had to do my fighting back on the snooker table. Attacking the newspapers through the courts could come later. The world championships weren't far away so my improvement had to begin there and then. I didn't want to put myself under that pressure, but there was no choice. Winning was the only thing which would silence the critics and the doubters. The second thing I learned was that I needed those two stiff drinks just before I played. The third was that I needed a new manager. Del and I had exchanged a few heated words at Warrington over the black eye business and it was obvious that we both wanted a change. Barry Hearn was the man I needed. He was the most professional man on the circuit. The Matchroom team deserved everything they got.

In the event, it was Howard Kruger who made me an offer I couldn't refuse. His Framework Management team was a big set-up and he'd recently become exclusive agent for Jimmy White. Howard offered me a three-month contract but I wasn't sure what was best. To give Del his due, he said he would carry on managing me if that's what I wanted, but if I thought I'd be better with a change he'd give me his blessing.

In the meantime, I had a resounding 5–1 victory over Mike Hallett in the Dulux and a thrilling 5–2 result against Peter Francisco in the next round. The whole evening was a high. Peter is a likeable young man – one of the Higgins Youth Movement I predicted would come good in the fullness of time. He'd modelled himself on me and played the type of snooker the audiences can respond to – quick and daring. If he hadn't been so headstrong, he could have made it closer than it was. I was in something like my old form and the crowd responded magnificently. I can't remember many matches I've enjoyed more. The banter was going on all the time between Peter and me and between us and the spectators.

I blew the chance of a televised 147 maximum but it didn't bother me. I'm not the sort to think 'There's £5,000 on this shot if I make it'. My mind doesn't work that way. I'd much sooner go for the risky one and the devil take the hindmost. I played my 'banana' shot bringing the cue ball spinning right up against the black after potting the red. It might have lost me the chance of maximum, but I enjoyed it.

The atmosphere in the dressing room was very cordial. Such a difference from the aggravation of a few weeks before. This was the Higgins the fans loved. They were all there: the little old ladies moving their heads from side to side in the front row and nearly putting me off, bless them; and the younger ones straining to give me a kiss after the game. I felt so good I was kissing everyone and everything that came near. I did a signing session for my followers and almost died from suffocation under the welter of requests. Anyone who can provoke that affection can't be all bad can he?

I took Peter Francisco with me to the press conference. I was back at my best, telling reporters I'd sunk that Portuguese man-of-war which wasn't bad for someone who didn't even swim! I asked Peter to come and practise with me for the world championships. He agreed. I thought we could both benefit.

Another lesson the trip away had taught me was that I had to get out of the rat race. I felt people were growing tired of seeing the same old faces year after year. I was certainly tired and jaded after fourteen years on the professional circuit. I gave myself four more years to get out. That meant I had to have a manager who would get me some lucrative contracts so that I'd be financially sound enough to call it a day soon after reaching forty.

For the time being, there was the prospect of going the distance in the Dulux tournament. Next man up was Bill Werbeniuk, but he perished 5–1 without a whimper. That put me into the semi-finals of the richest tournament in snooker history – my best achievement since winning the doubles with Jimmy White fourteen months previously. Curiously, despite my season of trauma, I hadn't failed once to reach the qualifying stages of the ranking tournaments.

The only fly in the ointment was failing to get a hotel room in town. It wasn't that they were fully booked – just that no one would take Alex Higgins. It's a recurring problem with me. You name a hotel in England I'm probably banned from it. I don't like hotel life and have made a rod for my own back by getting slung out of so many. Take the Friary in Derby. I was disappointed they wouldn't have me – and all because I tried to rescue a damsel in distress the previous year. I'd found her and a friend of Jimmy White's getting down to business in my bathroom. I was livid. The bloke didn't have a room of his own. I ordered him out. He threatened me with one of her bracelets which had a serrated edge, whereupon I personally escorted her to the hotel lobby. A bunch of blokes on a Cammell Laird business course baited me about the girl. They'd had a few drinks. I grabbed one of them by the lapels and said: 'I'd love to fight the lot of you, but I'm not not going to give you the satisfaction. If you hang on, there's a much angrier bloke coming down the stairs!' The manager told me to pack my bags. A shame because I liked the Friary. The nearest place I could get in was the Royal Hotel, fifteen miles away in Nottingham.

My semi-final opponent would be Steve Davis and there was no better time for me to meet the Ginger Magician. He'd been in spanking form mind you and seemed to have his name written on the trophy. Immediately before the match, I signed a three year deal with Howard Kruger in front of the television cameras. He was commissioned to revamp the Higgins image – no mean feat. He also had to face the prospect of two possible libel actions by me – one against the *Sun* for the 'Dirty Old Man' story from last September, and another against the *News of the World* for the drugs allegations. My first match under new management was a disappointment. I never got into my stride against Davis. He won 9–3 with some relentless play and, not surprisingly, went on to beat Willy Thorne, his new stablemate, in the final.

It seemed that two rival camps were now lining up – Barry Hearn who'd signed Thorne and Neil Foulds to boost his membership to six and Kruger who had Jimmy, Tony Knowles and me and planned to strengthen his squad still further.

There were two options open to me: either employ a secretary and manage myself, or join Howard Kruger. Once I'd sat down with Howard and Del to discuss a possible transfer, I realised this was my best course of action. Howard impressed me as a go-ahead fellah. He'd made his name in the music business and been involved with a string of famous performers like Wham, The Eurythmics, The Jacksons, Glen Campbell, Joan Armatrading etc. He'd also built up a sports agency over the last few years, dealing with Sharron Davies and Torvill and Dean among others. Snooker was new to him.

(*Howard Kruger:* It seemed a natural extension of what I was already doing. Snooker had become show business and I

felt, with my experience of promoting concert tours all over the world , that I could be of use. It started when I bumped into Tony Knowles on a beach in Spain. We both enjoyed water-skiing and developed a good friendship. Shortly afterwards, when I read the exposé about his antics with women's underwear, I telephoned him and suggested he needed a manager to keep him away from such stupid headlines. They could wreck his career. He agreed and asked me to take care of his affairs. The more I looked into the sport, the more I discovered that Barry Hearn had had it all his own way for a long time. There was plenty of cake for both of us. Besides, it couldn't be good for the game if there was only one management agency which knew what it was doing.)

I had to buy out my existing contract with Del which still had a year to run, then sell it to Howard. I received a tidy signing-on fee and Del was paid an amount to cover the goodwill for the work he'd already set in motion for me. Everyone was happy I think. I felt that at last I had someone working two hundred per cent on my behalf. I'm not convinced that was the case before. Because of his involvement with the WPBSA, Del's position was often difficult. He had to sit on the fence at disciplinary hearings and watch me hung, drawn and quartered. It didn't seem right somehow.

(*Del Simmons:* In many ways I was sorry to say goodbye to Alex. It was a bit like losing a son. I told him I was prepared to carry on despite our recent disagreements. But if he really wanted to leave, I wouldn't stand in his way. To be honest, I wasn't able to do as much for him as I'd have liked. He needed someone to devote more time to his special demands. I hope the new arrangement with Howard will benefit Alex. I wouldn't say he'd become an embarrassment to me, but I was unhappy about the black eye incident for instance. I shall never know why he didn't confide in me before making an idiot of himself. It was hurtful not to have been put in the picture by my own client.

If only he'd told me the truth, I'd have advised him to come clean, recite the story about the fight with Medati, and make light of it by telling the press if they thought HIS face looked bad, they should have seen the other guy! In the end he had to do that anyway, but only after he'd tied himself up in knots

163

with lies. All he succeeded in doing was putting even more pressure on himself. We saw where that led.

In the last ten years since I took over managing Alex, there've been dozens of things I've tried to blank out of my mind. People have said I must be mad to manage him, but, in many ways, he's been the easiest person in the world to deal with. It's all a question of timing. If you 'hit' him at the right time, he'll do anything for you. I learned very quickly that if he's just lost 5–0, that's not the moment to rush into his dressing room to speak to him. You've no chance! When he gets wound up, you have to leave him to cool down in his own time and realise that he's made a mistake. Then he's full of apologies.

Alex is a misunderstood person. He's done an awful lot of good which he'd never tell you about. I won't forget the time he went to Bristol to see a young lad suffering from leukaemia. Alex was the lad's idol. Instead of just signing an autograph and moving onto his next appointment, Alex astonished the boy by sitting next to him for two hours at a Boys' Brigade service at a local church. Those people and others like them will tell you he's a saint. We all know he isn't, but he does have redeeming qualities. Even with his busy schedule, he's opened scores of events and refused payment.

We've had our disagreements of course. There's one thing you can be sure of with Alex though – he doesn't harbour grudges. He'll murder you one day but the next day it's forgotten. Many's the time I've taken calls from him in the dead of night. Sometimes it's a plea for help, sometimes he's had one over the eight and he's in a vicious mood, calling me all the names under the sun and saying he wants no more to do with me. I just tell him to leave it out and go to bed. The following day, the call's not even mentioned.

When he first came to me, he'd been badly handled by Maurice Hayes who'd double-booked him for an exhibition when he was still in a tournament. He was earning about £50 a night in 1976, but had to pay a £960 fine out of his own pocket for the two nights he couldn't appear at the club in Harlow. That seems to have stuck with him. Only once after that did he ever miss an engagement. That was in his native Ireland when he'd made a mistake about the date. His lateness is legendary, but he would usually make it up to exhibition organisers by playing extra frames.

Alex thinks he should have had more money out of the game and made himself secure for life. What he can't accept is that he's lost out not because of management, but because of his nature. He should have been doing a lot more by way of endorsements but Alex is Alex and he should realise why he doesn't get the contracts that Steve Davis gets. It's no one's fault but his own. Against that, if you took away that fiery nature, he wouldn't be Alex Higgins the People's Champion. He can't have it both ways.

That temper of his has brought him more fines than anyone in the game. Some of the penalties meted out by the WPBSA might have seemed a bit severe but Alex is the first to admit that he's got away with a few things as well. On the whole I don't think he can say he's been unfairly treated though I don't suppose he'll ever concede that. From my point of view there's always been something of a conflict because of the two hats I wear. The Association has been left in no doubt though that as Alex's manager, my principal concern has been to act on his behalf. If they wanted me to leave the room while they discussed his misdemeanours, they only had to say. I've been allowed to vote on such matters, but normally decline. It hasn't been easy sitting there powerless while he's been tried and convicted.

Looking back, I don't know how he's managed to run around the country like he has done since 1972 and not keel over. The lifestyle would have killed a lesser person. He has quite incredible reserves of energy. When I started with him, I remember looking at a map and thinking it wasn't far between exhibitions in Manchester and Grimsby, and only a short hop down the east coast to Dover before popping across to London, and calling in at Leicester on the way back to Manchester. When you actually do the trip it's exhausting. For all his protests to the contrary I know he loves the travelling life, but my God, it doesn't half take something out of you.

The worst thing that happened to Alex was splitting up with Lynn. She's a strong woman, stronger than him. I was delighted when he married and settled down. I thought it was vital for him to have that base in his life and to have a family to go home to, not an empty hotel room. Without it, I feared he'd be lost. I just hope I'm not right. I'm godfather to his children and know how fond he is of them. Having said that, I can see why Lynn has got so upset so often. She's needed all her strength to come through the last few years, and she'll need more now they're apart. I know she'll cope. How will Alex get on though?

The day after his arrest when Dennis Taylor had crushed him in the Goya tournament, he broke down in tears in front of me. That's a side of him few outsiders have seen. He's very emotional and sensitive and cries easily. With the prospect of his family being split for good, he was inconsolable. Goodness knows how he ever managed to play that match against Dennis. Once again, I found myself wondering why he didn't confide in me until afterwards.

I can't see him ever retiring from snooker. His charisma is such that people will always want to see him. Even when he's on the way down, they'll still flock to see him before he dies. As long as they want him, he'll be there. I guess the day he dies is the day he'll put down his cue. We shall keep in touch, naturally. I can forget all the times I would happily have strangled him because, deep down, I'm very fond of Alex.)

Howard and I came to an understanding from the outset. I insisted that he never referred to me as 'son'. I'd spent the last ten years being Del's 'son' but when the chips were down, 'Dad' wasn't around to help. My new manager put his cards on the table by explaining that he wasn't necessarily out to create a team to rival Barry Hearn's Matchroom boys. What he specialised in was managing individual careers. To a certain extent, Jimmmy White, Tony Knowles, Joe Johnson and I would come together, but he didn't see us as a squad. Framework have now taken over all my financial affairs, although I don't work on the basis of a monthly allowance like Steve Davis and company. I'm not a baby. I can look after my own spending.

At long last I know someone's taking care of business. During the world championships in Sheffield, I spent at least a couple of hours of each day in Howard's company. If he couldn't make it, someone else from Framework did. There was always someone at my elbow when I needed them. Howard understands that I have to have some breathing space in between. I was chauffered everywhere, accompanied for interviews, escorted at the venue and had tedious things like hotels and flights sorted out for me. There was nothing to think about but snooker. It gave me a little bit of importance back. I began to feel like a professional artiste again. It's a long time since I could say that.

If I'd had this arrangement years ago, who knows what heartache it might have saved? Having the pressure of everyday chores removed would have enabled me to settle into a routine and could well have saved my marriage, I don't think there's much hope of that now. Lynn is adamant that she wants a divorce. I'd still like to keep the family together. At Sheffield, I persuaded her to come and watch me play and bring Lauren with her. I figured it might just trigger a few happy memories of four years before. I wanted her to bring Jordan as well, but she said it was too late at night for him. It was good having my daughter in the audience again. It's a shame it didn't work, Terry Griffiths knocked me out after I'd taken an early lead, and the brief reunion with my family turned out to be nothing more than that. Lynn was angry about the £200 a week I give her. She said it wasn't nearly enough. That's why she wanted the divorce.

I'm sure if Howard had been acting for me at Warrington earlier in the year, the 'black eye' episode would not have got out of control. I wouldn't have been left at the mercy of the press and the subsequent outburst would have been avoided. I know I'm a difficult bloke to manage but it's all about taking the pressure off me. Little things like organising autograph hunters have been taken care of. I like to meet the fans which is more than can be said of some players, but once you get swamped under a scrum, you've had it. Howard saw to that at Sheffield. The signing sessions were done on an organised basis. A quarter or half an hour at a time is enough for anyone.

One of the first things he did was arrange a bona fide Alex Higgins Fan Club, something new in snooker. He had a call from a Grimsby housewife, Gina Howes who volunteered to run the club. She ran a similar thing for Richard Claydermann, so she knew what she was doing. My fans will all have cards which will give them preferential treatment at tournaments. I suggested that once or twice a year the club has a get-together with a disco and maybe a mini tournament for members. I don't mind chipping in a couple of hundred quid for the bar and the prizes. I'll even present them and dance with the middle-aged ladies, fat or thin!

The purpose of the exercise is to change my image. It won't be easy. The secret is not to brush the past under the carpet and pretend I'm a goody-two-shoes, but to learn from the mistakes and start again. I can only change my spots within reason. I'm still Alex Higgins whatever they do to me. I still like female company and I still enjoy my drink. I can't see that changing. What I have to relearn is how to conform to a proper routine. Maybe then the aggression and the tension will subside. Next season we're working on the idea of four successive nights of exhibitions and shows, followed by three days off. That gets over the big problem in my life – playing exhibitions here, there and everywhere with perhaps one day in between in which there's no time to get back to base and relax. It's in situations like those that boredom sets in and the trouble begins.

(*Howard Kruger:* I moved in for Alex because I could see a lot of untapped potential. There's only one chap guaranteed to fill an auditorium and it's been that way for sixteen years. It amazes me that he's never got his act together before. I know he's a volatile person, in fact Knowles, White and Higgins are all that way inclined. That's partly what makes them so exciting as players. If you leave them to roam around without professional advice and guidance, you're bound to have outbursts and controversial incidents. Alex has been fodder for the press for a decade or more. He only has to trip up a nightclub step and he's 'in a drunken stupor', or accidentally bump into someone and he's accused of physical assault with attempt to cause grievous bodily harm!

I've seen it all before in the pop music world. What astonishes me about snooker is the amount of players who look after themselves. Tony Knowles never had an agent before I suggested it; Alex hasn't been properly represented either. It was a very loose arrangement before. Among those who were represented, there was a distinct lack of loyalty to one agent or manager. Players seemed to change at the drop of a hat. It was a complete contrast to the music world where artistes stay with the same agent all their lives because they trust them and have no reason to change. That's the stability I hope to give to Alex.

It's no good expecting the advertising contracts to come rolling in from day one. What I intend to do is progress slowly. A lot of harm has been done and it won't be repaired overnight. I plan to leave it for a good year before even thinking about marketing him the way Steve Davis has been marketed. Alex has to prove that he can behave in a civilised fashion and show that he still has plenty to offer at the table. If he can knuckle down, he'll make a lot of money. That's his incentive. If he can't, he's finished. It's as simple as that.

There are things I don't like about his behaviour. He has a habit of being too familiar in distinguished company. He has this penchant for touching people as if he's known them all his life. I was appalled once to see him take the Lady Mayoress by the arm at some function we were at. He was pulling her to one side to whisper something in her ear, the way you might do with an old friend. We can't have that. There has to be more decorum.

So far, he's been one hundred and ten per cent reliable and professional on business matters. Whenever we've had to meet people in the City, they've been amazed at his conduct. They wonder if this is the Higgins they've been reading about in their papers. When Alex wants to, he can carry himself in any surroundings. What he has to learn is how to trust people. He's a very lonely person and he's suspicious of everyone. That's a habit we have to break somehow. I think he trusts me now. I'd like to move him down from the Manchester area. He's too remote up there. I don't think London would be a good thing, but somewhere in the Midlands might be a better base. It would be convenient for the tournaments too.

Since I've known him, we've had a couple of outbursts. At the world championships he was extremely tense. He badly wanted to do well. We had a few heated words about trivial matters, usually when he'd had a drink too many. That's when he can fall foul of the press. They gobble him up when he blows his top and after all these years, he's still not learned to keep out of the way. He has to turn the press to his own advantage; to build up a relationship with them. It's easy. We have to show the big wide world that underneath the brash, rude exterior, there's a nice person trying to get out.)

Howard has quite a temper on him. I've seen it a couple of times but up to now we've got along okay. Temperamental stars like me will always be a headache to someone. It might as well be my manager. After all, I'm paying him for the privilege! The commercial side has been slow to develop. We haven't started to tap it yet. One of the first tasks is to reopen diplomatic channels with Australia. There's an embargo on me. It stems from a few drunken sessions and an incident some years back when I insulted a sports minister. They banned me from a tournament and I haven't been back since. It's important to resume relations because snooker can only get bigger there. They need entertainers, especially after a couple of decades of Eddie Charlton! In the meantime, I have to gear myself up for the next season in England. If Howard carries on the way he has been and if I can keep my end up as well, we can really go places.

Index

171

Irish Benson & Hedges Tournament 119
Irish Linen Company 34
Jacksons 162
Jagger, Mick 20
Jameson Tournament 118, 131
Jampot, Belfast 26, 27, 29, 36, 37
Johnson, Joe 74, 166
Jones, Mel 42
Jones, Wilson 63
Julie (niece) 10, 96, 109
Kelly, Billy 72
Kelvin School 26, 28, 37
Keogh, Mick 56
Khaled (Arab friend) 157–58
Kim (Bunny girl) 58–59
King, Warren 68, 123
Kirkwood, Geordie 27
Kit Kat Champion of Champions Event 144
Knight, Gladys 10
Knowles, Tony 114, 123, 162, 163, 166, 167
Kruger, Howard 20, 160, 162, 166, 168
Laverty, Vince 42
Leckey, Danny 37
Leckey, Ken 37
Leeming, Jack 20, 43, 44, 45, 48
Lomas, Geoff 19, 20, 136
Lomas, Helen 89, 128
Lorimer, Sir Graham 34
Love, Stewart 28, 29
Lowe, Ted 72, 73
Ludlum, Robert 10
Manchester Exhibition Hall 67
Manchester Hospital 155
Mans, Perrie 99
Margo 57–58
Martin, Campbell 37, 38
Martin, Dave 108
Masters Club, Stockport 123
Matchroom, Romford 115
McBride, Tom 37
McClatchey, George 29
McCreery, Norman 28
McEnroe, John 4, 12
McGuigan, Barry 14, 139
McLaughlin, John 20, 43, 44
McLeod, Murdo 72, 74, 123
McMillan, Harry 20
Medati, Paul 123, 149–50, 151, 152, 163
Meo, Tony 82, 118, 120
Mercantile Credit Classic 120, 149
Metcalf, Tony 75
Miles, Graham 45, 75
Miller, J.J. 62, 66
Morgan, Willie 11, 103
Mountjoy, Doug 72, 79, 98

Mountpottinger YMCA, Belfast 38, 40
Muhammed Ali 12, 13, 49, 50, 54, 97, 130
Nastase, Ilie 4
Northern Ireland Amateur Championship 39
Nottingham 162
Nottingham University 144
O'Beirne, Sheila 22
O'Beirne, Tony 22
O'Hara, Charlie 38
Owen, Gary 42
Owen, Marcus 42
Oxford Club, Belfast 37, 38
Park Drive 2000 Final 49
Parkin, Maurice 46
Parsons, Terry 42
Penygraig Labour Club 41–42
People's Palace, Singapore 59
Perrin, Reg 73
Piggott, Lester 12, 13, 22, 32
Players Number Six UK Team 1969 41
Pontins Open 1977 72
Portland Lodge, Manchester 103
Pot Black Series 39, 46, 49, 68, 71–72, 145
Potters Club, Stockport 86, 149
Preston Guildhall 122
Pulman, John 12, 40, 42, 46, 47–48, 53, 55, 56, 57, 59, 68–69, 153
Radcliffe Town Hall 49–50
Rae, Jack 46
Reardon, Ray 18, 48, 51, 55, 61, 66–67, 69, 70, 72, 73, 82, 95, 100, 102, 103, 106, 114, 117, 135, 145
Reavey, Eddie 31, 32, 33
Reavey, Jocelyn 32, 33–34
Redwood Lodge, Bristol 108
Reed, Oliver 17, 76–77
Robbins, Lynn *See* Higgins, Lynn
Ross, Diana 10
Rothmans Tournament 131
Royal Overseas Club 42
Selly Park British Legion 50, 55
Shannon, Jacky 39
Sheene, Barry 18
Shepherd, John 42
Simmons, Del 1, 20, 58, 66, 77, 103, 107, 112, 125, 143, 153, 163, 166; parts company from 160
Smith, Sidney 55
Smyth, John 131
Spencer, John 20, 42, 45, 49, 50, 51, 52, 53–55, 56, 65,

70, 73, 80, 93, 100, 103, 114, 117
Spencer (Hotel cat) 91
Stepney, Alex 61
Stevens, Kirk 11, 82, 99, 101, 114, 133, 134, 135, 154
Sunderland, Alan 79
Taylor, David 70
Taylor, Dennis 39, 40, 75, 80, 103, 114, 118, 120, 139, 143, 150, 154, 166
Taylor, Jim 30
Taylor, Joe 59–60
Taylor, Molly (sister of Dennis) 40
Thatcher, Margaret 15
Thickett, Smokey Joe 135–36
'This is Your Life' 22, 95, 96
Thompson, Geoff 79
Thorburn, Barbara 83
Thorburn, Cliff 69, 75, 82, 83, 99, 101, 131
Thorne, Willy 82, 99, 118, 120, 162
Thorpe, Jim 51, 69
Tolly Cobbold Classic 80
Torvill, Jane 162
Turner, Tina 10
2001 Club, Dubai 158
Ulster Hall, Belfast 80
Virgo, John 43, 92
Wake, Peter 22–23, 61, 62
Wallace, David 40, 41
Wally (owner of Ma Baker's Pool Club) 125
Warwick, Dionne 10
Watneys Open 69
Watterson, Mike 81, 108
Wembley 119
Werbeniuk, Bill 81
Wham 162
White, Jimmy 11, 99, 101, 114, 119, 144, 145, 154, 160, 161, 162, 166
The Who 61
Williams, John 81
Williams, Rex 48, 49, 55, 65, 69, 70, 125, 126, 133, 152
Wilmslow Conservative Club 5
Wilson Classic, Manchester 1980 80
Wilson, Phil 23, 60
Windmill Street Club, London 35
World Championship 1982 97–103
World Championship 1972 20, 45–54
World Professional Billiards & Snooker Association 43, 64, 65, 67, 70, 75, 80, 101, 133, 152, 153, 157, 163, 165
Worsley, Jimmy 42